The strange I

Wimblestone Road

Hamish MacNeil

By the same author:

Poetry

(Writing as Macaque)

A Man Remembers (2016)

Palimpsest of Ghosts (2017, 2021)

As one of the Writers in Stone

Driftwood (2019)

Cuckoo (2021)

10 9 8 7 6 5 4 3 2 1

ISBN 978-1-8384346-0-1

Cover design and photography by Wings of Weston

For Harry, Cameron, Ellis and Charlie

The real heroes of my story

Contents

Chapter One

Departure

The journey from London was full of mixed emotions for the boys. Their parents had made the move to the countryside sound as positive and exciting as they could, but everything was going to be unfamiliar, and they were all going to miss their friends. The family had spent the night at Grandma and Grandad's because their old house had been packed up, cleaned and locked for the last time in one very long, very busy day. Everything except the little suitcases the boys had packed themselves was now stacked and secured in the enormous removal lorry, which the boys had seen arrive before grandad had picked them up to keep them out of the way.

Jack, Alex and Max had set off with their dad just after breakfast, in the big family car with their suitcases in the boot, waved off from the kerb by their excited but tearful grandparents. It was a bit like going away on holiday, and they chatted excitedly to begin with, then sank into reflective silences for a while, which their dad tried to break with some observation or other about what they were passing, or what they could expect when they arrived. They waved goodbye to Heathrow as they joined the M4, waved to the sign for Windsor Castle and LEGOLAND, and then the monotony of the motorway took over, past Reading, past Swindon, past endless cars, caravans and lorries.

"Where will the removal lorry be now, dad?" asked Max.

"Oh, they might even be there by now. They probably travelled last night when the roads were quieter."

"Will they be sleeping in our new house?"

"No, they will have found a hotel, I expect."

"Some lorries have beds in the cabs, don't they? They might have stayed in the lorry overnight," said Jack, riding beside his dad in the front seat.

"True, but I don't know if there would have been room for four of them. Might be a terribly uncomfortable night."

"Bullaark" burped Alex, making the other two laugh.

"I do wish you wouldn't do that!" said Mr Pearson, glancing at Alex in the rear view mirror.

"And when will mummy and Sam be joining us?" asked Max.

"After all the hard work has been done and she can just complain that everything is in the wrong place," muttered Jack.

"They'll be with us before bedtime," said Mr Pearson, ignoring Jack's comment. "She's just keeping Sammy out of the way. And it will be good for Grandma and Grandad to have the day with both of them."

"Will we see Grandma and Grandad again?" asked Max.

"Yes of course! They might come up to see us in half term, if we're straight by then. And we'll be spending Christmas there as usual, I expect."

They passed signs for Bath and then the airport before they joined the M5 at Bristol.

"Is that where your new job is, dad?" asked Jack. "Is it far?"

"It's further than Heathrow was from our old house, but it is still quite close. We won't have any of the noise from the flight paths in the new house, though. It takes about twenty minutes, door to door, I'd say."

"Will we be at the new house in twenty minutes, then?" asked Max excitedly.

"A little bit longer than that, but not much."

"And will we go past the new airport? Shouldn't we have turned off back there?"

"No, we'll stick to the motorway around Bristol; don't want to get stuck in traffic. And we'll get to see the sea from the motorway!"

The boys cheered.

They cheered again ten minutes later as they crossed the river Avon where it runs into the Severn Estuary. From the top of the Avonmouth Bridge, they could see the docks where thousands of brand new cars and vans had been unloaded, their shiny paintwork gleaming in the sun, and the glittering expanse of sea beyond. The road climbed steeply uphill and the northbound carriageway dropped a few meters below as the motorway skirted the contours of the Mendip Hills giving them a clear view of little farms, hamlets and a densely wooded ridge hiding the Bristol Channel from view. They passed through a cutting, the angular rock face pressing right up against the hard shoulder, then began the descent towards Clevedon and Weston-super-Mare, where the see flashed once more like a mirror between two headlands. The holiday feeling took hold of them all again, and in no time at all, the car was pulling off the motorway into the lush, green countryside.

"Welcome to Somerset," said their dad.

"Are we nearly there yet?" chorused the children.

"Not far now."

The roads became narrower the further they drove from the motorway. The fields either side were as flat as cricket pitches, criss-crossed with little streams and canals. The children saw flocks of sheep, grazing cattle, free range pigs rooting in the dried mud, and two beautiful swans traversing the green pasture with their unhurried, stately countenance. The hills in the distance drew nearer, and they passed through little villages of stone houses with stone garden walls. They crossed an arched stone bridge and passed a garage with old fashioned petrol pumps on the forecourt, and a workshop that looked like it should have fallen down a hundred years ago.

"Time warp," said Jack.

"Urrlubok!" burped Alex, and the boys burst into laughter again.

Mr Pearson pointed out places and landmarks he thought were interesting, but it was all just countryside to the boys. "You see that last hill, there, with the funny little bump like the top of an old fashioned policeman's helmet?" he said, pointing ahead of them. "That's Crook Peak, apparently. We'll take a walk up there one of these days, it's not far from the village."

The road wound along the curves and contours of the hills, through tunnels of trees, then became a pass that had been gouged out of the rock in places, barely wide enough for the car to get through.

"Did the removal lorry come this way, dad?" asked Jack.

"I'm not certain, angel. I'm sure there are roads that are suitable for big lorries; they might have had to take a less direct route."

"This is the direct route?" questioned Alex sarcastically. "Jeez!"

"Nearly there now," said their dad, taking a left turn into another narrow road. A sign in the hedge, so overgrown it was barely discernible, claimed this road to be the High Street. The boys watched through the car windows as more stone walls, decoratively topped and festooned with creepers and wall flowers went past, some with little, arched wooden gates set in them. Many of the windows and doorways in this village were arched, giving all the properties a very quaint, fairy tale appearance. They turned onto East Street, where one little round house had a turret with narrow windows and a roof like a witch's hat. They passed The Old Vicarage and The Old Police House, large properties with large gardens, then they were back in a tunnel of trees that girded a steep climb. To their left, flashing between the tree trunks, their dad pointed out Weston-super-Mare again and the dull haze of the sea in the distance, over all the fields and waterways they had driven past. On the right, the woods gave way briefly to fields and farms with muddy yards and gateways, and ancient rusty tractors and other pieces of machinery. They came to some more buildings, like old fashioned station masters' cottages, and a pub called The Railway, then finally they turned right past a tidy-looking church yard with an enormous tree sheltering the wooden lichgate and cobbled path, and dad was telling them that this was it, this was their new village. The road climbed sharply, past large metal gates on the left covered with notices warning "Danger" and "Keep Out".

"What's in there, dad?" asked Alex eagerly.

"That's an old quarry," he replied. "I don't want you boys thinking you can play in there. Quarries are very dangerous places, not adventure playgrounds, ok?" There was a glum silence in the car, then their dad continued, "you're going to love it here, boys; Somerset will be a fantastic place to grow up: plenty of things to do outdoors; we've got the beach on our doorstep; there are the caves at Cheddar; they've got football and rugby clubs in the village, and mum's talking about enrolling you in the scouts."

"Have you got any more time off work now we're here?" asked Jack, pointedly, as they dropped down the other side of the hill amidst red brick semis and pebble dashed bungalows. This village was not the fairy-tale setting they had been presented with moments before.

"Here we are," said Mr Pearson as if he hadn't heard Jack's question, turning left into Wimblestone Road.

"Sounds like Womblestone," laughed Max, and his brothers joined him.

"There be Wombles in them there hills," said their dad randomly in some weird accent.

"What are you on about?" asked Alex, making a there's-another-one-of-dad's-lame-jokes face at Max.

Mr Pearson pulled the car into a parking space under a row of cherry trees in front of a brick and plaster semi-detached house with a banked lawn that swept round from the side and seemed to be lifting the house off the pavement like the skirt of a hovercraft. The removal lorry was parked along the kerb beside the house, with a wooden ramp making a bridge onto the lawn, and some of the boxes and furniture were already standing on the side path that led to a gate into the back garden. Across the road was a tarmacked quadrangle of garages, and Jack instantly wished he had a football in the car. Mr Pearson greeted the removal men and hurried to unlock the house.

The boys were eager to see inside, and raced up the stairs to check out the bedrooms. There were two bedrooms at the back of the house, and from the windows they could see the back garden which was level at the top then sloped down past an extension with a flat roof to a patio. There would be just about room to kick a ball once the shed and the baby's play house and slide were erected. Their neighbours must be keen gardeners because next door's garden was a series of flower beds and vegetable patches connected by a criss-cross of stone paths and steps, and to the side of the house behind them was a greenhouse. In London there had been a whole row of houses backing onto their street, and no elevation in the landscape, so apart from the gardens at the back and cars at the front, the only views were of windows and roofs. Here, as the houses climbed the hill they were staggered and set at an angle, so that behind the new house was a field that stretched past the side of their neighbour's garden and ran up past the houses behind to a farmhouse and woods at the top. Below the farmhouse was a jumble of farm machinery and junk, tractor forks, tyres and trailers half smothered in long grass and nettles. Max said they looked like dinosaurs floundering in a swamp. From the front bedroom they could see across the roofs of bungalows to more fields and the Mendip hills with that funny peak, and beyond that, through a gap in the hills, to what looked like the blue of the sea.

"Wait till I tell Liam and Perky that I can see the sea from my bedroom window!" said jack.

Chapter Two

Arrival

"Why don't you explore the street, see if there are any other children about?" said Mr Pearson, as they dodged around the removal men.

"On our own?" asked Max, who was only seven.

"You'll be alright here. It's much safer than London. Stay in the street, ok, and when you're hungry, come back and we'll go to the chippy."

The three boys dutifully trooped outside.

"I wish we knew where the bikes were," said Alex, looking down the hill where the quiet street branched off and became a narrow, winding lane beyond some bungalows. "This'll be awesome for bikes and scooters. Maybe we could build a go-kart, too."

"Let's go up this way for now," suggested Jack, "explore the cul-de-sac."

They set off, leaning into the gradient of the hill. The houses were cut diagonally into the slope, facing down the road like Easter Island statues, their back gardens rising above them, the front gardens falling away. Nobody had a fence or a hedge at the front, just neatly mown lawns and the occasional bush. Further up, one garden had a rockery with a little waterfall and a pond surrounded by gnomes. Everywhere seemed open and friendly and welcoming. As they climbed they passed cars with their windows down in the sun, and houses whose side doors stood open into utility rooms and kitchens.

"You don't get this in London," said Jack, "this is Freedom from Fear, this is."

"Stop trying to sound like dad," said Alex.

The road ended in a T shape with a row of houses along the top, surveying the whole road; indeed, the whole village seemed to lie before them, a patchwork of roofs and gardens and trees. There were houses tucked into the sides of the T shape, and through a gap in the left hand end, another quadrangle of garages was visible. They went and had a look round but there was nothing to see: all the doors were closed and intact, with no graffiti; nothing had been set on fire, and there were no kids doing tricks on bikes or smoking and listening to gangsta rap.

"I'm not sure there are any kids in this street," said Alex. "Looks like everyone is retired."

They walked to the other end of the T where a narrow set of steps led up between two high, wooden fences.

"Let's go up here," said Jack.

"I don't know. Dad said we had to stay in the street." Max pushed his glasses up his nose with a habitual, nervous gesture.

"We'll just see where it goes. It's still part of the street, really," said Jack.

"Yeah," said Alex, "dad probly just meant don't go too far. And he doesn't want us in the way right now, does he, so –"

"I don't know..." repeated Max, looking back down towards the house with the big lorry still outside it.

"Come on, don't be a wuss! You've seen how safe it is here."

Jack led the way without waiting for an answer from his brother. After twenty steps there was a level stretch and an alleyway of sorts led off to the left between the back gardens of the houses along the top of the cul-de-sac and the back gardens of another row of houses behind them. It was quite overgrown with brambles, and a couple of wheelie bins could just be seen protruding from the wilderness. The fences and gardens, and indeed the plasterwork and windows of these houses were not as well kept as the ones in their street. They carried on up and emerged onto a narrow path that ran along the front of this second row of houses. These houses seemed dark and miserable, in the shade of the hill above them, and the front gardens here were all divided by concrete block walls, with little iron or wooden gates off a narrow path. In front of the boys, another six steps led up to a road lined with parked cars, and from somewhere beyond the cars came the sound of a ball being kicked against a wall.

At the top of the steps the boys found the first litter they had seen in the village, along with some junk that had perhaps been left for the bin men but not collected: a child's car seat, a broken stair gate, and a bundle of plastic sheeting. This was more the sort of street the boys were used to. Across the road were dense trees and bushes, and another abandoned car seat, but this one was actually the front seat of a car. To their right, the road narrowed to a lane, and a track branched off down the hill, presumably to the farm whose fields bordered their new garden. To their left, the road ran down to the road they had driven up, past the quarry, and there were more steel gates with warnings about danger and private property. Another gap in the trees half way down was bordered with large blocks of black stone; that was where the sound of the ball was coming from.

The boys walked down to the boulders. There was a gravel area about ten meters by five meters cut into the hill and faced with ancient looking brick. There were three alcoves in the brick wall, and a girl about Jack's age was kicking a football, using the alcoves as goals.

"Hey!" said Jack by way of greeting, his brothers standing slightly behind him.

"Hey," said the girl, in a matter of fact tone, and Jack started to laugh.

"What's so funny? Never seen a girl play football before?" asked the girl defensively.

"It just reminded me of that bit in *To Kill a Mockingbird*, when Jem and Scout meet Dillon and they both say 'Hey!'"

"It's not very funny," said the girl.

"No; it just came to me. Sorry."

"Well, I suppose that would make me Scout, seeing as I live here and you're strangers. What's your name, Dillon?"

Now Alex laughed. "That's funny - what's your name, Dillon!"

"I'm Jack. This is Zander –"

"Alexander, really," said Alex.

"And this is Max."

"Maximilian, really," said Max, copying his brother.

"Shut up!" said Alex.

"It's what dad calls me sometimes!"

"As a nickname, you idiot, it's not your actual name!"

The girl looked at Jack, and Jack shook his head and rolled his eyes. "Well, I'm Poppy, I live in that house there. Where are you from? Are you brothers? I wish I had a brother."

"Trust me, you don't!" said Jack.

"What year are you in?" asked Poppy.

17

"Seven. Going to be starting at the Academy. Zan's in Year Six, and Max will be Year Three, now?"

Max nodded.

"We'll be in the same year, then. Do you know what house you're in?"

"No. It's all been a big kerfuffle. The council lost my application, or something. Mum's right stressed out about it. Can we play with your ball?"

So the boys told Poppy the story of their move from London while they tried to kick the ball into one of the alcoves. If it missed, the next person had to try before the ball came to a stop or they were out. In turn, Poppy told the boys about the village; what the rec and the skate park were like, what shops there were (not many), about the alcoves in the wall that had been lime kilns a hundred years ago, and about the quarry.

"Dad told us we had to stay away from the quarry because it's dangerous," said Max.

"It's safe enough if you're careful," said Poppy.

"You go in there?" asked Alex, full of admiration.

"All the time. I'll show you, if you like. Come on!"

It was too tempting to refuse, even though Max was worried what their dad would say. Poppy put her ball into the nearest lime kiln, and ran over to the trees at the side of the brickwork. There was a gap in the foliage where a rope swing hung from a stout branch, and a muddy path had been worn away. Poppy disappeared past the swing, and the boys followed. It was cool and dark in amongst the trees, and the boys followed Poppy up the muddy bank beside a wall built from the sort of stones they used for railway bridges and tunnels. At the top of the bank, where thick bushes met the wall, it was only about three feet high. There was a tree growing right beside the wall, and Poppy swung herself easily up onto the top of it using a branch of the tree. She waited for Jack and Alex to do the same, then leaned over and showed Max where he could put his feet to reach the branch. They emerged from the bushes onto a gravel track that led up from the metal gates they had passed earlier, and swung round in a hairpin bend just to their left.

"The quarry is divided into two main parts," said Poppy, walking backwards to talk to them like a tour guide. "You can see the lower part down there, look, but keep back from the edge."

The boys gingerly approached the edge of the track where a barbed wire fence and some gorse bushes marked the edge of the quarry. It was a long way down. The boys peered over into the enormous hole where the rock of the hill had been dug away in chunks like the boulders in front of the lime kilns. The floor of the quarry was about seventy meters below. The walls were sheer cliffs of rock. The scale of the hole was vast, and it took a while to appreciate that what looked like bushes on the far side and at the bottom were actually trees. And the more they stared at the rock, the more detail they saw; striations in the composition of the rock; places where structures had once been attached, rusty metal plates, grooves and pipes, patches that had been bricked up. About twenty meters in from the base of the cliff was a sort of platform, like at a railway station, probably used for loading the stone onto lorries or maybe even a train in years gone by.

"Wow!" said Alex, with Max once more emulating his brother a second later. "I feel like Barney at the start of

Stig of the Dump. I feel like I'm going to fall over the edge!"

"Except there's no rubbish down there; it's not a rubbish dump," said Poppy.

"Wait," said Alex, "you didn't say there were no cavemen down there!" They all laughed, although Jack noticed that Poppy's face bore a certain expression, as if she was about to say something in reply.

"How do we get down?" asked Alex.

"Not here," replied Poppy, starting to walk off along the track, "come this way."

To their right, a grassy footpath led off between trees and brambles, and the track led straight on to become the floor of the second level of the quarry. A cliff rose abruptly on their right, behind a scree of earth, rocks and bushes. To their left, another track, just wide enough for a car, curved around the top of the lower level, with trees on both sides, their branches touching in the middle. They walked on as the space around them opened up.

"This is incredible!" said Jack, staring all around him. "This must be what it's like walking out into Twickenham or Wembley!"

The floor of the upper level was a mixture of uneven mud and gravel strewn with small rocks, and swathes of long, course grass. At the far end was a hummock of earth with a tree growing on the top of it, and on the far side the track could be seen climbing the rock face at a gentle gradient. Above the cliff were more thick trees. It was a magical, secret place, Jack thought, like the tiny cove they had been to in Wales before Max and Sam were born, where he and Zander had had the whole of the beach to themselves.

"I can imagine a Stig living here," said Max.

"Yes; or trolls and hobbits and things," said Jack.

"What's in that cave over there?" asked Alex.

"Nothing, it's empty."

"How deep does it go? Let's go and see; it looks like Stig's cave!"

Alex ran to the far side of the quarry through the long grass. Not far from the tree on the mound of earth was a low cave in the rock. When the others arrived, Alex was stepping carefully over the loose rocks on the floor of the cave. After the glare of the open sky, it was very dark inside.

"Be careful!" came Max's shaky voice. "Poppy, is it safe in there? You hear about kids getting trapped in mine shafts."

"It's quite safe, and anyway, this isn't a mine shaft, it's a quarry. They're not the same thing."

"Hellooooo," came Alex's voice, like a ghost in a Scooby-Doo cartoon.

They all crept into the cave, Jack and Poppy having to crouch a little because the ceiling was so low. They hadn't gone more than five meters when Alex said he'd reached the end. They could hear him feeling along the cave wall, making sure there weren't any more tunnels.

"We'll have to bring torches next time," he said as they emerged once more into the sunshine, "have a really good look around."

"I can see why you come here to play," Jack said to Poppy, "it really is a fantastic place. Does anybody else ever come here?"

"I don't just come here to play," said Poppy, sounding a little bit indignant, "I come here to think and to be alone

21

sometimes. Not many people really come here that often. There are lots of footpaths and hill walks and so on around here, and one of them goes from the end of my road up that edge of the cliff and along the top of the hill to Churchill village. There's a pub there that all the walkers stop at. And there's an outward bound centre in Sandford, they sometimes do abseiling and climbing and stuff here, sometimes in the evenings with the scouts. I like to hide and watch."

"We might be joining the scouts, our dad said so," said Alex.

"I don't want to!" said Max.

"*I don't want to!*" imitated Alex in a whiney voice.

"Shut up, Zander!" said Jack, determined to keep the peace in front of Poppy. He knew how easily his brothers wound each other up. "You might be too young, Max, we'll have to see. But I bet it will be fun. I wonder what else they get up to. Camping, I'll bet; and lighting fires –"

"And helping old ladies cross the road," laughed Alex.

"Oh, shut up, will you, Zander!" said Jack, pushing him in the shoulder. "You're so lucky being an only child!" he said to Poppy.

"I'll show you the way down to the lower level," Poppy suggested. "We can climb up this bank to the track. It's a short cut."

"Is there anything up the top there?" asked Jack. The tracks seemed a little too well maintained to have been abandoned when the quarry closed.

"Not much," shrugged Poppy. "Rocks and grass, and a view of the sea. The gypsies camp there twice a year. They'll be coming again, soon."

She led them round the far edge of the lower chasm, where the track dropped more steeply through the trees and met the floor of the quarry by the main gates. The boys inspected some rusted cutting gear, abandoned and overgrown by the side of the track. Drums with large, metal teeth in a spiral pattern set on a huge pair of forks; the boys could just imagine them crunching away at the rock. This lower section was deeper and narrower than the upper section, and the boys felt a frisson of vulnerability with so much rock towering above them. Looking up at the edge they had first looked over, they could see coloured markers and metal clips, obviously used by the climbers and abseilers. 'How scary would it be to climb up there?' wondered Alex. Jack was marvelling at the sheer volume of rock that men had dug away and used to build who knew what.

They ran over to the brick and concrete platform, climbing onto it like kings of the castle. They had competitions seeing who could jump off it the furthest, and Poppy joined in. It was different sharing her special place with other children. It was fun. The three older children were all fairly evenly matched. Even though he was a year younger than Jack and Poppy, Alex was a very fast runner, and was fearless in his approach to the jumps. Max soon got bored because he was much smaller than the others and couldn't jump nearly as far.

"I'm hungry," said Max. "Can we go back now? Daddy said we could have fish and chips, remember!"

Alex started to imitate Max again, but Jack told him to leave their brother alone.

"He just wants to see if mummy has arrived yet, that's all!" he said, and Max lunged at him with his foot.

23

"We'd better get back," said Jack. "I'm feeling a bit hungry, too, and we've been out quite a long time for such a small street to explore," he laughed.

They followed Poppy back along the gravel track to the bushes at the top of the lime kilns, then one by one swung down from the tree branch, Jack taking Max by the waist as he dangled, and lowering him carefully to the ground. Poppy retrieved her ball from the goal mouth, and walked with the boys down the steps to the path that led to the houses.

"Can we see you again, Scout?" asked Jack with a smile.

"Sure. You know where to find me," Poppy smiled back.

As the boys descended the rest of the steps, they caught a glimpse of the removal lorry rounding the bottom of Wimblestone Road.

Chapter Three
Settling In

Jack had been right; their mum was in a bad mood when she arrived with Sam. After the excitement of the afternoon, and the delicious fish and chips, it rather spoiled the end of their first day. Their dad had decided that the bigger bedroom at the front of the house would be better for the three older children; the bunk beds and Max's single had fitted better in there, giving the boys more floor space for their toys and things. He and the removal men had built all the beds and put the double in the second bedroom, and Sam's cot and changing station in the smallest room, next to it.

"But the airing cupboard is in the front room, with the heating and hot water controls. How practical is it to have that in the children's room? And the wardrobe is much bigger in the front room; what about all our clothes? You just don't think things through, do you? Why didn't you consult me? Hmm? You could have phoned, couldn't you?"

When Mr Pearson was tired, as he clearly was after helping the removal men all day, he was no match for his wife; he just seemed to let her rant on at him with no defence. Not that there was ever much you could say to Mrs Pearson when she was on a roll. It wasn't that he stopped listening, though, because the children could tell that everything she said made him shrink a little further into himself.

"If I'm not here, nothing gets done, does it?" she continued in her high pitched drone. "And where was my

25

fish and chips? Didn't you think I might be hungry after driving all that way? Hmm? What do you mean 'you didn't know what time I was going to arrive'? Eh? You. Could. Have. Phoned. Couldn't you? Hmm? What do you mean 'I could have phoned when I was setting off'? Why do I have to do everything?"

And then, just like that, like a light switch being turned on or off, she could change completely and be a normal person, all sweetness and light, asking the boys what they thought of the new house, and how they had spent their afternoon. But the boys could still see the effect she'd had on their dad, and it kept them subdued. They just said that they had met a girl called Poppy, kicked a ball around, and explored the woods a bit. They wanted to keep the quarry a secret, and didn't want to get into trouble. They got washed and changed into their pyjamas, brushed their teeth, and climbed into their beds, Jack on the top bunk, Alex below, and Max on the other side of the room. Their dad had unpacked some of their toys and books, and arranged them in their Ikea units. Their mum chose a Famous Five story, one of Max's favourites, and read the first three chapters. The boys all felt a connection to the story, because the chapters dealt with the gang going to stay in a strange house, meeting new children, and wanting to explore. The tired boys fell asleep to the sound of more arguing and unpacking, all three of them thinking about the quarry.

The next morning they awoke to an eerie noise. There was no traffic, no shouts from the street, no aircraft passing overhead, just a low sort of moaning.

"Jack? Zander? Are you awake?" whispered Max. "What's that noise? Can you hear it?"

"I don't know. Maybe it's a bird." Said Jack, disinterested.

"Birds don't sound like that. Those other, chirpy noises are birds, listen."

"Don't know, then."

"Do you think it's a ghost?"

"Don't be daft."

"Oooh," moaned Alex, "I'm the ghost of Wimblestone Road, I'm going to eat Max, oooh!"

"Shut up Zander! I'm going to tell mum!"

"Don't wake Sam, Max!" warned Jack.

"Come on Jack," said Alex, a couple of minutes later, throwing off his duvet and rolling out of the bottom bunk, "let's get dressed and have breakfast, then maybe we'll be able to go back to the quarry."

When they went downstairs, Max was already in the dining room tucking into an enormous bowl of cereal, still in his pyjamas. Jack and Alex sat down and began to help themselves. Through the dining room window, the hill behind the farm crouched like an animal, the movement of the trees in the wind making it look like it was breathing.

"Dad said it wasn't a ghost, it was a wood pigeon," Max informed them through a mouthful of hoops.

"Doesn't mean it won't still eat you!" said Alex, making Jack grin.

Their mum came into the dining room and put Sam in his high chair. "Good morning, boys, did you sleep well? I couldn't settle for ages; I missed all the noise, isn't that strange?" She gave Sam a handful of dry hoops on his tray, while she went to prepare his breakfast puree. Sam

27

stuffed them into his mouth methodically, grinning and babbling at his big brothers.

"Right, boys," said their mum, pulling up a stool in front of Sam. "After breakfast I want you to unpack your suitcases and put everything away tidily. I've left some more boxes of your stuff in your room, and I want you to put it where you want it: and, Zander, the middle of the floor can't be where you want it, ok? I don't want you to take all day about it, either. We need to go shopping later. I thought we could see what's what in Weston."

The boys groaned in unison.

"The quicker we get settled, the quicker we'll be back to normal, and the sooner you'll be able to go and play and make new friends. You don't want to be looking for things in boxes once school starts, do you? And that reminds me; we need to get your uniforms sorted."

It didn't take the boys long at all to put their things in order. There were the usual squabbles as they got in each other's way or argued about whose things were whose and what could go on which shelf, but the incentive of the good weather they were missing and the freedom to explore the quarry again kept them more or less on task and unusually cooperative.

They all went into Weston-super-Mare after lunch. It was a typical seaside town, full of holidaymakers dressed for the beach: loud excited children and parents carrying far too much stuff. They followed the flow of traffic and ended up driving along the sea front. The tide was a long way out, and the golden sand was taken up with families enjoying the sun. There was so much beach, that even with the huge numbers of people, everybody seemed to have plenty of space, and it didn't look crowded at all.

There were a number of donkeys giving children rides on their backs, and quite a few pulling carts decorated like Thomas the tank Engine or space rockets. Lots of kids were kicking or throwing balls and flying kites. It seemed crazy to the boys that they weren't on holiday; this was their home, now, and they were just out shopping. They drove past the pier, past sweet shops and amusement arcades and countless fish and chip shops, then they pulled into a car park opposite a huge stone archway. Jack went with his dad to the pay and display machine while Mrs Pearson got the rest of them out of the car and put Sam in his buggy. There was a poster on the ticket machine for 'Circus Zyair', showing clowns, acrobats and three motorcycles under a traditional Big Top tent.

"Can we go, dad?" asked Jack.

"Maybe," said Mr Pearson, looking at the dates and prices, and also working out the charges for the parking.

"Meaning 'no'," muttered Jack.

"Meaning 'maybe'," said his dad. "Things are going to be different, now. Start of a new life. 'Maybe' means 'if we haven't missed it' and 'if it's not ridiculously expensive' and 'if there are tickets available', ok? Don't turn into a pessimist just because you're almost a teenager." He ruffled Jack's hair, then paid for two hours.

"We'll have a look along the front," he said, as he stuck the ticket on the dashboard, "see what's what, get an ice cream, then we'll park in Tesco's and do the important stuff."

"I saw you looking at the girl in the leotard!" said his wife, quietly but vehemently as they crossed the car park.

"I was looking at the poster. Jack wants to go."

"I know what you were looking at!" she said, and moved ahead to catch up with the boys.

"Start of a new life…" muttered Mr Pearson to himself.

Next to the car park was a playground with a waterpark, a fort, and a café. Children were running and splashing under an assortment of fountains and water jets, droplets sparkling like diamonds in the sunshine. It looked fun but was quite busy, and none of them had brought swimming trunks or towels. Mr Pearson got them all an ice cream from the café, and they carried on walking. Next to the waterpark was a crazy golf course, and Mrs Pearson sat with Sam eating their ice creams while the rest of the family had a round of golf. Jack and his dad were evenly matched. Alex was a bit overenthusiastic, spending half his time retrieving his ball from the flower beds, but also getting two holes-in-one by sheer fluke. Somehow, Max finished the round with the lowest score, and was really pleased with himself.

Beyond the crazy golf there was a row of noisy hotels and bars with outdoor dining areas. Most had music playing, and one had karaoke blaring, so they crossed over, through the arch, to the promenade. This side of the pier was like a little harbour, and there were boats lying keeled over on the wet sand, and what looked like a flat bottomed ferry lay moored to the sea wall that joined the promenade to a small island. On the other side of the road to the island was a lake with its own little beach. This small beach was much more crowded, with families just having picnics while mostly younger children splashed and paddled in the shallow water, quite a few using paddle boards and dinghies. There was a slipway down to the lake, and at the top, on one side was a hut selling

30

everything for the beach including paddle boards and all kinds of inflatable craft such as dolphins and crocodiles, and on the other side was a real life-boat next to an RNLI hut.

They walked down the slip ramp and around the lake in the hot sun. The far side of the lake was a dam with a causeway running along the top, keeping the water in the lake while the tide was out. Their dad explained that when the tide came back in, it would come right up to the causeway, and even completely cover it in a very high tide or a storm. This sounded very exciting, and Jack, Alex and Max all agreed they wanted to try and cross it during a high tide. Sammy was fascinated by the water, by all the bright sparkles on the little waves, and by all the children laughing and shouting. The air here was hot but fresh, different and more pleasant than London. There was room for the wind to blow, and there was that holiday aroma of salt and sand and chips. The three older boys were interested in the islands visible in the Bristol Channel, and what the land mass was on the hazy horizon.

"Is that Ireland, dad?" asked Jack.

"Is it America?" asked Alex.

Mr Pearson said that it was Wales, and that the buildings they could see might be Cardiff, but he'd have to look at a map to be certain. They climbed the steps at the end of the causeway, and walked round the island which seemed to be home to a hotel or flats and a couple of cafés. The sea air and the ice-cream must have been working some kind of magic because no one was in a hurry or a bad temper. All things considered, this was much more relaxed and cheerful than the trips to supermarkets in Hounslow and Isleworth used to be.

They walked along the beach past the ferry and stranded fishing boats. A stream came trickling out of a tunnel in the sea wall and meandered across the sand towards the incoming tide, and the boys jumped back and forth over it, laughing and measuring who had jumped the furthest. Alex wanted to explore the tunnel, but it was blocked by an iron grid half a meter from the entrance. Near the big stone arch the sea wall jutted out to accommodate another café, and Mrs Pearson used the shade of this feature to look at her phone while the boys climbed all over the granite slabs artistically arranged as seating.

"Right," she said to Mr Pearson, over the hubbub of the boys and the beach, "I've found the school shop, and the outdoor place for the scouts. Let's go to Tesco and I'll get them sorted while you buy the groceries. Then we'll head back. This sea air really takes it out of you, doesn't it?"

When they returned home, Jack helped his dad bring the shopping bags in while Alex helped his mum put the things away. Max set the dining room table ready for tea, and Sam sat in his high chair munching on some chopped up fruit. His attention seemed to be thoroughly fixed on something in the garden. Max paused to follow his gaze, and met the stare of a large, shabby cat sitting imperiously on the pile of wooden panels that would be their shed.

"Look at that, Sammy! That's a big cat, isn't it? What's it doing on our shed? Can you say 'cat'?"

"Ga!" said Sam, pointing a slice of squished banana with his chubby arm.

"And what was that?" mumbled Max going over to the window.

"Stop daydreaming, Maxie, and bring the beakers through, please. Plenty of time for gazing when the table is set," said his mum.

When he had finished setting the table, Max nipped outside and ran up the steps past the utility room to the top of the garden. The cat was still there, but it wasn't the cat that Max was interested in now. He went cautiously over to the hedge at the back of the bits of shed, and peered into the narrow gap beneath the leaves.

"Hello, young man," came a voice from the other side of the hedge.

An old man, heavily built, was smiling at him from the front of the greenhouse behind their garden.

"Lost something? A football? If I find any, I'll know where they've come from." He laughed.

"No, um, I was just...it's not a ball or anything." Max got quite shy around strangers.

"Where have you come from? Are you settling in ok?" The man seemed friendly enough, and now he had been joined by an old woman with narrow eyes and a nose like an unwashed parsnip.

"London," said Max. "We haven't seen much round here yet. Only the quarry and the beach."

"You be careful in the quarry, mind," said the man. "And you tell your dad, if he needs any help with anything, he just has to ask, ok? Here, give these to yer mum. Tell her Mr Dodds had too much ripen all at once in his greenhouse, an' thought she might like these." He handed Max two huge cucumbers and a tub of tomatoes.

Max had been taught never to accept anything from strangers, but he thought that probably applied more to drugs and things in London, not vegetables from a neighbour. He thanked Mr Dodds and took the surplus food into the kitchen.

"Oh, how kind!" said his mum. "Is he still there?" and without waiting for a reply, she hurried out into the garden to thank him.

When Max went back into the dining room, the cat had gone, and there was nothing to be seen in the garden.

Chapter 4

The Strawberry Line

The next day was Saturday, and there was a little bit more activity in the street. A woman from the house across the road came over to speak to Mrs Pearson while she was hanging the washing on the line. She had a son who didn't go to the local school and so didn't know many children in the village, and she wondered if he could come over and meet the new arrivals. Sam and Max were playing in Sam's little house on the patio, and mum invited him to join them. Stephen was a few months older than Max, but they were in the same school year. Stephen's mum worked away much of the time, and Stephen was often looked after by his Gran in a nearby village, so it was easier for him to go to school there.

"Can I take Stephen up to my room, mum?" asked Max, delighted to have someone his own age to play with. He loved Sam, but there wasn't much he could do without spoiling it and trying to bite it, and the older boys were always better at everything and teasing him. So at his mum's nod, the two raced upstairs to play with tanks and soldiers.

Jack and Alex were helping their dad to erect the garden shed. While he was holding the panels for dad to screw them together, Jack saw Poppy cycle past the fence, first one way, then the other. She cycled up and down the road a couple of times, looking like she was just casually riding around, but she kept glancing over at them as if she was hoping to make contact. When all four walls were up, Jack ran out onto the side path to see if he could catch her.

"Are you busy, yeah?" she asked, disappointedly.

"Just got to put the roof on, then we're probably done. Do you want to go to the quarry again?"

"No, the outward bound people are all over it today. I can show you the village, though. Have you been on the Strawberry Line yet?"

"The what?" asked Jack. "Why don't you come into the garden while we finish the shed?"

Poppy dismounted and wheeled her bike to the grass that wrapped round the side of the house, then followed Jack shyly through the gate. Jack introduced her to his mum and dad, and to Sam who came crawling through the door of his little house to see her. She immediately picked him up for a cuddle, and he chuckled and pulled her hair with sticky fingers.

"Would you like a cold drink, Poppy?" asked Mrs Pearson. "I was just going to fetch a jug of squash for the boys, they've been working very hard."

When the shed roof had been secured and they had finished all the squash in big, thirsty gulps, Jack asked mum if they could play on their bikes with Poppy.

"I was thinking of making sandwiches and going to the water park in Weston for the afternoon. You said you liked the look of it."

"Barlubaarpk!" burped Alex.

"Alexander Pearson!" said his mum sternly, while the three children tried to suppress their laughter with bursting cheeks. "Well, I suppose I could see if Stephen would like to come and keep Max company. What will you do for lunch? Will you wait while I make sandwiches for you?"

"Umm, could we have 'em later?" asked Jack.

"Alright. I'll leave them in the shed with an ice block, ok? Where will you be playing?"

"I thought I would show them round the village, Mrs Pearson," said Poppy. "There's a path that used to be a railway line; it goes the length of the village, so we won't be on any main roads. We'll be quite safe."

"Ok, then. Enjoy yourselves, and be careful. Don't leave Poppy – I don't want you getting lost."

"Yes, mum!" said the boys in a stop-embarrassing-us tone of voice.

They fetched their bikes and joined Poppy on the pavement. Poppy was staring at Jack's street BMX.

"I know, pretty sick, innit?" said Jack proudly. It was matt black with luminous green grips and pedals, and smooth, fat tyres. The seat was fixed as low as it could go, and set at steep angle.

"It'll be alright for the skate park," she said, "but you might be better with a mountain bike for the Strawberry line, if we want to go any distance."

"Distance?"

"The path goes all the way from Cheddar to Yatton, and it's not all smooth and flat."

"Oh, we'll be alright," said Jack, including Alex on his smaller BMX.

Poppy still thought they looked mighty uncomfortable. She set off down the hill, branching off past the bungalows to where the road became a narrow country lane. The boys followed, standing on their pedals to go up the hill, while Poppy rode easily, shifting down her gears. They crossed carefully onto Ibex lane, past a house whose gate was overgrown with ivy, and whose garage door had a small fir tree growing in front of it through the tarmac. There was no For Sale sign visible.

"Does no one live there?" asked Jack, "It looks abandoned."

"Don't know," said Poppy.

"There is that other property at the bottom of the hill, isn't there, that looks unfinished. Well, the house looks finished on the outside, but there is no driveway, and it's all overgrown and that. Seems odd when there are so many people looking for houses, building new estates everywhere, and these houses are just sitting empty, not even up for sale?"

"I suppose. But there are a few more in the village, we'll see a couple from the Strawberry Line. I guess it is a bit weird."

"Do you know what I think?" asked Jack.

"Here we go!" said Alex.

"I think houses like that, that appear derelict or abandoned but never have anything done to them by the council or whatever...I reckon they're wizards' houses, charmed to look abandoned so the wizards can live there undisturbed by muggles."

"Like Grimald Place in *The Order of the Phoenix*?"

"Yeah, exactly, you've got it!"

"It's a good theory, I'll give you that." Said Poppy. "I love the Harry Potters; have you read them all?"

They talked about the books they had read as they cycled over an arched bridge with stone walls like the side of the lime kilns, then Poppy slowed to a halt. Before them, the road became a rutted earth track between fields that filled the valley between two sets of hills. There was a wide gate leading to a cemetery and remembrance garden on their left, and just between that and the bridge was a narrow footpath.

"Look, there's Crook Peak," said Alex to Jack, as he skidded to a stop next to his brother.

"Up there's Banwell Castle and the old bone caves," said Poppy, pointing to the hill on their right.

"A castle? And bone caves? Like the one in the quarry?" asked Alex excitedly. "Where? I can't see anything."

"That's because you're a muggle," laughed Jack.

"Behind those trees. And they're bigger than the Stig cave, that's just a hole, really. These are more like grottos, like the cave systems in Cheddar. Apparently, when the lord of the castle found them in the 1800s, they were full of bones."

"Human bones?"

"No, prehistoric animals. They think bears must have lived there, and the bears ate lots of other animals and left their bones lying on the floor of the cave."

"Wait till we tell Max tonight!" cried Alex, gleefully. "He won't sleep! Yesterday, he thought the wood pigeon outside was a ghost come to eat him!"

They all laughed, then Poppy set off again along the footpath by the cemetery. The narrow earthen path dropped quickly down to a wider track of packed stones that obviously came from under the bridge behind them.

"This is what they call The Strawberry Line. It used to be a railway line that took strawberries and other fruit from Somerset up to Bristol, then on to London. Most of it has been converted into a path, now, and you can go pretty much from Cheddar to Yatton. I think they are planning to open it up further, too. The old line went as far as Wells, I think, and maybe Clevedon, right on the coast."

The path took them past the backs of large houses with balconies and long gardens to their left, and fields of cattle on their right. There was a little kink in the path, a blind corner past a tall garden fence with an apple tree overhanging it. Poppy rang her bell and pulled tight to the fence before going round, and a brown nose bearing white teeth barked furiously through a hole at the bottom.

"You can tell it used to be a railway by how straight and flat most of it is," shouted Poppy, as the houses and fields dropped away from them, and they were now on a high embankment looking over the roofs to the Hills beyond. Between two small housing estates, a stone cottage stood in a large garden full of apple trees and meadow flowers. Steep steps from the estate joined the path, and then there was a thick bramble hedge along the top of the bank, and a small wood below them on their right. They were just level with the tree canopy.

Poppy pulled over and began to pick blackberries from the hedge. "These are delicious," she said, "try some. I eat them every day."

The boys tried them, and they were indeed delicious. They ate the berries for a few minutes, while some people with dogs passed them and said a friendly 'hello'.

"I think we should rename this the blackberry line!" said Alex, his mouth and hands full of fruit.

Trees grew up the bank on either side now, and the embankment widened out, although the path itself didn't change. A worn line in the grass broke off diagonally and ran past some old railway sleepers around a rusted crane pedestal, and Poppy took it, effortlessly shifting down a couple of gears. The boys followed, jumping their bikes over the uneven ground, and standing on their pedals again to keep up. They passed a concrete sculpture set in the long grass, which Poppy said had been built for the millennium, and then they were on a wide expanse of packed earth with a few benches and a sign warning that no cycling was allowed on the station green. Poppy wheeled to a halt under an expansive tree which looked great for climbing, and put her bike down next to a bench.

"This used to be the railway station for the village. Now it's a picnic area and where they hold the village fetes. Down that path, there, is the community centre and playing field; there is a youth club there on Thursdays during term time, and it's great fun. You can see the fire station there, too, with its training tower. Come this way, we can leave our bikes here, they'll be ok."

Further along station green, the original platform rose out of the ground. There were a set of old buffers in a siding, with a silver birch tree growing in front of them, and then the platform with its paved edge running alongside the cycle path. There was a commemorative information board which the boys looked at, and brass strips set at uneven intervals into the paving slabs, marked with dates and historical events. In the centre of the platform, the original front of the station had been preserved, laid flat in the ground, so that you could walk over the bricks and balance along the window ledges. Alex got down into a crouch and pretended to be spider man walking up the wall, and Jack pretended to be embarrassed by him in front of his new friend.

Poppy led them down what would have been the station road but was now pedestrianised with wide wooden barriers. They came to the main road where there were some terraced houses, an optician's and a travel agents, and some public toilets surrounded by a small garden.

"Hang on a sec, you two," said Alex, disappearing into the gents.

"Typical," said Jack. He and Poppy sat on a bench by the garden to wait for him.

"Do you believe in wizards, Jack?" asked Poppy, swinging her feet self-consciously, and not looking at him.

"Um, yeah, kind of," he replied. "You know, when I'm reading something like Harry Potter I like to immerse myself in that world, really believe in everything, you know. And part of me wants it to be real, to be true, even the story about Harry and Voldemort and everything; part of me likes the idea of a wizarding world and being able to use magic, even if there's a rational side of my brain that says it can't be, it's just fiction." He paused for a second, looking up into the sky, then carried on. "But if you think about it, the idea must have come from somewhere. I mean, every culture in the world has tales of magic, wizards, magicians, witch doctors; people have believed in magic for centuries, probably longer than they've believed in god. I mean, how old is Merlin and the legend of King Arthur, the sword in the stone and all that? Then there's ghosts and vampires and werewolves. All the modern horror story stuff isn't modern at all. That's got to count for something."

"And do you believe in ghosts as well? And vampires and werewolves? What about Hobbits? And Stig?"

Jack laughed. "I think Stig and the Lord of the Rings are just stories, but I think Tolkien's ideas came from older notions. I think he created Hobbits as a kind of symbolic representation of how he wanted people to be, but he didn't invent elves or dwarves or dragons or any of that stuff. And, yes, I think I do believe in ghosts and parallel universes and all sorts of things that maybe most people can't see. Don't you?"

"You two comfy there?" asked Alex.

"You took your time!" said Jack.

"Right," said Poppy jumping up from the bench, "come on!"

She led them up the main road where they could see a barbers, butchers, pharmacist and a Co-op on the corner.

"Wait, I know where we are!" said Jack, gleefully. "The chippy is just round that corner, innit?"

"That's right. This is the centre of the village." She crossed over near the pharmacy, and walked up round the corner. "Here is the library, and there are a couple of good charity shops to buy cheap books. You'll have seen the Indian next to the chip shop, and there's a good Chinese up there. That road at the end of the street goes down to the rec, but we're going to carry on along the strawberry line and get to it that way. There is a Spa shop there which is good for sweets, cheaper than the Co-op, but the bakery is even better. Got any money on you?"

"No," said both boys together.

"Don't worry, you can pay me back another time."

They crossed back over the road in front of the 'Caxton Library', some sort of newsagent with brown painted woodwork and a shop window so dusty and dirty it was tinged yellow, the old and faded magazines on display only just visible – it had to be a wizarding shop. Jack half expected the Weasley twins to emerge through its brown door, sharing Every Flavour Beans or something. Next to this, however, was Poppy's favourite shop in the whole village, the bakery. The door stood open in its little mosaic recess, and as Poppy entered, she was greeted by the lady behind the counter.

"Hello, Poppy, my dear, how are you today? Brought some new friends, I see. Well, well."

The glass counter was full of buns and cream cakes, slices, flapjacks, enormous scones, doughnuts, dough rings, muffins and gingerbread shapes, all freshly baked, and the boys were practically drooling. It suddenly occurred to their stomachs that they hadn't had any lunch.

"Can I have a Danish, please, Mrs Bradley?"

"Of course, my dear. And anything for these two?"

Feeling very awkward that they hadn't got their own money, and secretly wishing they could have one of everything, Jack and Alex chose a Mars muffin and a jam doughnut. Poppy paid, and Mrs Bradley put each cake in its own striped paper bag, and handed them over the counter.

"Thanks very much," the boys said as they all left the shop and walked back down to the strawberry line. They could see that the road ahead narrowed through an old bridge just past the public toilets, and people were cycling over the bridge along the line. Through the archway, Poppy pointed out the other wizards' houses she had mentioned. The structures looked sound, but uninhabited, half hidden by very overgrown gardens, but not vandalised or turned into squats like they would have been in Isleworth. Just ignored. It really was very peculiar, Jack thought; they were inconspicuous enough to go unnoticed as the average person drove past, but to a mind as curious and observant as a child's they stood out like sore thumbs. Definitely a magical conspiracy of some kind!

The children took their buns up to the picnic area and sat at one of the benches in the shade of the hawthorn tree. They could see that their bikes had been left untouched under the climbing tree, and as soon as he had gobbled his doughnut, Alex was aloft himself.

"You never answered my question, you know," said Jack, as they ate their buns more slowly.

"What question?"

"About whether you believe in ghosts and wizards and goblins."

"No, I didn't, did I?" she teased. "I think I can trust you," she said, "I'm just not sure about anyone else." She looked at the tree, whose upper branches were shaking with Alex's explorations.

"So you do then?"

"Oh, I don't know. Yes, I agree with what you said about believing it on one level, getting absorbed in a story or whatever. And, in church on Sundays, I used to pray to Aslan rather than God. But, there are also things I've seen that I can't explain. Or maybe I've just imagined it. It sounds stupid when I say it out loud. But, yeah, I think you're right, you know, about how old the legends all are; and maybe they must have come from somewhere other than people's imaginations."

"What about UFOs? Do you believe in aliens?"

"Yeah, I guess so."

"Do you want to know a strange fact?"

"Ok." Poppy's attention suddenly sharpened.

"You know my dad works at the airport, yeah? Well, you know they have radar screens and that to show the positions and trajectories of the planes? I bet you didn't know that those radar screens are filtered."

"Filtered? What do you mean?"

"Well, when they first started using radar to track planes, obviously there weren't so many planes flying in those days, the screens would sometimes pick up images that couldn't possibly have been planes: things that weren't where any of the planes should have been; things moving too fast to be planes; things changing direction too sharply, you know? So now, these things are so common and so distracting to air traffic control that they have computer programs that filter them out and only show actual known, terrestrial aircraft. But they are there. In the background. And the military keep track of them, but it's all classified, and people like my dad are just told to forget about it. But dad's got lots of books on sightings and research and so on."

Poppy was stunned. She looked at Jack in awe.

"So I kind of think that there could be anything, you know, extra-terrestrial or supernatural, or 'magic', and the general public wouldn't know about it."

"There's something I really want to show you," said Poppy, eagerly, "and so much to talk about, but it's in the opposite direction to the rec. Do you think your parents would let you come on another bike ride tomorrow?"

"I don't see why not, if the weather stays like this."

"Great. Let's get the bikes and I'll show you the skate park."

"Cool! And thanks again for the muffin a[nd] doughnut," said Jack, scrunching up all their p[...] and posting them into the litter bin.

"There's a café where the strawberry line joins the s[...] at Yatton; you can buy me a coke tomorrow, if you li[...] She smiled as she picked up her bike.

"Come on Zander, you great baboon, we're going to the skate park," shouted Jack.

e Discovery

waterpark, guys," said their
and Alex were in the back
up Sam's slide. They had eaten
out of the cool bag about half an hour
having spent most of the afternoon at the rec and
cycling with Poppy. "So what did you pair get up to?"

The boys told their parents and Max about where they had been in the village; about the strawberry line, the blackberries, the library and the bakery, and about the station green and the youth club.

"And there's a wonderful climbing tree at the station, even Max could get to the top," said Alex.

"Then," Jack continued, "when you go further down, over the bridge on the main road, you come to the rec. The football, rugby, cricket and tennis clubs are there, and there is a playpark, too, with great things for Sam and Max, and a skate park with half-pipes and boxes and everything."

"Yeah," added Alex, "and it wasn't crowded, and I did some awesome jumps, dad!"

"See, we're not so far from civilisation, are we?" Laughed Mr Pearson.

"I dunno," said Jack, "I think the comics in the newsagents were probably on sale when you were a kid."

"Then, if you carry on past the rec," continued Alex, "first you go into this steep cutting, and there are tracks up the bank which are great fun on a BMX, then you go through this long, dark tunnel, then you come to some woods, and there is a path through the woods that takes you out onto the Mendips and all the way up to Crook Peak, Poppy says."

"And apparently, in the other direction, you can go all the way to Yatton, and there's a café at the station there. Poppy has asked if we can go there tomorrow."

"Can we, dad?"

"Well, let's see," he said, as their mum disappeared into the kitchen. "I think mum had something exciting planned for tomorrow, but maybe you two have outgrown soft-play. And it's good that you're making friends already. We'll discuss it over dinner."

Mrs Pearson came back into the garden, looking very business-like. "Right, lasagne's in the oven, dinner will be in three quarters of an hour. Can you three sort the DVDs and PlayStation games out? The boxes are in the lounge. When you've put everything away, you can choose a film for movie night tonight. I'm going to feed Sam now."

"Yay, movie night!" cried Max.

"So did you have a good time at the water park with Stephen?" Jack asked Max as they went through to the lounge.

"Yeah, he's pretty cool, and he gets lonely in the holidays. We played in that fort we saw, and dad took us to the crazy golf again, and I beat Stephen, even though he's been there loads of times. Sam just stayed in the water park with all the fountains and jets. We played there for a bit to cool off, but the fort was better. Stephen likes Ninjago, too, and the fort was our temple."

"We're not watching Ninjago again tonight," moaned Alex.

The next morning, Max was excited about going to the adventure park, and little Sam was picking up the vibes. Mr and Mrs Pearson seemed happy, too, which was refreshing. Apparently there was much more to the park than a soft play area; there were farm animals and outdoor attractions, too, and Mrs Pearson thought it would be educational as well as fun, and it was right on their doorstep. She had taken a little bit of convincing to let the older boys go cycling with Poppy, but eventually they had all agreed in the end that the adventure park would be there another day, when it was raining, perhaps, or when Poppy was unavailable.

Mr Pearson gave Jack two ten pound notes, which Jack put in his London Wasps wallet.

"You don't have to spend it all, ok, but if you want to have some cake or something in the café, or browse the charity shops or whatever, that should be enough for the three of you."

"Thanks, dad," he said, stuffing the wallet into the back pocket of his jeans.

"Are you sure it'll be safe in that pocket, while you're riding your bike? Why don't you take a rucksack with a couple of water bottles and put it in there?"

"Because I don't want to look like a geek!" said Jack.

"Well, let Zander have the bag. He can be quite sensible, sometimes. You should always have a drink with you, anyway. And take some sun cream, too."

"What about some flares and a first aid kit? And a tent in case it rains?"

"Don't be cheeky," said Mr Pearson, good-naturedly. "Right, I don't know how long we'll be, a good couple of hours, I suppose, but I'm sure we'll be back before you.

Unless we go somewhere else afterwards," he muttered as an afterthought.

"If I had a phone," began Jack for the umpteenth time, "you'd be able to let me know if you were going to be late."

"Hmmm, maybe," said his dad. "We said we'd get you one for the start of term, didn't we? Maybe it wouldn't hurt for you to get used to it now. I'm just worried you'll lose it out of a back pocket."

"Dad, I'm not a child anymore, I'm thirteen," protested Jack.

"Nearly thirteen," corrected Mr Pearson. "I'll talk to your mother about it, ok?"

Max appeared in the doorway. "Mum says we're waiting in the car and it's hot. Sam's getting wriggly. Can you hurry up?" He trotted back out to the car, and Mr Pearson gave Jack a pat on the shoulder as he turned to leave.

"Ok, have a good time, you two. Zander, can you go and get one of the rucksacks from your bedroom, please? Don't forget to take water bottles and sun cream. Lock the back door and take the key with you. And don't lose it!" he called through the front door as he locked it behind him.

Alex came bounding down the stairs with a union Jack backpack, and the boys went to fill their water bottles at the kitchen sink. Jack zipped the wallet into the front pouch of the bag, and gave it back to his brother.

"You can be in charge of the bag. It's got the money in, so it's very important."

"Ok," said Alex, feeling very mature and responsible.

'Sucker!' thought Jack, with a little smile to himself. He locked the back door and shoved the key right down in his pocket, below his handkerchief, then helped Alex get their

51

bikes out of the shed. There was a large, mottled looking cat sitting on the shed roof. Not basking in the sun on the hot felt, but sitting upright, watching them. And for a strange cat, trespassing as it was, Jack thought it peculiar that it could sit there so calmly as they extracted the bikes and locked up the shed.

At the side of the house, as they closed the garden gate, another cat was watching them from under the large bush. It didn't seem any more bothered by them than the first one. Alex was just asking Jack which way they should go to Poppy's house and whether he thought they could get up the narrow steps with their bikes, when, with a squeak of breaks, she was there at the edge of the pavement. Alex was pleased to see that she had a rucksack over her shoulders, too.

"Hey," she said with a smile.

"Hey!" the boys replied.

"Which way shall we go, Scout?" asked Jack.

"We'll go the way we went yesterday. Fewer hills and no roads. Saddle up, come on!" and she started rolling away from the kerb. The boys jumped on their bikes and rode them down the bank of lawn, past the ever watchful cat, and jumped them off the pavement onto the road, peddling energetically. They zoomed past Poppy, laughing and calling for her to catch up.

When they reached the strawberry line at the bottom of the narrow path, Poppy turned 180 degrees and took them under the bridge they had just crossed. It was shady and cool in the cutting. Trees grew close on either side, and a stream ran along next to them. They rode side by side where they could, tucking in behind each other when it narrowed or when they encountered other people.

"This feels just like Middle Earth," said Jack, "it's like we'll emerge into Hobbiton in a minute, or meet Gandalf with his horse and cart."

The three of them sped happily along, splashing through puddles where the stream had overflowed its ditch. "That's Sandford station up there," said Poppy as the land on their left dropped down and the trees gave way to fields. The track made a bit of a dog-leg and descended in line with the farmland, while on their right they could see an old stone building with some cargo trucks lined up outside, and a development of new houses and flats. "The original building is a museum for the old train line, and these are all retirement homes for old fogeys. It's like a little community. There are a few places like this where the original route of the track has been taken over for other uses since it was abandoned, and so the cycle path has to make a little detour. But you can still get in there to the museum."

They passed through a metal frame designed to reduce cyclists' speed, and free-wheeled down a steep road past a few nice houses. At the bottom of the hill was the road to Banwell and a pedestrian crossing. Across the road, there was a tarmac ramp that led through a wooden zig-zag onto a track of packed earth past another strawberry line information board. This path was clearly still not part of the original track as it wound past the ends of gardens, through an apple orchard, down a valley and up the other side, then came to another lane. Poppy checked for traffic, and turned left, leading the way past a couple of farm houses and more orchards.

"These are all Thatcher's orchards around here, where they grow the apples for the cider. My dad drinks a lot of cider." Poppy couldn't help being a tour guide at times, observed Jack, and the two boys followed her without comment, taking in the smell of the trees and the sight of them, row after row after row. Poppy shifted through her gears again as they climbed a hill that turned out to be another bridge. She stopped at the top, and they all leaned on the stones and surveyed the view.

Away from the hill they lived on, the land was so flat that they could see for miles. It was like looking at a lake with trees and hedges sprouting from it. Straight ahead was a small church with a squat little tower leaning forward at a very dangerous angle. It gave Jack the impression that it was sinking. They looked from both sides of the bridge, seeing where the farms had taken over the original line of the railway that would have run underneath, and where the cycle path re-joined it further along.

"So what are your brothers doing today? Have they gone back into Weston?"

"No, Mum heard of some adventure playground place, something Park? They've gone to see what that's like."

"Puxton Park? I used to love it there. Puxton Farm is just behind those trees over there, look. You turn left by the leaning church, then, if you're on a bike, you can take the second lane on the right and climb over a couple of gates to get into the car park. It's a great place. Mostly for younger kids, but you should check it out, sometime."

They set off down the other side of the bridge in a controlled descent, because the cycle path continued through another metal frame before the road levelled out. Their tyres crunched on the loose white gravel that made up the next section of the path. It was wide enough for the three of them to ride abreast. A copse of trees on their

54

right and a giant oak on their left plunged them into cool shade again, but soon they had to squeeze through a gap in the hedge on their left and ride single file over a stretch of bumpy earth that rose and fell unevenly, worsened by rabbit holes, until they came to an old cattle bridge over the stream. From there, they could see the gravel strawberry line stretching straight ahead in the distance, edged with tall stands of cow parsley and juniper bushes. The path was on an embankment roughly two meters above the fields on either side, and through the gaps in the trees they could see cattle, farms, and the occasional church tower. They passed a bench made from an old railway sleeper, and every few hundred meters there were wide tracks leading down to gates in the fields. One of these tracks ran alongside an algae covered stream, a 'rhyne' as Poppy called it, deep wheel ruts cutting through the lush, long grass. All the time, the only sound was the crunch of their tyres or their own voices. At one point, by a farm gate with mature trees leaning over the cycle path, a lane led off on the right, to the village of Congresbury, Poppy told them. It was cool under the trees, and the children stopped for a drink of water, before setting off again.

Before long, the embankment they had been on for three or four kilometres broadened out, and the path entered a small wood of slim trees and dense ivy. Another information board gave details of birds that now frequented the old station due to the conservation of the trees. Poppy pointed out the edge of the old platform running alongside the path, just like the one at Millennium Green, but this one was overgrown with ivy and only just visible through the waxy green leaves. Above the platform, hidden by more trees and thick creeper, the old station building looked like another wizard's house. "It's like Godric's Hollow round here!" joked Jack, as the three children emerged from the trees at a point where the cycle path came to a crossing over a main road.

"Where's the café?" asked Alex.

"This is still Congresbury. Yatton's not far, now."

Poppy pressed the button on the crossing, and they waited as a tractor and trailer went past. Across the road, the cycle path zigzagged up onto another embankment that followed the road for a couple of hundred meters before crossing a wide river via a narrow bridge. The river was deep and slow flowing, and willows leaned over it, trailing their branches in the water. To their right, vehicles streamed over a stone bridge, and a pub called The Boat had sun umbrellas set out on the bank. A pot holed private road led them past some houses and stables, and the children rode side by side up to a footbridge over another rhyne, and they were once more on the original train line for another kilometre or so. This section seemed popular with joggers and dog walkers, and families with toddlers on balance bikes. Across the fields, they could see Yatton drawing ever closer, the church with its ugly truncated steeple rising above the houses, gardens and allotments. Tall grasses, stands of teasels, and all kinds of wild flowers bordered the path, and butterflies meandered drunkenly through the warm air. The path skirted the village in a gentle arc as the trees once more multiplied into a wood with enticing footpaths leading off the main track. Coming into a clearing, the children passed under a metal outline of an old steam engine decorated with birds and animals, like a shamanic gateway, then they arrived at Yatton station, where the strawberry line would have joined the main line from Exeter and Cornwall to Bristol and beyond. They cycled into the gravel car park as a passenger train arrived from the south.

They leaned their bikes against the aluminium stand by the entrance to the platform, and Poppy chained them together, then led the way into the cool interior of the café.

The café was small inside, and the tables were quite close together. A few customers were leaving through the platform door to board the train, and the children were now the only ones in the café. Alex ceremoniously removed the rucksack and handed Jack his wallet.

"What can I get you, Poppy?" he asked. "I think I'll have a slice of cake. You can have anything you want."

They all ordered a cold fizzy drink and a slice of chocolate fudge cake, and sat down at the largest table. The boys' eyes began to roam over all the black and white photographs framed on the walls, showing the old steam trains and views of the village before pavements and street lights.

"Have you heard of Goblin Combe?" asked Poppy while they waited for their orders to arrive?

"No. What is it?" asked Jack.

"It's a valley the other side of Cleeve, between here and the airport. It's like a nature trail or whatever, and there's an old Iron Age fort on top of the hill."

"And is it full of goblins?" asked Alex excitedly.

"Well, there is an old legend about a little girl who got lost up there while picking primroses with some friends. She started to cry, and a rock opened up and some fairies or goblins came out to comfort her. The story goes that they gave her a golden ball to stop her crying, then, because she was a gentle soul and was carrying primroses, they took her back to her friends, all safe and sound. And when they all got back to the village, an old man heard about the goblins and the gold, and thought he would go and get himself a lot more than one gold ball. So he picked some primroses and sat down by the rock. But the story goes that when the goblins came out of the rock, either he hadn't picked enough primroses, or they could tell he wasn't a gentle soul, because they took him, and he was never seen again."

The two boys didn't know what to say.

"And look. I found this book in the charity shop near the Spa." She pulled an old paperback with a worn, faded cover out of her rucksack, and showed it to the two boys.

"A Somerset Sketch-book by H Hay Wilson," read Jack. Is it drawings?

"No," said Poppy, "the sketches are folk tales a bit like the goblin one, all about people and places in Somerset. Most of them are a bit odd, without real beginnings, middles and ends, even the one about Goblin Combe, but all together they paint a picture that I thought you might find interesting."

She paused while the waitress deposited their drinks and cakes on the table, and they each said 'thank you'. Then there was silence while the three of them sucked hard on the straws in their drinks after the long ride.

"Anyway, the story in here about Goblin Combe isn't the longest or most fascinating one, but it is stated so matter-of-fact. Actually, I think that's what strikes me about these stories; they are more like diary entries really. It's got so much food for thought, and it's so local." She was clearly excited. She hadn't even looked at her cake yet. "I don't know anyone else who likes books and folklore as much as I do, but I think you're like me."

She flipped quickly through the old book, the page she wanted falling open almost immediately.

"Right, now this is interesting, because it starts off by saying that when Christianity came to Britain, paganism ceased to be a religion and became the stuff of legends and fairy tales, and the old gods, like Pan and all the nature spirits retreated into the shadows and went underground; now, people today would interpret that as meaning out of public view, you know, like underground organisations. But I think it is talking about them literally going under the earth, listen," She put her finger to the words on the page and began to read: "'in the days before the seen and unseen world were parted as widely as they are now, the entrances of the elder world were wide and sure.' Then it says here, 'the wild places were full of mystery, and all the solitudes peopled by ghostly presences, friend or fiend.'" She went on to the next page, sweeping her finger over the text: "'When mythology grows old it becomes romance, and this beautiful West Country became the hunting ground of romance in later days. Avalon and Camelot are both in this county of Somerset...' You both know about Camelot?" she looked up at Alex and Jack. Alex nodded, taking the fork out of his mouth and returning it to his half devoured cake; Jack had eaten a couple of bites, but was listening with interest.

"Yes, King Arthur and the round table. I thought that was in Cornwall, though. I'm sure there was stuff about King Arthur at Tintagel when we went there on holiday," he said.

"I think there have been lots of theories, same with everything else, but a number of them point to Glastonbury and the Somerset levels. They think Avalon refers to the river Avon, and the North Somerset county of Avon. Tintagel might just be a castle that he lived in for a while, or even laid siege to; I'm not really sure."

Jack had some more cake, then asked "so what does it say in the book about this Goblin Combe?"

"It says that a man was walking around the Combe and lost his way, when he met a funny looking boy with big ears. The boy smiled, but when the man asked for directions, he didn't reply, just smiled. And when the traveller asked him his name and where he'd come from, he still wouldn't speak. I don't know; there's something about it that just makes me wonder. I mean, as it stands, it's hardly worth writing down, let alone printing in a book. It's as if he wants to say something but is holding back."

"Like what's not being said is more important than what is? It's all implied but not specified?" put in Jack.

"Exactly."

"What are you two on about?" asked Alex, his plate empty, fork licked clean.

"Ugh, brothers!" said Jack, rolling his eyes at Poppy.

They both tucked into their cakes, and Alex watched another train come into the station, this time from the North. Poppy seemed to have run out of steam on the subject of goblins and mythology, possibly because of Alex, who was clearly getting restless now that the cake was finished. As they were leaving the café, Poppy quietly made a detour to a Cancer Research collecting tin, and dropped some coins from her purse into it, with that shuttered, pensive look that often came over her. Jack held the door open for her, but didn't say anything. When she had unlocked their bikes, and while Alex was pulling wheelies around the bottom end of the car park, she suggested to Jack that he might like to borrow the book of sketches.

"It's full of strange characters," she said, "children who appear quite wild and otherworldly. Mysterious places and roads that vanish. Proper folk tales, not just stories."

"Um, yeah, thanks," he said. "Zander," he called, "I'll take the rucksack now, ok? Fair's fair." He caught the bag as his brother cycled past and flung it to him, and zipped the book inside the front pocket with his wallet. "Right, let's go!" he said with a smile.

On the way back, fuelled up with sugar from the cake and fizzy drinks, they raced along the gravel track, overtaking each other and laughing wildly, the boys confident now that they knew the route. From the station to the road, across the wide river, there was enough of a breeze to cool them down, but once they passed the wizard's house, the close cover of trees stifled them.

Alex called out "Can we stop at that bench and have some water?"

Poppy called back, "I've got a better idea." But didn't explain what it was. Before they reached the bench, she gave the hand signal for turning right, and slowed down at a gap in the trees. The boys followed her down the side of the embankment to the track beside the rhyne they had seen earlier.

They leaned their bikes against the hedge at the foot of the slope, just out of the way of the track, and Poppy led them along by the stream.

"Where are we going?" asked Alex.

"Got something else interesting to show you," she said. "And we can sit and have a drink."

Now that they had stopped cycling, the only sounds audible were the birds singing and the wind strumming the leaves of the trees. The air was so fresh, and everything was so green, a million different shades of green that the boys had never really noticed before. There were different greens of grass: broad, dark blades and light, thin blades, and shorter blades in a deep mid-green hue; the leaves of the different trees were different shades, and the same leaves were different colours on the underside when the wind turned them. Then there were sunlit greens and shaded greens. It was incredible. And all this green was broken in places by the dried mud of the track and the dark water of the rhyne. It was a shame about the water, Jack thought. He stepped over to the edge of the little canal, and took a closer look. He was surprised to see that the water was crystal clear, and that what he had taken to be a scum of algae on the surface was in fact the small leaves of a water weed lying flat on the water like a film of suds in the sunshine. He could see the stream bed and the stems of the weeds clearly through the water, like looking into an aquarium.

Across the rhyne, the long, broad blades of grass shone silver as the wind brushed them back, glistening like the water on a lake. To complete the image, there appeared to be a rowing boat under a stand of trees in the middle of the field.

"What's that over there? It looks like a wooden boat, but it can't be."

Poppy laughed, "It is actually; that's what I wanted to show you. Come on, we can cross further up."

Jack and Alex followed her along the tractor path, Poppy balancing along the ridge between the ruts, the boys on either edge. Just on the bend of the rhyne, there was a footbridge made from an old log that had been embedded in the banks for stability. It was about twenty five centimetres in diameter, and mossy. Poppy nimbly traversed it in two strides; Jack, more cautious, edged his way over to the middle then took a big stride and jumped to the bank. He turned and steadied himself with one foot on the log and one on the bank, reaching his arm out for Alex, who looked disdainfully at him.

"Careful, Zan, don't fall in. Again!"

"Get a grip!" said his brother, and stepped across almost as neatly as Poppy had done, then they all made their way across to the boat. It was a full sized rowing boat, weathered and worn, the paint mostly gone from the gunwales and upper boards. It had a bench fitted round the stern, one in the middle for rowing, and a short plank in the prow, big enough for one person. Both sets of rowlocks were in place although the forward pins were broken in half, but there was no sign of any oars.

"Why is it here?" asked Jack. "I mean, at all, not just so far from the stream. Surely a boat this size would be useless on such a narrow, shallow waterway?"

"I haven't the faintest idea, but it's great for picnics. And I think it's kind of romantic; not in the soppy sense," she added, as Alex mimed retching, "but in the sense of romance like it said in the book – King Arthur and Lancelot and so on."

"We saw an old black and white film once, with dad, do you remember?" said Alex. "It was set in the war, but it was a comedy. There was a soldier called Arthur King, and another one, Lance Elliot, or he was a lance corporal called Elliot, I can't remember. But they were digging a trench or something, and they dug up a sword, and one of them joked that it was Excalibur, and history was repeating itself. Anyway, the sword brought them all good luck, and Arthur really believed he was King Arthur reincarnated. And I think, at the end, one of them said it was just a sword, and they had made up the connections with the names, and Arthur threw it into a lake cos he was angry and disappointed, and a hand came up and caught it like in the legends."

"And that's sort of what I'm trying to say, with the book and Goblin Combe," said Poppy. "I think people have just forgotten their past, and certain things have become seen as legends and myths. But deep down, they are real. The magic is still real, it's just been lost."

The three of them climbed into the boat, Poppy in the prow, Jack in the middle, and Alex on the Bench in the stern. They took out their water bottles and sat there, in the shade of the trees that were like a wild island in the middle of their green lake, watching the wind blow the grass like choppy waves.

Chapter Six

Crook Peak

The following day, Mr Pearson put on his best suit, because he had to drive up to the airport for a meeting. He would be starting his new job this week, now that the move was complete and the family were settling into their new surroundings. He seemed quite tense, checking the time on his phone every few minutes, and Alex asked if he was nervous.

"We are always a little scared of the unknown, aren't we?" he said, with a smile. "Like the start of a new school term. It's all a bit daunting until we get established. But like you guys and school, I know everything will be fine when I get there."

"When do we start school?" asked Max.

Alex groaned and rolled his head around his drooped shoulders. "Next week, Max. We've told you a thousand times," he moaned.

"Have not."

"Have."

"Have not. Not a thousand. Liar!"

"Alright, you two, put a sock in it, please," said Mr Pearson. "You all start next week. I'm on the early shift this week, so I'll be on the late shift next week. On Monday, mummy will take you to the village school, ok? And I will drop Jack off at the Academy until he gets his bus pass sorted. Then it will be just like the old routine: I'll take you in the mornings when I'm on lates, and I'll pick you up when I'm on earlies. Now, I've got this weekend off, and I was talking to Terry next door yesterday, and he said that the rugby season starts on Sunday, so we'll have to get you all down to the club for ten o'clock." He looked at his phone again. "Right, well, I'd better get going; don't want to be late. It's just a meeting today, so I'll see you this afternoon, but I'll be gone when you wake up in the morning, alright?"

He checked the knot of his tie in the hall mirror, then gave the boys a smile and a wave as he went out through the front door. The boys went to the lounge window to wave him down the road.

On Tuesday morning, Jack and Max were up at their usual time while Alex remained dead to the world. They set all the breakfast things on the dining room table, and helped themselves to bowls of cereal, then went through to the lounge and turned on the television at a low volume.

"Yay! Scooby-Doo!" said Max, jumping onto the sofa.

"Sure you won't be scared?" joked Jack.

"Of course I won't, it's only a cartoon. And anyway, it's never a real monster, is it? It's always just a miserable grown-up in a mask."

"Or maybe a wood pigeon," Jack said, giving Max a big smile. "It's always clever how the grown-up creates the effects, isn't it?" he said. "They always manage to convince everyone else until the gang turn up."

"Jack? Do you actually believe in ghosts? Seriously, I mean. No joke."

For all that Max was young and could be annoying much of the time, especially when Alex was around, Jack genuinely cared about his brother. Because of his age, Max could sometimes take a joke the wrong way, or take a flippant answer too seriously; Jack felt it was important to be serious with him now, but on a serious level, this was a very difficult question.

"I do believe, Max, but I don't want you to be scared. Belief doesn't alter the truth, as dad says. What each of us believes can be real to us, but it doesn't mean it's actually real. I could be wrong. But, yes, ghosts and aliens, even wizards, the existence of true magic, and all the things in ancient myths and folk tales, are things that I want to believe in, deep down. But the ghosts I believe in aren't the frightening ghosts – that's just for horror stories and television and stuff. I think that if ghosts are real, they are just people's spirit or life force that has been trapped in this world after the person has died. Or sometimes, they are the spirits of family members who want to look after you from heaven. Like when dad told us about feeling tired on a long drive, and sensing the presence of his dad, the grandad we never knew, keeping him awake and focused on the road. And like that video of your first birthday, when you're batting a balloon towards the fireplace and smiling, and the balloon keeps coming right back to you every time, even though you didn't have the control to hit it in the same place every time, and dad said he thought grandad was playing with you."

"So you do believe they're real?" persisted Max.

"What I'm saying, without trying to frighten you, is that I am open to the idea that ghosts and magic really exist, just like I believe dad when he talks about the probability of aliens being real, but I'm aware that many of the stories, and most of the clips on YouTube are either fake or have some other, logical explanation."

"So you think aliens are more believable?"

"Yes. I think it's easy to believe that, just as life has flourished on our planet, given the trillions of other planets in all the other galaxies in the universe, that life might also have developed on other planets. And just as we have travelled to our moon and sent robots to Mars and so on, other lifeforms might have travelled further and come to Earth, and if they have developed tech to travel that far, they might have the tech to remain invisible to us, or even possibly live among us undetected. You should have a look at some of dad's books. Anyway, I think that kind of belief is quite scientific and based on probability, supported by the fact of our own existence. Ghosts, the spirits of dead people staying around after the body has been buried? Emotional vibrations being trapped in buildings or whatever? It sounds plausible, but it's harder to support with science. So I don't feel quite as certain."

"But perhaps," said Max, "if someone saw an alien who hadn't quite made himself invisible, might they think they had seen a ghost? Or might an alien pretend to be a ghost if it had accidentally been discovered?"

"Well, that's an interesting idea, certainly. We could ask dad when he gets home." Jack could sense something in Max's preoccupied expression. "Why are you so interested all of a sudden?"

"You'll think I'm crazy."

"You're my younger brother, I already think you're crazy," laughed Jack, "it's part of the package."

"I keep seeing things. Things that aren't really there, or that vanish when I try to look properly."

"Maybe you need new glasses."

"I knew you wouldn't take me seriously," said Max, instantly angry.

"No, I am, it was just an automatic joke, Max. Tell me what you thin..." he stopped himself; "what you've seen."

"Well, I saw something in London a year or so ago, which I never told no-one about. Not a ghost, but maybe an alien. I called it the invisible dragon at the time, just to myself. You know ice sculptures, or those glass ornaments? Well, it was like one of them, so it was totally see-through, but it kind of had an outline, had some substance to it, but like invisible substance, like a raindrop on a window. So it was one evening when we were at the park, you know, near the airport, and I saw this thing, like a giant lizard but running on two legs with long arms and a tail, and like wings or fins or something on its back, just the outline of this thing running very fast across the park, from the main road towards the airport. I remember just standing and watching it, then looking around and realising none of you had seen it."

Jack was speechless. Surely this was far too complex for Max to make up?

"Then, since we've been here, I keep seeing things in the trees and bushes, just out of sight like they're hiding and watching us, and once I've spotted them, they just disappear, and I can't really tell what they looked like."

"Where do you see these things?"

"I first saw them around the quarry, and once in the hedge behind our shed, and sometimes out of Sam's window, in the field. Do you believe me?"

"Yes, I believe you, you sound very convincing. I certainly believe you feel it's something that can become invisible, like a ghost or an alien. And I want to believe in it, too, but

I have to say that because you wear glasses, just from a practical scientific point of view, it could be your eyesight, or a reflection off the lens, or even a smudge on the lens –
"

"I knew you wouldn't take it seriously!" cried Max, and he jumped up off the sofa and stormed out of the room.

"Morning, Max," Jack heard Alex say in the hallway.

"Go away!" shouted Max angrily, and stomped up the stairs.

"What's up with him, now?" asked Alex.

"Oh, nothing," said Jack, but he was busy mulling over what Max had told him.

When their mum brought Sam down for breakfast a few minutes later, she was full of enthusiasm for the day. "I've joined a Facebook group for the school, and some of the mums are going for a walk up to Crook Peak this morning. I thought we could all take a picnic, and you older boys can bring your kites. It will be a good way to meet some more of the children in the village."

"Can't we wait for dad?" asked Jack. "I know he was interested in visiting the peak."

"He can come another time. It'll be too late by the time he's got home and changed and everything."

When breakfast was over, their mum turned the television off and chivvied the boys upstairs to get dressed, then they each had their jobs to do to prepare for the picnic. Max had calmed down again, and gave Jack a smile when he asked if he was ok. Somehow, they both felt closer for having talked so openly earlier. Max rinsed and filled their water bottles, and chose a packet of crisps for each of them while Jack chopped up some carrots and cucumber to go with the sandwiches. Alex found the kites and put them in the boot of the car along with the picnic stuff.

There were half a dozen cars in the little car park. Other mums were lifting rugs and cool bags out of boots, and children were running around by the stone wall, waving sticks. Mrs Pearson went to introduce herself to the adults, and left the boys to get Sam's all-terrain buggy out and stow the picnic things underneath. When everyone was ready, they all moved off in two groups, the children leading on energetically, the mums plodding behind. Immediately through the iron gate in the stone wall were some large oaks with huge canopies spreading over the bare earth. A path led steeply down to the left, broken by exposed roots that made rough steps to walk down. Joining this path was a deep ravine with tracks worn between some smaller trees running along the top. A group of teenage boys Jack didn't know were using these tracks as ramps to do some pretty impressive jumps.

"This must be the wood Poppy said is just off the Strawberry Line," Jack said to Alex. "Hey," he called to one of the boys in the picnic group, "does the Strawberry Line come past here?"

"Yes," replied the boy. "The long tunnel goes right under the car park back there, and comes out at the bottom of that hill. There is a gate just past the jumps, where that path goes down through the trees. Takes you down to the Strawberry Line right at the end of the tunnel."

They walked on up the hill, where the trees grew closer together and the undergrowth became thicker, with a few less-worn paths leading through into the unknown. Gradually, the boys introduced themselves to the other children. Most of them would be in Max's class, but there were some older and younger siblings. They all seemed friendly and excited to make new friends, and they pointed out the places where they had made dens or found a dead squirrel, and where the Scouts did backwoods cooking on open fires.

After a while, the path emerged from the woods onto the spine of the hill, and the wind that blew unchecked across the flat fields took the heat out of the strong sun. They walked for another half hour, then they could see the distinctive bump of the peak as they approached. To the south of the peak was an escarpment which dropped steeply towards the M5. The children ran on ahead, racing to reach the mound of the peak. Jack, Alex and Tom, the boy Jack had asked about the Strawberry line, were the winners as they were the oldest. They stood proudly atop the mound, surveying the low land for miles around.

Jack could trace part of their route from the motorway junction when they had first arrived and their dad had pointed out the peak, past the farms and the little rivers. He could see Banwell Castle, too, and the woods surrounding their quarry. Max arrived with some of the younger boys, and seemed to take quite an interest in the mound itself. It was a promontory of rock, mostly covered in short, coarse grass, but the exposed rock wasn't smooth as is often the case with such features that are constantly groomed by strong winds and harsh downpours. It was quite jagged in places, like a higgledy-piggledy heap of the sort of stones that made up the crenelated garden walls in the area. Like when builders have knocked something down and left it for so long that the grass has moved in and reclaimed it.

The parents with the picnic bags and pushchairs finally joined them, and after a brief look at the view, started to spread out the rugs and unpack the food a little below the top of the hill, out of the wind, but safely away from the cliff. Alex took charge of Sam, sitting him with his toys on the rug and playing with him while their mum unpacked the plastic plates and all the food. Jack, Max and some of the other children followed Tom around the edge of the escarpment where the beginning of the cliff was accessible before the ground sheered away. Tom quickly climbed up the cliff where it was only about two meters high. The cliff was very jagged and full of easy hand and foot holds, and Max went up next under Jack's watchful eye. Their mum called them to eat their sandwiches, and so the pack of children settled down for a few minutes, eating and drinking and laughing in the sunshine.

When the food had been devoured and the adults were chatting, the children once more dispersed over the peak, playing, exploring and climbing. Jack fetched the kites from Sam's buggy, and helped Max unwind the line on the biggest one, while Alex laid out the smaller one and got his line ready. Soon, both kites were soaring in the blue Somerset sky, watched by some of the other children. The peak was an excellent place to fly, much better than the beaches or the parks where they had flown them before. Jack and Max kept theirs steady, flying it as high as they could on the strong currents. Alex, however, was making his swoop and dive, whooping and laughing, until it went down over the north side of the brow and didn't come back up.

"Look," said Alex, straining to see where the kite had gone, "there's another quarry down there." The others came and looked. It was only a small quarry; tiny, compared to the one behind their house. If it hadn't been for the way the rock had been cut in exactly the same way, it might have been a natural dent in the hill. The bottom of it was much more overgrown, with small trees and bushes covering much of the ground.

"Let's go and explore!" said Tom, as Alex wound in his line and hauled the kite up out of some low bushes at the top of the quarry. Two of the bridles that attached to the wings were broken, but they could easily be fixed.

"We'd better just tell our mum where we're going," said Jack, running back to the picnic area with both kites, and leaving them in the compartment under the buggy.

Mrs Pearson was talking to a couple of the other mums, asking questions about the primary school and nurseries for Sam. Sam was being entertained by a couple of girls Max's age; one of them was blowing soap bubbles from a pot, and Sam was bursting them and chuckling.

"Is it ok if we go down the hill with Tom, mum?" asked Jack. "There is something he wants to show us."

Mrs Pearson looked doubtful for a second. "Is it safe?" she asked the other mums.

"As long as they don't go as far as the road, they will be fine. It's too steep for the buggies, but there is a path going down that way, so it's alright."

"Well, just be careful," said Mrs Pearson, "and look after Max. We'll be heading back in about an hour, alright?"

When Jack re-joined the others, Tom was telling Alex and Max about the cooking he had done in the woods with the scouts. He continued as they made their way down the steep path, the three brothers listening attentively; they loved anything to do with barbeques and bonfires.

"When we had collected the dry twigs, we arranged them by thickness. We made tipis of thin ones about the length of a small ruler, and placed the smallest twigs like matchsticks in the middle with special cotton wool soaked in paraffin. Then we struck sparks with our flint and steel to light the wool, and gradually added thicker sticks until we had a good fire going. Then we prepared the bread while the flames died down. We measured out some flower into a freezer bag and added enough water to make a paste that we rolled up in the bag and squeezed until it was a firm, sticky roll of dough. Then we had to take the dough out and wrap it round the end of a stick and hold it over the fire until it was cooked, then we ate it with our fingers."

"And what did it taste like?" asked Alex.

"Actually, it was the nicest bread I have ever had. We get sliced bread at home, so I've never had it fresh from the bakers or anything, but it was delicious. And I've made it a few times at home, whenever we have a barbeque, or if dad will let me build a camp fire. You really have to join the scouts, it's wicked."

"And it's just flour and water?" asked Jack.

"Umm, there might have been some sugar in the flour. And I think it has to be self-raising. But, yeah, it's as simple as that."

"But didn't the stick make it taste dirty?" asked Max.

"The cooking sticks aren't ones off the ground, silly, you have to snap off a live one and then pull the leaves off or strip it with a knife. Howling Wolf said you should lick the stick to make sure the tree isn't poisonous, but there aren't any poisonous trees round here. If the stick tastes bitter, you shouldn't use it, though."

"Howling Wolf?"

"He's one of the leaders. They've all got names of Indian chiefs."

They had reached the trees at the bottom of the path where a style gave access over a fence onto the road. There was a gravel space to park on the opposite side of the road, but there were no cars in it. Tom turned left, winding through the trees, holding the slender branches out of the way as he went. There was no path, and the grass here was long and wispy with shaggy seed heads. There was no noise apart from the rustle of their passage through the branches and the crack of the occasional twig. After a couple of minutes, the boys came out into the sunlight again in front of a high cliff of dark rock. They excitedly explored all around, and Tom had a go at climbing on the exposed rock, but it had been cut away too smoothly to find many good holds, not like the natural escarpment above. Alex was disappointed to find there were no caves, and Jack had been hoping for some abandoned machinery, but there was just a scattering of boulders and the trees.

"It would be a great place for a scout camp," said Tom. "Pity it's so close to the road. You could build a decent fire just here, and all sit on these boulders and tell ghost stories and eat backwoods bread."

"Do you believe in ghosts, Tom?" asked Jack, and caught sight of Max looking over at them.

"Nah," said Tom in a mature, dismissive tone. "I like spooky stories and that when we're out somewhere like this, but to tell you the truth, I only like 'em cos I know they ain't real," and he laughed.

Jack gave Max a shrug, which Max copied, then he looked at his watch. "We'd better head back up, I reckon. They'll all be heading home soon."

When Mr Pearson got home at three o'clock, Mrs Pearson had a job for him to do.

"Come on, Maximilian," he said to Max, who was sitting at the dining room table looking out at the woods at the top of the hill, or staring into space in a catatonic trance as it appeared to his dad, "I need a strong pair of arms to help me take all this cardboard to the tip."

As the unpacking had progressed, more and more empty boxes had been flattened and put to one side, and had quickly taken over the utility room and the hallway. There was now a cardboard carpet 5 centimetres thick from the stairs to the kitchen preventing access to the toilet under the stairs, and nobody (i.e. Mrs Pearson) could get to the washing machine. So Max and his dad dragged as many of the boxes out as they could and filled the large boot of the Galaxy. Mr Pearson moved Max's booster seat to the front so that he could collapse the rear seats and make more room. Max always felt very special when he was allowed in the front.

They drove down the hill past a farmhouse with a scarecrow in the window, past a field of long pasture with highland cows blending into it. They passed an old cottage set in a large garden with the biggest 'For Sale' sign Max had ever seen. "What does 'development opportunity' mean, dad?" he asked.

"Well, it means two things, Max. Firstly, that I will never buy or sell a property through that estate agent. Secondly, it means that the agent thinks it would be better for that lovely cottage with its garden where kids could play football, or the adults could host a summer fête, grow vegetables or put in an outdoor swimming pool, would be better turned into a mini housing estate of half a dozen small boxes with no gardens."

"Would they do that?" asked Max, shocked.

"Yes, it's all too common these days. You look at street names or place names sometime. Anything with Meadows or Orchard in it – Green Meadows Drive, Simon's Orchard, Apple Tree Close; they would all have been open fields or orchards of fruit trees twenty to a hundred years ago, and now they are streets or cul-de-sacs of houses. Yew Tree Gardens in Sandford would have been the gardens of the houses opposite the church. Shepherd's Bush in London would have once been just that, a bush that shepherds sheltered under while tending their sheep in open pasture. And all the different areas of modern Greater London would have been small villages a few miles outside the old city of London: Richmond, Kingston, Wimbledon, and Isleworth. Gradually, all these places, these rural, bucolic places have been developed and built on and become unrecognisable."

"What about Wimblestone Road?" asked Max.

"Hmm, I don't know about that. Maybe after a Mr Wimblestone, although it's not a name I've ever heard of, but he could have been a prominent person in the area. Or maybe there was a local stone by that name, like the Blarney Stone or the Stone of Scone."

"What's a blarney stone?" asked Max.

"It's a stone set in a wall of a castle in Ireland, and according to legend, if you kiss it you will become a more eloquent speaker."

"Ugh, kiss a stone? That's gross! But why would someone want to build lots of houses in that garden back there?"

"Money and greed," replied Mr Pearson with a sigh. "If you bought that house and built four more houses in the garden, then you could sell all five houses and make a big profit. If you built five houses, you would have even more profit. And just to give you some idea, if you managed to do all that building in one year, which wouldn't be hard, you'd probably make ten times what daddy earns every year."

"Wow! So why didn't you become a builder, dad?"

"Well, I did think about becoming an architect, someone who designs buildings, but I realised that I didn't want to be involved in any way with pouring more and more concrete over our beautiful countryside. Remember, Max, art and literature are man's greatest achievements, not buildings and monuments. It is art that sets us apart from animals. And just to be clear, if I ever become the mayor of Weston-super-Mare or any kind of local dignitary, I'd rather have a park or a forest named after me than a brand new street, understood? I'm going to leave you in charge of that, Max, ok?" He smiled at Max in the front seat beside him, and Max grinned back.

"Ok, sure!" he agreed, and they both laughed.

"I think it's probably time we read The Hitchhiker's Guide to the Galaxy." Said Mr Pearson.

"Is that a car manual?" asked Max, suspiciously.

When they got home, Stephen was playing with a football in the quadrangle of garages opposite the new house. Max asked if he could play with him for a while, and scampered across the road under Mr Pearson's safety-conscious gaze.

79

"Alright, Stee?" he said, excitedly. "Want to play one-on-one?"

"Yeah, sure. Where were you just now?"

"We was at the tip in Cheddar, getting rid of all the removal boxes, you know."

"You should of gone to Weston, their tip's much better. It's bigger, and there's stuff that's not rubbish but just what people don't want, and you can get toys and that really cheap." Stephen nutmegged Max, and booted the ball against the brick wall between the two slim buttresses that served as goal posts. "I love going to the tip, but dad hardly ever takes me. I think your parents are really cool. We hardly ever go to the beach or the waterpark or anything."

Max was concentrating on dribbling in a zigzag towards Stephen. "They're ok, I s'pose," he said, and suddenly chipped the ball past Stephen, sprinted after it and walloped it into the green garage door of number twenty six.

"One all," said Stephen, matter-of-factly. He brought the ball back to the drain in the middle of the quadrangle, as Max continued to talk. Although shy with people he didn't know, Max could be quite talkative at times, but he often got the impression that nobody was really listening, which added to his sense of frustration at being stuck a few years younger than Jack and Alex, and much older than Sam. It felt good to finally have a best friend he could share his thoughts with.

"Mum does do lots of stuff with us, but she loses her temper a lot for no reason. Dad's ok, but he's quite boring most of the time. Like, when I say 'what can I do?' he's always like 'read a book' or 'practice your guitar' and stuff.

And he doesn't listen to what you say, he just corrects the way you say it." Stephen tried the outside chip that Max had used, but Max's quick reflexes stopped it, and the race was on to see who could reclaim it first. Max won, because he was facing the right direction, and the green door shook again with a loud bang. "You know, like I'll say 'I should of done this', and he'll say 'you should *have* done it', then he'll go on and on saying '*of* you finished your homework? *Of* you been to school today?' just to ram it home, you know? And, like, one time back in London, I asked him for some money cos I wanted to buy summink, and he said he had lots of ink, did I want a bottle or cartridges. And you gotta say 'bottle' and 'water' not 'bo'le or 'wa'er'."

Stephen laughed. He found the way Max spoke funny sometimes, and he still thought Mr Pearson, for all his bad habits, sounded interesting and more caring than his own dad. "Where are your big brothers?"

"Dunno. Probly in the quarry with that girl from up the top, there."

"Wanna go and spy on 'em? See what they're doing?"

"Nah." Max didn't really want to share his new friend with his brothers. He was quite happy being the focus of some decent attention, and having a bit of independence from them.

"We could go up to my room and build one of the Scalextric sets," he suggested.

"Yeah, ok. Actually, Max, I'd really like to see your guitar. Is it electric?"

"It's only a classical," said Max, as they looked up and down the road, then walked across to the open back door, "But dad's taught me some blues tunes, and some bits of

Metallica." The boys dashed past Mrs Pearson, and bounded up the stairs to the front bedroom.

Chapter Seven

Portents

The boys spent the next three mornings with their mum and Sam. Once they had finished breakfast, cleared the table and washed up, and once Sam was dressed for the day, Mrs Pearson would announce what they were going to be doing. On Wednesday, it was Puxton Park. When Sam and Max had been on Sunday, Mrs Pearson had thought it very expensive, but the mums at the picnic on Crook Peak had said that they all had family membership, which made it very reasonable. They all went at least twice a week, apparently, and bought all their meat from the butcher in the farm shop on the way out.

Bearing in mind that Poppy had said she enjoyed the park, Jack and Alex were quite keen to see what it was like. Max was very excited as soon as his mum had told them, and Sam started making lots of enthusiastic noises as they drove down the long drive past wooden cut-outs of cows and sheep and owls.

Once inside, Max shot off like a rocket. "Follow me, you guys!" he called to Jack and Alex, and he disappeared into the maze of soft play tunnels. Mrs Pearson took Sam to the toddler area, where there was a mini version of the soft play maze, but also Sam's favourite thing: a ball pit with an air jet that made him look like a sky diver when he put his face over it, his chubby cheeks flattened out and vibrating in the wind. The three older boys would peep in at their brother every now and then as they came down slides and chased each other up and down the padded

83

towers and walkways. All three of them watched in awe as other children came hurtling down the death slides, but, although they went up and had a look, none of them were quite brave enough to try it themselves.

On Thursday, Mrs Pearson took them all to the beach at Brean. It was much less commercial than Weston-super-Mare, although there was an ice cream van that drove up and down all day. They parked the Galaxy on the sand, set out their fold-up chairs and a rug for Sam, and unloaded all their spades and buckets and diggers and footballs. They made some sandcastles for Sam, and used the flats of their spades to create roads between them for him to drive his diggers and cars, then they marked out a pitch and played football and touch rugby.

As the tide came in slowly over the hot sand, the inch or two of water was very warm, and they all splashed about, kicking and throwing balls to each other, and helping Sam take a few steps, listening to him chuckle as the warm waves splashed him.

On Friday they went into Weston again to buy some stationery for the start of term, and to get a phone for Jack in case he was going to be late home from school for any reason.

On Saturday, the whole family went to the matinee showing of Turbo at the Odeon. When they came out, the boys said they wanted tacos for tea, just like in the film. Mr and Mrs Pearson didn't know where they could get tacos in Winscombe, but agreed that they could all have a Chinese, with prawn crackers and sweet and sour sauce.

On Sunday morning, the boys got up and ate their cereal in a nervous silence. Their dad cooked them bacon and scrambled eggs with melted cheese to prepare them for the morning, then Alex and Jack took their dad and Max down the strawberry line to the rec. They were too full to eat any blackberries, but they did show Mr Pearson the brass timeline at the station as they passed. "Look," said Jack, "this one says '1476 Caxton Starts Printing'. I reckon that's the same Caxton that runs the newsagent; the date looks about right!"

When they got to the rugby club, Max became very shy. Stephen had said he didn't play rugby and didn't really want to, so Max was worried he might not know anybody in his group.

"I'll come with you and meet your coaches," he told Jack and Alex, "then I'll stay and watch Max, make sure he's alright. Any problems, just come over to the Under 8's pitch, ok?"

Jack's coach was a tall, bald man with a strong Somerset accent. He smiled kindly as he shook Jack's hand, a strong, firm grip, saying how pleased he was to have some new blood on the team. He told Jack to find a ball and warm up with the other boys, jogging round the pitch, throwing the balls up and catching them. The club kit seemed to be black with two thin white stripes, although not everyone was wearing it. Jack had on his London Wasps replica shirt, and thought he would fit in well, but as he jogged round the first set of posts, two boys who looked identical caught up with him.

"Brave wearing that shirt," said one.

"Why?"

"Looks like a Hornets shirt. The Hornets are our rivals; they're in Weston."

"They're pretty mean, no one likes them much," said the other twin.

"What are you wearing?" asked Jack, throwing his ball up with a tight, practiced spiral, and gauging his pace to catch it again.

"These are last year's tour shirts. Every year the club goes on tour in the Easter break. There's always a theme and a special shirt."

The twins accelerated round the corner flag ahead of Jack, and he saw on the backs of their shirts an image of a goblin doing what looked like a jig. Around it were the words Winscombe RFC Dorset Tour 2014. Jack caught up with them and asked what the theme was.

"Anything to do with goblins or Thatcher's Cider."

"Why Thatcher's cider?"

"They're our sponsors, and they make Green Goblin cider. Most people dressed as Lord of the Rings characters."

"Coach was Gandalf; he was awesome."

The coach's whistle blew, and they all sprinted over to huddle round him. There was a welcome back to the new season speech, and a welcome to the club to Jack, then they started some training exercises. The coach focussed his attention on Jack, finding out what he could do and what position he was best suited to.

In the half time water break, the twins approached Jack again. "We saw you last week," said one. "With that girl, Poppy, on the strawberry line."

"You got a brother?" said the other.

"Yeah; well, I've got three, actually. What do you mean you saw us? Where were you?"

"Up our tree. We're building a tree house at the end of our garden."

"Have you got a psychotic brown dog?" asked Jack.

"Yeah, but he's just a puppy, soft as anything, really."

"Bark is worse than his bite!"

"What were you doing with Poppy?" asked the first twin.

"We weren't doing anything. She was just showing us around."

"Well, you wanna watch her, she's a bit weird, that one."

"Yeah, away with the fairies!" The twins laughed in unison. For the last forty five minutes, they played a mini match. Jack was on the twins' team, and they played quite well, fearless and competitive, but having a laugh together at the same time. A few of the other team seemed to put in some extra hard tackles on Jack, either to prove something to the newcomer, or because the wasp on his shirt reminded them of the Hornets. 'Show no fear, show no pain' was a slogan Jack had picked up from a Garfield cartoon. It had been funny because of the pictures: a fearless, leonine Garfield striding towards an adversary in the 'show no fear' cell, and a battered and bedraggled Garfield in the 'show no pain' cell, but Jack had taken the words as something of a mantra during any tough situation, and they helped him overcome any negative emotions. At the final whistle, the coach said Jack had done well, and told him to get a Winscombe jersey from the kit cabin for next week.

"Coming to the hut, Jack?" asked one of the twins. They had told Jack their names, Sean and Kyle, but he couldn't tell them apart. They really were identical.

"What's the hut?"

"Tea hut. They do bacon and sausage rolls and that. Makes all the pain worthwhile." He laughed.

When they got to the hut, Jack recognised Terry, their next door neighbour, putting some fresh bacon on to the hotplate.

"Alright, Jack?" he said with a big, friendly smile. "'Ere, that ain't a Hornets top, is it? Glad you came down, lad. Did your brothers come, too?"

"Yes, they're probably with dad at the Under 8's pitch. Don't know where that is, though."

"It's down past the first pitch this year, over there, look. Now, what can I get you boys?"

The twins both had bacon rolls, but once again Jack hadn't brought any money.

"Oh, that's alright. Here's what I'll do: I'll let you have this sausage roll here if you say you'll take Max for a walk, how's that?"

"Max? My brother?" said Jack in confusion.

"No, my Labrador!" laughed Terry. "Are you ok with dogs? He's no trouble; he's getting old, like me."

"Thanks very much!" said Jack, salivating as Terry handed him a bread roll with 2 sliced sausages in it.

"Ketchup's on the table there," he said.

Jack found his dad and brothers at the kit cabin.

"Come and see if there is a second hand shirt in your size," said his dad.

"Have they got any goblin shirts?"

"You'll need a home shirt for matches," said the man in charge of the cabin, "and you'll get your own tour shirt if you come on the tour this year."

"What's the theme this year?" asked Jack, doubtful that it would be goblins again. He would have loved the chance to dress up as Aragorn.

"You'll have to wait and see. Details usually emerge around Christmas and New Year time. Here, this one looks about your size: try it on."

When they got back home, their mum was stressed. Alex had made friends with some of the boys who would be in his year at school, and Mr Pearson had been chatting to some of the parents of the Under 8's, but there was no chance of relaying their news or showing off their new kit.
"What's up?" asked their dad.
"We had a visit from the police." She said.
"Is everything alright?" asked dad, instantly worried. "What's happened?"
"Your delinquent kleptomaniac son happened, that's what."
"Eh? Which one? I mean, who? I mean, what?" He looked at each of them in a panic.
"I bathed Sam and put him in his room with his toys while I had a bath myself. I put his gate across the stair so that he wasn't shut in, and could come and find me if he wanted. So, there I am, relaxing in the bath when the doorbell rings, followed quickly by a pounding on the front door. And the pounding continues, really urgent, frightening me to death, I thought maybe the house was on fire. So I run downstairs all wet with just a towel round me, and there's two police officers at the door, and quite a few inquisitive neighbours in their front gardens. "What's the emergency, madam?" asks one of the policemen. "What do you mean?" I say, "you're the ones hammering on the door for dear life." "We received a silent 999 call from this address. Can we come in?" One of them then goes round through the side gate to check the back garden. I let the other one

in just to get the door shut, and he goes from room to room looking for whoever might have been holding me hostage or something. "Are you alone, madam?" he asks, as he heads upstairs. And that's where we find Sam; sitting in his room with the phone from the bedside table next to him."

"Sammy called the police?" laughed Alex. "Was the bath water too cold, Sam? Did you get mummy arrested?"

"It's not funny, Alexander!" said his mum, crossly. "What a great introduction to the local community!" she fired at their dad, "*that new family from London with the four kids – already had the police round, you know.*" I can hear it, now!"

"Look, it'll blow over. No harm done. We can explain to the neighbours, it will be an ice-breaker."

"If you say we'll look back on this and laugh in a few years –"

"Of course we will! Just like Zander falling in the lake."

"I still don't think that's funny at all! And anyway, it'll be hard enough for us to fit into a small village like this after London, without alienating the locals. Especially when they find out why you've really transferred to Bristol."

"Oh, don't start that again."

The boys knew it was time to take Sam outside and play in the garden. As soon as they were out there, Stephen appeared at the gate, wanting to know about the police car. They all had a laugh about Sam calling the cops. From the kitchen, they could still hear the raised voices of Mr and Mrs Pearson; mostly Mrs Pearson.

"Why has dad really transferred to Bristol from Heathrow?" Alex asked Jack.

"I'll tell you later," said his brother, quietly, glancing around in case the neighbours were in their gardens.

"Can we get the tractor out?" asked Max.

"Adga!" said Sam in agreement.

So Jack opened the shed and fetched the ride-on tractor and trailer. He sat Sam in the trailer and secured it to the tractor, then Max and Stephen took turns pedalling Sam about the top half of the garden.

"Don't go down the hill with Sam in the back," warned Jack. "It's too steep, and he'll fall out."

Over the hedge, Jack saw Terry come around the side of his utility room and climb the steps to his shed. Unlike the Pearsons' shed, Terry's had tall windows of little square panes, and glazed doors in the side. It was the sort of shed you could sit in, like a summer house, and look out at the garden. Jack watched as terry carried two deck chairs down to the patio, one under each arm. As he erected them near the hedge, Jack called over to him.

"Hi Terry, would you like me to walk Max for you this afternoon?"

"That would be lovely, Jack. All's I want to do right now is rest in this 'ere chair and watch the flowers drink in the sunshine."

"I'll have to just check with mum and dad that it's ok," said Jack, "but I don't think we're doing anything else this afternoon."

Just then Mrs Pearson came into the garden to check on Sam, who was now being driven around an assault course devised by Alex.

"Is it ok if I take Terry's dog for a walk, mum?"

"Well, I want you three rugby players to have a shower first. There'll be time to walk him before tea, if that's all right with Terry."

"Yes, course it is, course it is. That will be perfect, in fact," said Terry, settling himself down in his deckchair.

Jack had dressed and was drying his wet hair with his towel. Max was under the shower singing 'Rock you like a Hurricane' by The Scorpions, and Alex was towelling himself off on the landing.

"Do you want to come with me to take Terry's Max for a walk?" asked jack.

"Yeah, alright," said Alex, pointing towards the bathroom and doing an impression of Max singing.

"Well, hurry up and get dressed, then, stop messing about."

"'*Stop messing about*'," imitated Alex in his whiny voice.

"God, you can be so immature!"

"'*You can be so immature*'. Anyway, I thought you said I was juvenile?"

"They mean the same thing! Ugh!" Jack threw his towel at his brother. "Just get dressed!"

"Hey, Jack, watch this!" Max had turned off the water and was climbing over the side of the bath. Alex flicked his towel at him and caught him on the back of the thigh. Alex laughed.

"Ow!" Screamed Max, rubbing himself vigorously, and starting to cry. "What did you do that for? I'm telling mum!" and he ran past Alex, down the stairs, wet and naked, into the kitchen.

"Now you've done it, you idiot!" said Jack, as they waited for the consequences of Alex's action to erupt up the stairs. "What did you have to go and do that for?"

"Because it was funny," laughed Alex. "He shouldn't be such a wuss."

"He's only seven. You know what he's like."

"Alexander! Get down here this instant!"

Alex wrapped the towel around himself, and went downstairs, grinning. After a minute or two, Max reappeared and fetched his towel from the bathroom.

"Are you ok?" asked Jack.

"Yeah. Mum says I can watch TV. Zander's got to stay up here and have time out." He was smiling.

Jack shook his head to himself. 'Brothers!' he thought, then went downstairs.

Terry and Max met Jack at their side gate. Max was wagging his tail with a slow vigour that suggested he was keen to go out in spite of his age.

"I usually take him up to the pet food shop and then down the steps from Quarry Road. That's usually enough for him in the evenings. Or up to Sandy Lane and back down past the bungalows. It's entirely up to you."

Terry handed Jack the lead, and Max led him down the hill past the cherry trees, stopping at the kerb on the corner.

"You want to go that way, today, do you, Max? Ok, then. Cross over." And the pair of them crossed the road and rounded the corner, heading up the hill towards the pet food shop and the quarry. A tractor went past with a trailer full of turnips or sweet potatoes or something, muddy brown shapes piled high, shifting and rolling as the trailer bounced over a manhole cover. A grubby looking teenager waved at Jack from the top of the pile, looking like he was riding a rodeo bull. Jack was impressed, as he's never seen anybody riding on a trailer before. He wondered if he might have been one of the gypsies. When they reached Quarry Road at the brow of the hill, Poppy was there, picking up a couple of the vegetables that had fallen off the trailer.

"Hey!" She said. "Is that Max?"

"Hey! Yeah, do you know him? What are you doing?"

"Just collecting these; saves us having to buy them." She hid the sweet potatoes under a bush on top of the retaining wall. "Bring him this way, I've got something to show you."

They checked the road for traffic, then crossed towards the shop. Max trotted eagerly, clearly hoping they were going to buy treats. But instead, Poppy turned at the pavement and led them down the hill towards Sandford.

"Have you had a look at that book I lent you yet?" she called over her shoulder.

"Yes, I have. And I've been thinking a lot about the quarry. About the cave and all those blocked up holes on the lower level? I don't think they should be there."

Poppy nodded and continued down the hill.

"It's like you said that first day, when Zander went into the cave. It's a quarry, not a mine. There shouldn't be any tunnels or shafts or anything at all."

Poppy was smiling. "So, what do you make of it?"

"Well, I don't know. With that and the book, and something Max told me,"

"What, are you Doctor Doolittle, now?"

"Not the dog, my brother Max. The one with glasses, remember?"

Poppy laughed. Max shook his head and plodded on.

When they reached the bottom of the hill, Poppy opened the lych gate and held it for Jack and the dog to go through into the churchyard.

"So, what about the cave and the tunnels?" she asked.

"Well, I don't think they're part of the quarry. I don't think the cave is really a cave at all. I thought at first, maybe, like people have been looking for something. Something they think might be buried or hidden in the rock. But then, with the stories in the book, and everything, I think maybe it's a doorway for, well, maybe goblins or something. Sounds stupid, I know. Anyway, why have we come here?"

Poppy took them along the cobbled path to the entrance to the church. Max spotted a cat behind one of the grave stones, and gave an excited bark. The cat escaped into the bushes by the fence, and Jack wrestled with the lead to stop Max bounding after it. The church door was set back in a large stone porch where there were notices pinned to cork boards. The door itself looked old and heavy; medieval; like the door to a castle. It was crossed with beams to form wooden squares, reinforced with black ironwork. She pointed at the door handle. The handle was a black Iron ring, but it was mounted on a piece of ironwork that didn't appear to have any purpose other than decoration. It was in the shape of a figure; there was a pear-shaped head with a tall crown, a slim oblong body, arms that seemed to be bracing themselves, lifting up the shoulders with hands sticking out at right angles, and short legs bending out at the knee, with either no feet or else the feet were pointed like a ballet dancer. It looked like one of the Roswell aliens, and it looked like it was doing some kind of tribal dance.

Jack was astounded. It looked like the green goblin on the tour shirts, doing its little jig. Was this what his little brother kept seeing in the bushes?

After a minute's silent staring, Poppy said "I thought you'd like it," and when Jack turned around, her face was dominated by a big, satisfied smile.

"Hello, Poppy," said a slim man dressed in black, with a white band under his collar. "Hello," he smiled at Jack.

"Hello, reverend," said Poppy, "we were just walking Max."

"And admiring my door, I see."

"Is this a very old church?" asked Jack.

"Not really, no, as churches go. Not nearly as old as St James' or Banwell, for instance. In fact, the oldest part of the whole building is this door."

"Really?"

"Yes. Well, the centre of it. You see the middle section inside this outer frame, held in place by the ironwork and these batons? That apparently came from a very old local house when it was demolished. Doors were much smaller hundreds of years ago because people were not as tall as they are now. Someone obviously kept the door, a good, strong bit of oak, and then when this church was built, they made it fit the new doorway. Not really sure why, seems like a lot of effort, doesn't it? But it's a nice feature, and something a bit different. I think there is only one other door still in use in the country that is older, and that's in Westminster Abbey."

"Wow!" said Jack, stroking the ancient wood. "Incredible."

"Now, if you'll excuse me, I have things to prepare. Very nice to meet you...?"

"Jack," said Jack, and the reverend shook his hand firmly, then pushed open the heavy door, and entered the church.

Jack couldn't wait to tell Max about the figure on the church door, and what it might mean. He urged the Labrador back up the hill, but the old dog sat down at the entrance to the pet food store, and wouldn't budge. Poppy laughed at Jack's attempts to coax him homeward, then she dug in her pocket and gave the dog a few broken bone-shaped biscuit pieces.

"People drop these in the entrance sometimes," she explained. I usually have some in my pockets. I like meeting friendly old dogs." She gave Max's head a rub, and he happily got up and crossed the road with them. Poppy retrieved her sweet potatoes, and they headed along the path in front of the houses. When they reached Poppy's gate, she went through, and turned to close it.

"Well, see you at school tomorrow, I suppose. Are you catching the bus?" she asked.

"Not tomorrow. We didn't have time to apply for my pass. I'll have to see the secretary about it in the week."

"O.k. Well, see ya then, Dillon."

"Yeah, bye Scout! Come on, Max."

Jack took Max home and told Terry that everything had been fine, and he'd really enjoyed walking the dog, then he ran round to his own garden gate, and went in through the back door to the kitchen.

"There you are, I was getting worried," said his mum through a cloud of steam as she drained the vegetables. Mr Pearson was carving the chicken on the other side of the kitchen. It all smelled delicious. "Go and wash your hands and sit at the table. I don't want you having a late

97

night tonight. First day of school tomorrow," she reminded him.

After dinner, and rather theatrically, Jack thought, his mum presented him with his mobile phone. It was just a basic model, but he would still be able to play games and watch videos on it.

"We've put our mobile numbers and the landline in it, ok?" said his mum. "Now, this is just for emergencies, really, you understand? If you're going to be doing something extra after school, or you miss the bus or something. If we think you're abusing it, we'll take it off you."

"But I can text my friends, can't I? And download some games?"

"Yes, you can message your friends, but only up to bedtime. It stays in the kitchen overnight, agreed?"

"And decent games," added Mr Pearson, "I'm not having you waste your life matching four fruits in a row, or whatever."

"Yes, dad! And thanks, mum. It's great. And I'll be sensible with it. Promise."

Jack wanted to get Max alone for a quiet word, to tell him that now he genuinely believed that he could see things that other people missed. But he didn't get a chance. Their mum fussed about, making sure they had everything ready for school in the morning, and making sure that Max was settled in bed early for a good night's sleep. Jack and Alex were allowed to watch one hour of television before they, too, were sent to bed at a reasonable hour.

Jack was too excited to sleep, however. Thoughts about the figure on the church door, the goblin on the tour shirts, the stories in Poppy's book, and the strange tunnels in the quarry cliffs, rolled over and over in his mind. Then came the noises of another argument downstairs. Something to do with dad looking at one of the nursery teachers.

"Of course I was looking at her. She was talking to us about the nursery."

"No, you were *looking* at her."

"That's ridiculous!"

"Oh is it? Hmm? So you didn't happen to notice *at all* how young and slim and pretty she was?"

"Oh, for pity's sake! What's that go to do with anything?"

The sounds became a bit muffled then; dad had obviously moved to the dining room, maybe thinking of keeping the noise down so as not to wake him or his brothers. After some more murmuring, accusations and denials, Jack heard the back door, then a car door and an engine over-revved in anger, and his mum's footsteps coming up the stairs. He feigned sleep while she looked in on them, much easier for him being in the top bunk where she couldn't really see without climbing up a couple of rungs on the ladder. He heard her shuffle off to bed, and relaxed. But he was still unable to sleep.

Chapter Eight

Through the Window

Jack heard the car return about an hour later. He crept downstairs and poured himself a glass of milk as his dad came in quietly through the back door and into the kitchen.

"Hello, what are you doing up?"

The fact that Jack was clearly pouring himself a drink must have meant that more of an explanation was required. "I couldn't sleep, so I came down to get a drink of milk." He said. "Where have you been so late?"

"Oh, I just had to go out for a bit." He started to be vague as adults can be, then he let out a sigh and seemed to deflate a little. He looked at Jack as if seeing him afresh, as the teenager he nearly was and not as the little boy he had assumed him still to be. "I went for a drive to unwind, calm down a bit before bed, you know; otherwise I wouldn't have been able to sleep either. And, do you know what? I'm glad you're still awake, Jack; I want to share with you what I've just seen."

"A U.F.O.?" asked Jack eagerly.

"No. No, not quite. But something that has had just as profound an effect on me. Maybe you'll understand. Come through to the lounge."

Jack took his milk into the sitting room and sat on the sofa. His dad went to the cupboard under the stairs and came through with the spare duvet and a pillow.

"Are you going to sleep down here, dad?"

"Yes, I thought I would; don't want to wake mum up, do I?"

"Is everything alright?" asked Jack shyly. "I heard you and mum arguing before."

"Yes, of course," came the immediate, automatic reply. There was a pause. "It's not easy being an adult, being a parent, you know; no easier than growing up yourself, I suppose. I know we seem like we know everything and have all the power, we make the rules and all the decisions, but none of it comes naturally. None of it is easy, Jack. And mummy and I have our differences, just like you and Alex –"

"And Alex and Max," put in Jack, with understanding. His dad smiled, and put his arm around Jack's shoulders.

"These things often sound worse than they are; like when I come into your room when you and your brothers are fighting, and I go all over the top, all upset and stressed that you can't just get along, and I take your toys away and ground you or whatever, and you think I'm overreacting because you were just having a disagreement, yeah? Arguments always sound worse to those who overhear them. But I want you to know; we keep saying it, don't we, but it's the truth: mummy and I both love you all - you, Alex, Max and Sammy - no matter how cross we are with each other or about something one of you has done; we will always love you, and support you, and any decisions that we make will always be what is best for you; what is best for all of us as a family, yeah? Even if those decisions are hard for a while, it's ultimately what is best in the long run, you understand?"

"Like moving away from London?"

"Exactly. Prime example, Jack. You do like it here, in the village, don't you? You're settling in ok, making friends? And keeping in touch with your old friends, the good ones?"

"Yes, yes, all the good ones. And it is nice here, and I can see how it's better for Max and Sam to grow up here and everything." His dad gave his shoulders a squeeze. "So, what did you want to tell me, anyway? What was it you saw?"

"Well, you heard the argument with mum; I just had to get away and unwind, so I drove out of the village, not consciously heading anywhere, just driving to relax, you know, and the moon was fantastic: perfectly full, amazingly bright, clear black sky, all the trees and buildings painted silver and black; magical. So I kind of followed the moon. It was ahead of me, slightly to the right: two o'clock as we say; so I crossed the A38 by Murphy's, and then the road wound a little more to the left, so now the moon was at three o'clock, to my right. Then there was a turning on the right to Burrington Coombe, so I turned up there. After about half a mile, the road goes into a gorge with trees on one side and steep stone cliffs rising suddenly on the other, and the road winds sharply through the rocks. So I came round one sharp bend, where there were cliffs on both sides and fewer trees blocking out the sky, and it was the most unexpected, incredible, mystical sight: the rocky cliffs with steep sloping grass at intervals, like balconies, looked like they had been etched in silver, and there, on the grass, just at the side of the road, not behind fences or anything, in the bright silver light of the moon, were white, long-haired goats, about a dozen of them, just standing like sentinels all up the gorge, staring down serenely at the car with the moon herself high above. It was most unearthly. It was incredible, and I'm glad I could tell someone about it; someone like you who can appreciate it; your mum wouldn't have understood at all." "Wow! That does sound incredible." Jack tried to picture the goats in the moonlight. It sounded very curious; it sounded…he couldn't quite put his finger on how it sounded.

"Right, have you finished your milk? It's been a long day, and I think we both need to get to sleep now. Do you want me to come up and settle you down?"

"No, thanks, it's ok. Good night, dad."

"Sweet dreams, Jack. Love you. See you in the morning."

Jack crept quietly upstairs, listening to the sounds of his dad sorting the cushions and the duvet out on the sofa. He crept past Sam's door and his parents' bedroom where, increasingly, his mum slept alone; he listened, then crept on to the front room, certain that his mum was asleep.

Moving slowly and carefully, light on his feet and sure of his fingers, he quietly found clothes for Max and Alex, and laid them at the ends of their beds, then got dressed himself. All their outdoor shoes and boots were in the utility room downstairs, past where dad was probably not quite asleep, but he found their rubber soled beach shoes in the bottom of the wardrobe. Then he waited as long as his patience would let him, wondering whether or not his dad would be asleep yet. When he could bear it no longer, he stroked Max's face to gently wake him up, then whispered to him to get dressed. He sat on Alex's bed and gently shook the mound of duvet. "Sshh! Get dressed. Quietly," he whispered, as Alex started to object to being woken. "This is important."

"What is? What's going on?"

"I can't explain it. I've just got this feeling that tonight is really important," whispered Jack. "Tonight is a magical night, I know it, and we have to go to the quarry."

"The quarry? Now? Are you mad?" whispered Alex.

"Come on!" whispered Max excitedly, "it will be such an adventure! Like The Famous Five!"

"What are these for?" asked Alex a minute later, holding up the beach shoes.

"Dad's on the sofa; we won't be able to get our trainers from the utility room."

"Then how are we going to get to the quarry if we can't go downstairs?"

"Put these on, and come with me, quietly."

The three boys crept along the landing to the top of the stairs, hardly daring to breathe. Jack swung his long legs over Sam's security gate then passed the plastic step to Alex, who used it to silently scissor over the gate himself. Finally, Max stood on the step, and Jack lifted him over the gate, setting him silently down in Sam's room, before reaching over and retrieving the step. With the greatest of stealth, the boys tiptoed past Sam's cot to the window. Jack climbed carefully onto Sam's wooden toy chest, pushed open the window, and climbed through, letting himself down onto the flat roof of the utility room and placing the plastic step under the window to make the return journey easier. Alex followed, then they both helped Max down so he didn't make a noise. Jack pushed the window to within a finger's breadth of being closed, then he jumped off the roof onto the upper part of the back lawn. Alex jumped after him, landing with a stifled exhalation of breath, then before he could think of the best way to fetch Max down, their brother had jumped too, and was rolling like a paratrooper on the silver grass beside them.

As he often did, and much to the annoyance of their mum, Mr Pearson had left the garden gate open, so with no further obstruction nor potentially dangerous noise, the boys were on the street, heading up the hill.

It was almost as bright as day, but all the colours were muted and the shadows accentuated. It was dream-like. One or two houses had lit bathroom windows, but all the other windows were dark. There was no noise, not even birdsong. The boys felt as if they were the only ones awake anywhere. It was thrilling and scary. They walked softly and silently up to the cul-de-sac, and approached the steps up to Quarry Road. The passageway between the high fences was in utter shadow.

"I should have thought about torches," said Jack, cross with himself.

"I've got my keyring torch," said Alex, digging in his pocket.

"Oh, brilliant! You're a star!" said Jack.

The small Maglite cast a narrow but strong beam, enough to illuminate the steps safely but not make the boys too visible. Alex went first, now, lighting the way, Max behind and Jack bringing up the rear. As the moonlight lit up the last few steps, Alex put the torch back in his pocket. Jack looked across to Poppy's house, half expecting her to be there, answering the moon's call, too, but all was in darkness, and nothing moved in the shadows of her garden. They crossed to the lime kilns, trod softly over the gravel, and through the gap in the trees. With the aid of the torch again, they climbed up onto the track, and stood for a minute, listening. But for what?

Each of them was hypersensitive with nervous excitement. Was this how Julian, Dick and George felt on Kirin Island or Mystery Moor, Max wondered? If only they had a Timmy for support and protection. The silence around them was as thick and strange as the moonlight. There was a strong sense of something magical and immense, something of great importance that had brought them here after midnight, just them, with no adult supervision.

A sudden breeze brushed their faces and animated some of the leaves and grasses to stirring. The deep shadows were playing with their perception, the monochrome landscape looked like a Magic Eye picture; the leaves on the bushes swam in and out of focus as if they were going to reveal some hidden image.

"Come on," said Jack in a low voice, "and keep away from the edge. We all know where we're going."

They rounded the corner that overlooked the lower level; the rocks on the far side looked like beaten silver, and the floor shone like mercury. They kept close together, each of them feeling the comfort the others provided, each looking rather fearfully at the bushes to either side of the track. Then they were in the quarry where they had first come with Poppy, and the great mottled disc of the moon looked down from above the far cliff. The landscape itself looked lunar, and the boys felt weightless with adrenalin.

The little tree looked ghostly, swathed in the shadows at the foot of the cliff. "Guys," said Max, urgently, grabbing each of his brothers at once. "There's something there, on the mound under the tree. Can you see it?"

The boys were terrified. They were out in the open, in the glare of the moon, nowhere to run for cover for a hundred meters on any side. And as their eyes strained, they could make out, on the top of the earth mound, a small figure, quite still, like a dog sitting to attention as they do with their front legs straight. The boys stared in silence while their hearts beat furiously, and their palms became sticky with sweat. None of them moved. The figure on the mound didn't move. Was it an animal? Was it just their imagination or a trick of the light?

"What should we do, Jack?" asked Max.

"I don't know. It must have seen us, if it's alive. We're much more noticeable out here than it is in the shadows. I think we should keep going, but stay alert; be ready to run."

"What if it's a trap? If it's waiting for us to get closer?" asked Alex.

"If it was a trap, why show itself at all? Why not just ambush us out of the darkness? Why not stay hidden in the cave or the bushes?"

"Do you think it's Stig?" asked Max in a tiny voice.

"I don't know, let's go and see. But be ready to run home if I say so, right?"

"Why don't you go, and we'll stay here, ready to run for help?" suggested Alex.

"Alright," said Jack, surprising himself with his bravery. "You look after Max, ok?"

So the two younger boys stood holding hands in the moonlit expanse of the empty quarry, while Jack kept his eyes focussed on the figure under the tree, and confidently made his way towards it. "Show no fear, show no pain," he whispered. Somehow he had known something would be here, something would happen. He had been convinced of the need to come by his dad's description of the goats. Somehow, he wasn't afraid now, he was only excited.

If it had been daylight, he could have made out the nature of the figure from much further away, but in the subtlety of the moonlight he was about twenty meters from the dark shape when it seemed to unfold and grow, like a transformer, and step towards him, out from the shadows of the cliff and the tree.

"Poppy!" he said in amazement and some disenchantment. "What are you doing here?"

"Waiting for you. What took you so long?"

"How did you know we'd come?"

"I felt it, didn't you? Isn't that why you're here?"

"I suppose it is. Weren't you scared on your own?"

"Nothing to be scared of out here," replied Poppy in that tone that seemed to imply an unspoken element to her words.

Jack turned and beckoned the others over.

"Did you know Poppy was going to be here?" asked Alex, "did you arrange this?"

"No. Like I said, tonight is full of magic or something; Poppy felt it too. Right, now, are we going to explore this cave? Alex, get your torch out."

The four of them followed the beam of the torch into the cave. "Why are we going in here?" asked Max.

"You're not scared, are you?" teased Poppy.

"Because," cut in Jack protectively, "I don't think this is a cave. I think it's something else: a tunnel, or a gateway, or something."

"Did anybody bring any primroses?" joked Poppy, and Jack wondered if she might have a point.

Alex swept the torch across the floor, like a searchlight, so they could all see where they were treading. Soon, they had reached the back of the cave; all their senses tingled with the thrill of anticipation, of expectation. They cast their eyes about the cave; the floor, the walls, the ceiling, following Alex's torchlight, not knowing quite what they were looking for. Jack turned and looked back through the mouth of the cave at the dark tree and the silver grass swaying gently. Max was peering intently at the scene outside, too.

"Aarlubbock," burped Alex.

"God!" said Poppy, startled, as Max laughed and the tension was broken. Then they all stopped still in fear, for there came a rumbling from the back of the cave.

The children huddled together, even Poppy, and Alex shone his torch in the direction of the noise. Something was happening to the rock of the cave wall. The torch beam couldn't focus on it; it seemed to be dissolving, evaporating, melting away, and there was a mineral glow coming from behind it. Then, quite suddenly, the noise stopped and there was a tunnel leading further into the hill. Gem stones set into the sides of the tunnel seemed to be illuminating it like the safety lights in a cinema auditorium. The children stood enraptured, unable to move or speak. Alex switched off the torch, and the glow from the tunnel was sufficient to see each other and the floor of the cave.

"I guess you were right," said Max, the first to recover his powers of speech. "What now?"

"Erm," said Poppy, pointing like someone in a trance. Four small figures with green skin and wearing simple tunics of leather and animal fur were standing in the tunnel.

"Greetings, emissaries of the overworld. Enter and be welcome."

Chapter Nine

Cave Painting

The children were dumbfounded in shock. Now that the something magical and important had actually happened, Jack couldn't believe it. He was, in fact, the most surprised of all of them. Max was the first to take a step towards the creatures, who remained on the edge of their tunnel, standing in a welcoming formation a bit like the handshake tunnels at the end of rugby matches. He looked at Jack with a triumphant expression that said 'Now do you believe me?'

"My name's Max," he said to the one who had spoken the greeting.

"Be welcome, Max, one who has eyes to see," said the green creature.

When Poppy didn't move, Alex stepped forward and told the creature his name.

"Be welcome, Zander, one who speaks with our tongue," said the creature.

"I'm Poppy," said Poppy next.

"Be welcome Poppy, one named in remembrance of the dead and for the life that rises from the soil."

"And I'm Jack."

"Be welcome Jack, one with strength in his arm and a good heart. Be welcome, all of you; but are there no more?"

The four creatures looked out towards the entrance to the Stig cave, expectantly. They lingered at the mouth of their tunnel, reluctant to close the rock too soon, it seemed.

"No, it's just us," said Jack.

The creature took just a moment or two to register this, then he gestured with his slender, root-like arms, and the eight of them walked deeper into the hill as the fissure in the rock healed itself behind them. "I am Sostror. My companions are Tibigar, Bauzon, and Minador. We have waited a long time. Come."

"Where are we going?" asked Poppy.

"To our chambers," said Sostror. "We have much to share, much to share, and not much time."

The four green creatures led the children down the tunnel which opened out into a large cavern, with alcoves set in the side, and two more tunnels leading deeper into the hill. On the floor of the cavern, boulders like the ones outside the lime kilns, only smoother, were arranged in concentric semi circles facing a stone dais which lay between the two tunnels at the opposite end of the cavern to where they had entered. The seats in the chamber, for that's clearly what they were, were all empty, but more of the creatures were sitting in the alcoves, which looked like large café or restaurant booths; they had low benches carved out of the walls, and little stone tables in the middle. In one, a stream of water spilled out of the wall into a carved stone basin. By the side of the basin, vessels were stacked like cups and bowls on a draining board. The children could see more of these vessels on the little tables in the other alcoves. There was a stirring of interest among the creatures as they watched the children being led across the chamber, but none of them came any closer.

Sostror took the children to the first row of boulders in front of the dais. "Be sitting," he said, gesturing with his thin arm. Tibigar and Minador brought them cups of water from the stream. It was deliciously cool, with a rich aftertaste of crisp, fresh apple, although there was no texture of cordial or anything artificial. They all drank deeply, although none of them had been feeling thirsty before. Sitting on the stones, the children were all about as tall as Sostror standing in front of them.

"What exactly are you?" asked Jack, hesitantly.

"We have been given many names by your kind: Elves and Goblins have been the most common, and Goblin has lasted longer in these parts."

"Of course, the Green Goblin!" said Jack. "I can't believe it!"

"We call ourselves Elder-iche, from a time when we lived more closely with your kind, the Awer-Iche. We were not so very different, once upon a time. But your kind were controlled by desires we did not share. Desires for wealth and strength and power over your fellows. Dividing up the common land, building houses and castles with walls round everything, claiming ownership of the trees and the rivers, the very rocks beneath the soil, and the bright rocks, the gemstones, the wimblestone. Wars were fought against your fellow man and against us, and so we retreated into the earth which has always been our home."

"Did you say wimblestone? What is the wimblestone?" Interrupted Alex.

"The wimblelstone is why you are here, young Zander. Why you are all here. And why we, we creep and hide at the margins of the overland, powerless against the forces of evil. Over a thousand years ago, there was one of your kind who was strong but not cruel; rich and powerful but not riddled with greed; a king who held his court at a table with but one side so that all his knights were of an equal with him. He had the strength of arm and head and heart to unite our worlds in harmony, and we surrendered our magic to aid him to this end. He had a sword that only he could wield, a sword that could not be defeated, for at its hilt was set the wimblestone, the Elder-iche stone of life. After his death, the sword was returned to The Lady of the Lake, and the stone should have been returned to us. But it was taken and never seen again. Without the wimblestone, our kind cannot survive much longer."

"Erm, sorry, what does this have to do with us?" asked Poppy.

Sostror stepped up onto the dais and beckoned the children to join him. "This image has been here for fifteen hundred years, since the time of Merlin and Morgana. It shows the sacred five who will restore the stone to the Elder-iche." He made a gesture with his arm, and the glow from the crystals set in the walls and the roof of the cavern intensified. On the wall behind the dais was a set of figures, pale yet distinct in some ancient pigment. Five figures, like people, but one with an exaggerated mouth, one with enormous ears, one with bulging eyes, a fourth with a torso like a body builder, and a fifth diagram like a human spider with four arms and four legs. Above their heads was something like the sun or a comet, with rays of light coming from it, clearly representing the magical stone.

"And you think that's us? And some kind of monster?" asked Alex.

"Zander, this is you, the one who speaks our ancient tongue, who opened the door in the rock; Poppy, we have watched you for many years, and I think you sensed this.

Now you will be given gifts beyond your understanding. Max, you have the gift of sight to see the hidden realms of the world, you are very special. And Jack, you are strong and with a good heart, your help will be crucial in the times ahead. And there is one other whom you must find, the one like this; without their help you will not be able to complete your task."

"Our task?" said Poppy.

"You must find the stone and return it. It is your destiny and our fate. Time is running short and our powers dwindle every day. We grow fewer, and we grow weak. We grow old, and there are none growing up who can replace us. The wimblestone to us is like the sun in the sky, it gave us what we needed to live and grow. Our powers are not strong without it. We have dwelt in a dark age for centuries, but now we must have light once more."

The children were incredulous. They looked from each other to the paintings to Sostror, unable to take it all in.

Sostror sat on one of the rocks behind the children. "For many centuries we were part of your community, part of the world of the Awer-Iche. Some of the ancient local families had Elder-gates in their garden walls, and welcomed our visits and our counsel. There are still some descendants of mixed blood from long ago, Awer-Iche who are small, and green-fingered. Yes, that is where the expression for a good gardener comes from; someone with Elder-iche blood, an affinity for nature, an understanding of the plants and the animals. We shared our knowledge freely, and the kind folk of the overworld revered and respected us; protected us as much as they could. But the overworld changed quickly, too quickly for us. People started to move away from their ancestral homes; strangers arrived with no knowledge, no understanding, no sight. They turned away from nature; built machines. Gone were the old ways, the quiet ways, respectful ways. All about greed and profit. The farmers had machines to do everything. Used chemicals on their crops and on their animals. Forgot about the other creatures in the hills and hedges, in the streams and rivers and pools. Poisoned everything! Dug up our hill. Cut down our trees. Heard rumours about the wimblestone, and tried to find it, burrowing into our home, seeking us out. We had to retreat; we had to hide. Stay underground, out of the way. Until we were all but forgotten to your kind, except in tales and superstitions of The Green Man, of sprites and pixies and fairies. And now we are weak. We will last but another century here, unless you can return our life-stone. You four chosen ones, and the fifth whom you will need to find. Now, drink up. It is late. You must get home. And, Poppy, remember to keep well with the gypsies. It will soon be time for the gypsy fayre."

Jack was looking up at the mural again. Now that his eyes were fully adjusted to the light in the chamber, he could see that there were brushstrokes above the five figures, forming a pattern.

"Sostror? Is that writing at the top, there? What does it say?" he asked.

"Between the dream time and the now is never and forever," said the goblin, solemnly.

"Right." Said Jack. "And what does that mean?"

"What it says," replied Sostror, a puzzled look crossing his green face.

"Ok," said Jack, none the wiser. "Can we come back and see you? What if we have questions about this quest? There has been so much to take in."

"Will we be able to open the tunnel any time?" asked Alex. "Or was it you who opened it tonight, because of the moon?"

"You have the power to open the rock whenever you choose, young Zander," said Sostror, "but soon the winter time will be here, when the trees sleep, and the animals hide in their dens until spring. We, too will pass the dark months nestled in slumber, for without the stone of life we are too weak to face the winter. Even now we prepare for the long nights. But you may find us awake still, for a few more weeks."

The goblins led the children back through the tunnel, and opened the wall into the Stig cave. The children stepped out into the moonlit quarry, feeling like they were waking from a dream. They walked silently back to the lime kilns together, climbed down into the trees and crept slowly out past the boulders. There was nobody around, just a cat sitting on the bonnet of a car outside Poppy's house. They crossed the road to the steps, then said goodbye to Poppy.

"See you tomorrow, Jack. Don't be late for school!"

The boys crept down the steps, down the silvery road, and in through the garden gate. Jack helped Alex and Max climb quietly onto the roof of the utility room and back in through Sam's window. They undressed without a word, hid their clothes under their beds, and were soon fast asleep. In a little under five hours they would all need to be up again.

When their dad woke them the next morning, they didn't feel tired at all. It felt like Christmas morning, they were so excited.

"Guys, did that really happen last night?" asked Max in a whisper, "Jack, you really believe me now that I could see those goblins in the bushes? They must have been watching us when we came to the village, sure that we were the chosen ones."

It seemed crazy, in the normality of their bedroom, with the sounds of their dad downstairs in the kitchen, the aroma of simmering porridge oats rising up to their nostrils telling them that it was a school day. They looked at each other's faces, then each retrieved the clothes they had taken off and hidden in the night. Their beach shoes were all scuffed and covered in fine grey dust from the quarry. They put the clothes and shoes away properly, and got dressed in their new school uniforms.

"I wish Stephen was going to be in school today," said Max.

"Listen," said Jack, very seriously. He put his hands on his brothers' shoulders, and looked at them both in the eyes. "You cannot tell anybody about this, ok? This has to stay our secret, just between us three and Poppy. You get me?"

"Why?" asked Max.

"Because no one will believe us. Ok? Not even Stephen will believe you, and if you tell anybody, you will be made fun of; everyone will think you're weird, that we're all a weird, crazy family, ok? Trust me. Some guys in the rugby team told me to stay away from Poppy just because she talks about folk tales, myths and legends. They told me she was weird and crazy, and that's even before we knew that the goblins are real. So promise me you won't tell anyone. Either of you."

"Porridge is on the table, boys!" called their dad.

"Promise? Just for now, we keep this our secret, yeah?"

"Ok," and "Promise," replied his brothers.

"Good." Said Jack with a broad smile.

As they passed Sam's room, they saw him standing up in his cot, clinging to the bars and making noises at them. They could hear their mum getting out of bed in the next room, ready to come and get Sam dressed. Jack quickly whispered to Alex to stand by the cot and say good morning to Sam, and while their mum was distracted by the delightful brotherly scene, Jack quickly took out his handkerchief and wiped three sets of dusty footprints off the toy chest and the windowsill. Then they all went downstairs together for their porridge.

Chapter Ten

Gypsy Fair

The next couple of weeks ticked by in a clockwork pattern of increasingly complex routine. Jack got his bus pass at the end of the first week of school, and from then on, every morning, he would walk down the hill to the bus stop near the wizard's house, waving at the faces of his mum and Sam in the big lounge window. The twins would already be on the bus, which picked the majority of children up outside the pub opposite the chippy, collected the twins at the bottom of the hill opposite the highland cow field, then went on with Jack and a couple of older boys, adding Poppy at the top of the hill by the pet food store. Jack had got to know the twins, Kyle and Sean, a bit better at the second rugby session, and he thought they were alright, but Poppy wouldn't have anything to do with them. She just glared at them before taking her seat, and they would laugh and make quiet comments about her to themselves. Jack was torn, but because the twins were already in their seats when he got on, he went and sat either next to or just in front of them, and Poppy always sat nearer the front. He had tried to explain to her about it at break time on the first day he had caught the bus, and she had said it was fine. Boys would be boys, after all, she knew, and there were already rumours going round the village about Poppy's boyfriend, the new kid from London, so she said it was best if they weren't always seen together. She sounded a little disappointed, but not, Jack thought, with him, just with the way things were.

Being new, Jack had expected to be something of a novelty in a small community, but Churchill academy brought together a large number of primary schools from the surrounding villages, and many of the children had been split into houses and tutor groups with children they didn't know. A few of the boys seemed to know each other from rugby or scouts even if they had attended different schools, but initially there were lots of strange faces for everyone to get to know, and Jack was just one of them. He noticed, however, that Poppy didn't seem to have any particular friends. Didn't seem part of a set or crowd. She tended to be by herself in the less structured parts of the day; always quiet and unassuming; often with a book or notebook, when others were just chatting or playing games.

Alex and Max enjoyed their walks to and from the village school, and didn't miss the noisy, busy streets of Hounslow at all. On their first day, they had seen two girls waiting with their mums to cross the road ahead of them. When they reached the pavement, they all disappeared into the hedge. Mrs Pearson walked Alex and Max up the quiet roads that wound round the estate of bungalows, and as they reached the school gates, they saw some more children emerging from a narrow gap between two gardens. When their mum came to collect them, they asked if they could explore the secret passageway, which was like an overgrown jungle, twisting and turning between trees and bushes all the way through the estate, and they took great delight in showing their dad when it was his turn to take them in the mornings.

The boys' classrooms were in different parts of the school and so only saw each other at assembly and lunch. Their differences in temperament and age kept them apart at these times, too, but even so, Alex did keep an eye on his younger brother, and knew just when to give him a bit of reassurance if he was looking lost or upset. Both boys liked their teachers, and the classes were much calmer than they had been in London. Break time was also much better. There were still clear friendship groups and hierarchies, and Alex in particular suffered some exclusion and mean behaviour for being new and sounding different, but it was nothing like the extent of bullying that he was used to seeing. By the end of the first week, though, he had been accepted by the majority of the boys for introducing them to a song about a fart. The school was divided into four houses, named after key milestones in the history of transportation, and the Pearson boys were both in Brunel, named after Isambard Kingdom Brunel whose famous bridge spans the gorge of the Avon in Bristol. Most people thought Zander was a cool name when they first heard it, but Alex was suitably impressed by Isambard Kingdom. That was something else entirely. But he had to admit in class that he had never seen the bridge, and not yet visited Bristol at all.

"I can't believe you've never been to Bristol," said Marlon, whose name Alex thought was also quite cool, when they were standing in the playground watching some of the girls playing hopscotch.

"The only time I'd ever heard of Bristol till we moved here was in a song the older boys used to sing on the coach on school outings."

"What was the song? Go on, sing it for us."

"I can't remember it all, just the bit about Bristol, cos it was the funniest. It's about someone who does a fart, and it escapes. It goes like:

> The fart went rolling down the street,
> Parlez-vous!
> The fart went rolling down the street,
> Parlez-vous!
> The fart went rolling down the street,
> Knocked a copper off his feet,
> Inky, stinky, parlez-vous!
>
> The copper got out his rusty pistol,
> Parlez-vous!
> The copper got out his rusty pistol,
> Parlez-vous!
> The copper got out his rusty pistol,
> Shot the fart from here to Bristol,
> Inky, stinky, parlez-vous!"

All the boys thought this was hilarious, and by the second week, the whole school was singing it at break times and on the way home. In assembly that Friday morning, Mrs Williams, the head mistress, banned the song with threats of punishment for anyone caught singing it on the school premises, but Alex's reputation as a playground hero in the eyes of the other children was established.

Gradually, the weeks filled up with activities and commitments. The first Thursday, Poppy took Jack to the youth club, and this became a regular thing. A handful of adults supervised the club, providing hot and cold drinks, toast and biscuits, and organising board games and table tennis, but a lot of the kids just ran around outside playing tag and chatting. For some reason, Poppy was much more sociable in this environment, willing to participate, and also not shy or self-conscious around Jack. She seemed much more at ease with all the children who came, apart from the twins who showed up occasionally. All she would say when Jack asked her about them was that they were mindless thugs without a brain cell between them.

Jack and Alex joined the Scouts and Max joined the Cubs, taking up Monday and Tuesday evenings, and there were swimming lessons for all of them on Wednesdays. Now that they were living so close to the sea, Mrs Pearson thought it essential that they were all strong swimmers. A fun and friendly touch rugby tournament started up on Thursdays, finishing just in time for Jack to go to the youth club, and by the third week, karate lessons in Weston were taking up Friday evenings, too. Mr Pearson had the idea of sampling a different fish and chip shop every week on the way home, because there seemed to be hundreds. When their dad was working the late shift, their mum could sometimes be persuaded to carry on the tradition, but generally defaulted to the village chippy because they were very good and parking was easy. The bodywork of the big family car was a testament to the importance of this factor.

Jack asked the boys in his tutor group about football, and heard that the Winscombe team were not as well organised as the rugby club, but were in the process of appointing some new coaches, and they were excited about the new season. Jack and Alex went along to the club on Saturday morning, and due to the size of the club, and a lack of players Alex's age, were both added to the under 13 squad, while Max preferred to have at least one day without any commitments so that he could play with Stephen.

All these activities left very little time for visiting the quarry or even thinking about goblins and where to find the wimblestone. Then there was still the mystery of the fifth picture on the wall of the cave; the spider-like creature that was supposed to help them. The boys would sometimes have whispered conversations in their bedroom after the lights had been turned out, and Jack would pick Poppy's brains on Thursday nights, but they all felt that the task was impossible. If the stone had been missing for a millennium, how were they supposed to find it now? Jack was overwhelmed with sympathy for Bilbo Baggins and Harry Potter, and any other characters he could think of being given such responsibility. At the start of October, as they were cycling along the strawberry line from the youth club, Poppy asked Jack what he was doing on Saturday.

"I've got football in the morning. It's a home match, so I'll be finished by half eleven. Then mum will have made lunch for twelve, I expect. Why?"

"I want to show you and your brothers something, that's all. Could we meet by my house after lunch? Say one o'clock?"

Jack and Alex were in a good mood after football on Saturday. The new coaches were very enthusiastic and encouraging, galvanising the team that had evidently been a little lacklustre in previous years. They had won their game against Portishead 2-1, and the boys gave everyone at the dining room table a full breakdown of their key moments in defence. They were so engrossed in their victory that Jack almost forgot about meeting Poppy.

When lunch was finished, the boys excused themselves, and walked up the hill, up the narrow steps, and out onto Quarry Road.

"Come this way!" said Poppy, who was waiting for them. She led the boys away from her house and the lime kilns, up the road towards the farm. There was a footpath by the side of the turning area in front of the farm gate, doubling back towards the lime kilns, past an overgrown area of bricks and concrete that Poppy said had been a forge, probably at the same time as the kilns had been operating. The path then turned steeply uphill, and they scrambled up in silence, saving their breath for the exertion involved. The path turned to the right and levelled out again, ascending gradually towards a wider track, but at the corner there was a steeper shortcut worn out of the undergrowth, and Jack could see something that interested him.

"What's that up there, Poppy?" he asked, already stretching his legs and pulling against the trunk of a tree to hoist himself up.

"Oh, that's nothing, let's go the easy way," she replied, but Alex and Max, always keen to sniff out adventure, were already following their intrepid brother.

They came out onto a smooth gravel track, rather like the strawberry line, although thick moss was encroaching here from either side, and the edges were more overgrown. A little way to their left was what had caught Jack's eye. Half hidden at the far side of the track was an old railway box

126

car, the metal frame rusted, and the wooden panels rotted and broken. Half the roof was missing, too, the remaining boards blackened and covered in creeper.

"Looks like it's been burned," observed Alex.

"That's right," said Poppy, joining them.

"Did this used to be a railway line from the quarry?"

"Yes, I think so," said Poppy, looking at the box car with a sad expression.

"And what about this?"

"That used to be my special place, my secret hideaway. It was all in good repair round the front here, but there was a hole in one of the panels round the back. I found an old kitchen worktop to use as a door, and I had cushions and a little table and an old paraffin lamp, and I would come here and read my books and that, even in the rain. It was ace."

"What happened to it?" asked Jack.

"The twins trashed it and burned it down."

"What!? Why?"

"Dunno. Jealous, I guess. I see they've built their own tree house now. They're just mean. I hate them." Poppy kicked a large grey stone into the bushes, and turned moodily away, walking back up the old train line. "Come on," she said. "This isn't what I was going to show you."

Poppy wouldn't explain where they were going, just led them up along the track with the trees arching overhead like a tunnel. When they emerged into the sunlight again, they were all amazed at the sight before them. A dozen or so old fashioned gypsy caravans, like giant, colourful barrels on wheels, were grouped in two rows that curved around the lip of the upper level of the quarry. They formed a kind of street of wooden houses. The caravans

127

had wooden steps at the front, leading up to little doors. Some were closed, some wide open with curtains hanging across the entrance, and some were open at the top like windows or stable doors. Chairs, tables, small fires with kettles warming, and sometimes richly patterned rugs lay before the caravans, and gypsies were sitting in the sun, drinking and talking, or busying themselves with the fire, or engaged in craftwork, while dogs lazed in the sunshine or ran between the settlements chased by groups of small children. The brow of the hill rose another two or three meters above the gypsy camp, and horses were visible there, grazing contentedly, tethered by long ropes.

Poppy was already walking slowly between the rows of caravans, smiling at the gypsies, who seemed to recognise her. Certainly, nobody shouted at her for intruding, and so the boys followed, taking in all the colours and beautiful decorations. They soon noticed that some of the villagers were also here, inspecting wares and chatting to the travellers. One caravan was selling decoratively painted pottery, another fine metal ware, a third freshly caught pheasants and rabbits, and items decorated with fur and feathers. There were a couple specialising in gold and silver jewellery, and Max noticed that there were a number of stones arranged on the wooden steps of one of them. A gypsy with a leather hat, long black hair tied in a ponytail, and thick silver hoops in his ears watched Max looking at the stones and gave him a smile that showed his gold tooth. At the far end, near the thick trees that covered the northern slope of the quarry, was a caravan with a bubbling cauldron set over a fire. A pretty woman with her long, coal black hair kept back from her face by a bright red headscarf was stirring the cauldron as the children approached.

"Hello, Poppy!" called the woman, "I bin 'spectin you. And who's this ye've brought, some friends, is it?" She gave them all a welcoming smile and brushed her hands against her skirt. Poppy introduced Jack, Zander and Max, and they all sat down on thick logs that had been arranged around the cauldron. "Spect you'd like some tea, eh?"

"What is it today, Bethany?" asked Poppy.

Bethany was already dipping a copper measure with a long handle into the centre of the cauldron and filling small tin mugs with a pungent green liquid. "Nettle and mint, my dear. This'll open your minds," she chuckled.

"Are you a witch?" asked Max and Jack quickly shushed him. "But there's a witch in the village, Stephen told me; and she's using a cauldron!" protested Max in a whisper.

"It's alright," laughed Bethany with a genuine smile, "I's no witch. A cauldron's just a useful travelling pot is all, my dear," she said to Max, handing him his mug. Poppy was the only one who was sipping at the tea. "Drink up! Best while it's hot."

The boys tentatively sniffed the green tea steaming in their mugs. It didn't smell bad. It was just that word 'nettle' that was putting them off.

"Haven't you got any milk?" asked Alex.

"Oh, we doesn't put milk in 'em," laughed Bethany, "spoils the taste," she said, "and dilutes the magic." She winked at Poppy and smiled at the three boys. "'Spect you all know somethin' 'bout magic, now, don't you?" She sat down on the tallest log with her own mug of tea, and smiled at them all.

"What do you mean?" asked Jack, nervously.

129

"Well, we comes to this 'ere place twice a year, see. Every spring and every autumn. We bin comin' here for generations, and we knows a lot about the old places like this ancient hill. We knows a lot about what most folks don't see or don't believe in. Secrets and ancient ways. I thinks you knows what I's talkin' 'bout, Jack. Am I right?"

Her voice was soft, and her accent thick and warm. Her smile came from her eyes as well as her lips, and Jack felt he could trust her. He looked at Poppy and his brothers, but saw no warning in their expressions.

The green tea reminded him of Sostror and the other goblins in the cavern. He took a sip, not looking at Bethany. It was like nothing he had ever drunk before. He could taste the mint, but it was not sharp like mint sauce, and not exactly like mint chocolate either, just fresh, like a Trebor mint, and underneath was what must have been the taste of the nettles, but it was a gentle taste, not sour as he had expected. Combined, the sensation was like walking into a cave and breathing the air from the rocks, not the hazy air of summer. Although it was steaming hot, he felt like he was diving into a cold pool. It certainly did open one's mind.

He looked up at Bethany again as he surfaced from his mug, and said he thought perhaps she was right. Bethany nodded, and turned to Poppy.

"I 'spect you saw Django as you came through? He'll be along of a minute, shouldn't wonder. Got something for you, 'e 'as." She poured herself another ladle full of tea, and offered to top up the children's mugs for them, then she hung the ladle over the handle of the cauldron, and sat back down on her log. "Tell me about this witch in the village, then, young 'un," she said to Max.

"Well, my friend Stephen was showing me some donkeys up Sandy Lane, and we was coming back when suddenly he says to me 'quick! Hide in the hedge!' and when I asked why, he pointed to this woman, and he said she was the witch of Woodborough Drive."

"Did she look like a witch? With a big, hooked nose and everything?" asked Alex.

"She had white hair, but she looked ordinary. Anyway, I asked why he called her that, and he said that one time his mum needed to get something from the Co-op, some everyday thing, you know, like bread or milk or cheese or something, and it was busy and the car park was full, and it was raining, so his mum just parked up Woodborough Drive, past the car park. Anyway, when she got out of the car, this old woman had a go at her for parking opposite her house. It's not double yellow lines or anything, it's ok to park there, but this woman was really nasty about it. So Stephen's mum explained that she would only be a few minutes, she was just going to the shop, and the witch said to her 'it won't do you no good, misses'. So she went to the Co-op, but they didn't have any of the basic things she needed, so she walked up to the Spar instead, but they didn't have no milk or cheese or whatever, either. So she came back to the car, absolutely soaked cos of the rain, and no shopping to show for it, and the old witch was still standing in her garden, in the rain, laughing at her. I mean, how creepy is that?"

"Which is her house?" asked Alex, captivated by this tale.

"Dunno," said Max. "We was near our house when we saw her walking up the lane."

"You can just see it from the Chippy," said Poppy. It's the one with the grotty yellow van on the drive, and a little black Smart car."

"Instead of a black cat!" exclaimed Alex, laughing.

Bethany looked like she was deep in thought, as the children discussed the tale of the local witch.

"I wonder if she does have a cat," said Alex.

"Oh, yes, there'll be cats, alright," said Bethany, still gazing far away.

"We keep seeing cats around the garden," said Max, but just then, a man's voice cut into their chatter with:

"Hallo there, Poppy my girl! Bin lookin' fer you since morning, I 'as."

"Hello Django," replied Poppy brightly, "these are some friends of mine. They moved to the village in the summer."

"Well, well, owdyer-do?" said Django, touching the brim of his leather hat, and nodding to the three brothers, who each said a shy 'hello' to the stranger.

"Here, Poppy, I made these for you a long time ago, bin waitin' fer right time to give 'em you. Think you must 'ave yer ears pierced by now, eh, my girl?" Poppy nodded, an astonished smile on her face, and Django handed her a black leather pouch tied with a cord. "Now, ye' must keep 'em safe, y' unnerstand? And keep 'em in that pouch when you'm not using em. Got that? Very important, that is."

Poppy nodded again, undoing the cord, and shaking the pouch over her upturned palm. Two gold earrings fell out. They were shaped a bit like the nativity star, with the bottom point longer than the rest. And set in the centre of each was a fiery red gemstone.

"Django! They're beautiful! They're absolutely amazing! Thank you so much!" She gazed at them in disbelief for a

132

minute, then took them in her fingers and pushed the gold hooks through her ears. "How do they look?" she asked, her face glowing as fiercely as the gemstones.

"You do look a picture, my girl!" said Django proudly. "Now, look after 'em, mind, and don't lose that pouch, neither."

"I won't, I promise!" said Poppy, and she gave the gypsy a big hug.

The boys all had lots of questions about the gypsies and their way of life, but were a little bit shy to ask about most things. Django sat down on one of the big logs, and Bethany poured him a mug of tea.

"Django," asked Jack, "how did you get all your caravans up here? Surely not along the old railway track that we followed?"

"We calls 'em 'vardos' not caravans," said Django kindly, "and we come by the gypsy road." He touched the side of his nose with his one finger, confidentially, and smiled. "Aye, we'll be gone by the morn, and you'm won't see us go."

"And you'll be gone, then, until the spring?" asked Jack.

"Aye. An' sometimes we leaves messages behind, if ye knows how to read 'em."

"Patrins?" asked Max, who had been keeping an eye on Django since he had joined them.

"Why! Yes, young sir, that's right!" he said, astonished. "And how comes you knows so much about 'em at your age?"

"From The Famous Five book about Mystery Moor," said Max, excitedly. "It's my favourite, and there is a gypsy boy who shows the Famous Five how to read the patrins that his family have left behind. We used to play gypsies in the

133

woods in Center Parcs, where one of us would run off into the trees and leave patrins made of twigs and leaves and stones for the others to follow a few minutes later."

"Well, well. And is that why you was a-looking at my stones afore? You'm got good eyes behind them spectacles, 'avent ye, young man?"

"That's what Sostror said, too," blurted Max without thinking.

There was a sudden silence around the cauldron.

"Aye, happen 'e did," said Django with a smile.

"So you know about the goblins in the quarry?" asked Jack.

"Aye, young man, an' more besides. There's much truth to be found in many an old folk tale or superstition, ye know. We gypsies live apart from society as ye can tell. We're closer to nature and the old ways."

"So why haven't they asked you to find the wimblestone?"

"Because it wasn't gypsies foretold as the saviours. It was regular folk with good hearts. And that's you."

They all fell silent again, thinking about the task they had been set, and gazing around them at the wonderful sight of the gypsy vardos, at all the wonderful colours and beautiful decorations, and the craftwork for sale. Alex saw their neighbours, Mr and Mrs Dodds, talking to the people selling pottery.

"Django, you see that woman, there, the sort of round one with the big nose?" he asked. "Sostror told us that some people had goblin ancestors, and you could tell by the way they look. I was just wondering – "

Django laughed, a big, booming sound that tipped the brim of his hat back, made his silver earrings jangle, and showed his shiny gold tooth. "No, lad," he said, then he

134

leant in towards the children for confidentiality. "Her mum brought her here from somewhere up north fifty year ago. No, I'm afeared Mrs Dodds there is just ugly, that's all."

Some gypsy children came hurtling out of the trees beyond Bethany's vardo, and ran through the encampment up to where the horses were grazing.

"Where did they come from?" asked Alex of no-one in particular.

"You can get to Sandford rec down the hill, there," said Poppy, "They'll have been on the swings and the climbing frame. I can show you, if you like. I ought to be heading off soon anyway."

The children stood up from round the camp fire, and thanked Bethany for the tea.

"It was lovely to meet you," said Jack, politely, and Bethany gave him a beautiful smile.

Django gripped hold of Jack's forearm in a strong, traditional handshake, and wished him luck on his quest, then he did the same to Alex and Max, before giving Poppy a hug and saying "take care, my girl."

The boys followed Poppy into the trees and down the steep hill towards Sandford. Through the trees, they could see the houses, the orchards, and the flat plain of farms and rhynes, with the straight line of the old railway cutting across it. At the bottom of the hill, was a dry ditch, and then a nominal fence made of three strands of wire fixed between round wooden posts, which the children quickly climbed through.

Sandford rec was a sloping field with a zip wire, a pirate ship climbing frame, some swings, and a basketball hoop. It wasn't much to write home about, not compared to Winscombe with its skate park. Jack wondered why Poppy had decided to bring them this way rather than the direct route to Quarry Road. Perhaps she was keen to avoid the old box car, he thought. He stood and watched as she and Alex took turns on the zip wire, and Max captained the pirate ship in his own little world of make-believe. Only, he reflected, what everyone had always thought of as Max's world of daydreams and fantasies had, for once, turned out to be true. Jack turned around and scanned the trees and bushes behind him, wondering if anyone were watching them now.

Then he heard Poppy calling, "Come on, I'll show you the way home."

Chapter 11

An Unexpected Journey

The following morning, Jack was not looking forward to going to rugby. He sat quietly at the breakfast table and didn't make much of a hole in his porridge. He felt bad about what had happened to Poppy's box car, and he didn't know how he could still be friends with Kyle and Sean. They hadn't seemed like the sort of thugs who would damage someone's property like that. Had he misjudged them? But then he also hadn't managed to ask Poppy how she knew it was the twins who had done it. Did she even have any proof? These thoughts buzzed round and round his head while his brothers chattered and squabbled, and his dad told him to eat his breakfast or he wouldn't have enough energy to run around for an hour. He didn't know how he was supposed to be part of a team with boys who were capable of behaving like that.

Everyone else on the team seemed in high spirits during the warm ups. Jack tried to keep out of the twins' way as much as possible, without making it look too obvious. He felt queasy with nerves and couldn't concentrate. He fumbled a catch and the ball bobbled over to Kyle. Jack had learned to tell the difference between them on Sundays at least, because Kyle wore red boots while Sean's were blue.

"What's up Jack? Split up with your girlfriend?" he said in a jokey, not unkind tone.

Jack picked up the ball and looked at Kyle, who was smiling in his usual, carefree manner as he passed his ball to Adam, another boy in Jack's tutor group at school. He took a deep breath, then said what was on his mind.

"Look, you know Poppy..."

"Your girlfriend."

Jack gave Kyle a look that shut him up and made him listen. "She said you and Sean trashed her den and burned it down. Is that true?"

Kyle suddenly looked uncomfortable.

"Yeah, no, we didn't mean to. It was an accident, yeah?"

"An accident." So, he'd admitted they had done it.

"Yeah. We knew the old shed thing was there, but it had this ancient great padlock on it, all rusted up and that. We never paid it much attention. Then one day we came down the hill from where they do the abseiling sometimes, and we saw this bit of wood leaning against the back of it, like a door. We didn't know it was Poppy's or anything, we just wanted to explore, youthful curiosity, you know? Anyway, we squeezed through this hole in the back, and I heard Sean knock something over. It was all dark inside, so I lit a match, and we could see that it was someone's den. The thing we had knocked over looked like a lantern, so Sean said we should light it to get a better look. I mean, we were quite impressed, you know, we wouldn't have deliberately trashed it. So I picked up the lamp and put it on the table, but we didn't realise that the fuel had spilled out of it, so when I lit it, the flames went straight from the lamp all across the table, down one leg and onto the floor – whoosh! It was so sudden, there was fire everywhere, we thought we were going to be burned alive! So we panicked, and just scrambled out of there. Didn't have time to think about putting it out or rescuing anything. Like I say, it was just an accident. We didn't even know whose stuff was in there. And it was pretty dangerous having that old lamp like that, anyway. I mean, we could have been killed."

Kyle seemed genuine, and Jack had always thought they were decent guys to begin with. He felt a lot better now that he had spoken to Kyle about it. He just wished that Poppy could see the good side to them as well.

Sean came jogging over and pointed to the corner of the pitch by the kit cabin. The opposition team were arriving. Coach blew his whistle, and they all jogged over for the team talk.

"This is going to be a walkover!" said Sean as they all got down on one knee. "Look how small they are."

"Never underestimate that which you haven't tested," said the coach. "Backwell might look small, but maybe they're fast; maybe they can move the ball well between them. Maybe they are all demon tacklers. We don't know, because we haven't seen them play yet this season. So don't go making assumptions, ok? Jack, are you back with us, now? You ok, lad?"

"Yes, Coach!"

"Right. Let's take it to them, then, boys. Remember, focus; keep onside; move it out to the wings, ok? Eyes on the ball. Who are we?"

"WE ARE WINSCOMBE!" shouted the team.

After the match, Jack fetched his dad, Alex and Max over to Terry's tea hut for bacon rolls. The twins were already there, adding ketchup and brown sauce to theirs.

"Listen, guys," he said, "where did you get the wood to build your tree house?"

"From the tip in Weston. Hey, you should come over and see it, now that it's finished."

"Yeah, ok. Have you got any bits left?"

"Some. I'm sure your dad could get more from the tip, though. They don't charge much," said Kyle.

"You thinking of building your own?" asked Sean. "We could help, couldn't we? We're experts, we are."

"Here's your sandwich, Jack," said Mr Pearson. "How was your match, boys?"

"It was pretty close," said Kyle. "They didn't look much, but they played well as a team, and had some really fast runners in the backs. But we still won five tries to three."

"Dad, is it alright if I cycle back to their house for a bit. I won't be long. They want to show me their tree house."

"Ok. Sure. But just for half an hour, alright? Mum's cooking a roast and she won't want it spoiling."

"Thanks, dad. See you at home, Zan, Max!"

After lunch, Jack went to see if he could distract Poppy for a couple of hours while the twins put his plan into action. He cycled up the main road and turned right onto Quarry road, wheeling past the lime kilns on his low seat. He lay the bike down on the wide pavement near the telegraph pole, and jumped down the steps onto the path to the houses. As he reached her front gate, Poppy came out of the house and shut the front door behind her.

"Hey!" they both said.

"Want to go for a bike ride?" asked Jack.

"Yeah, ok. Get me out of the house."

Her bike was standing against the wall in the front garden, and Jack held the gate open for her. He noticed she was wearing the gold earrings from Django. They seemed to brighten her face, making her look less gloomy and pensive than normal.

"Where do you want to go?" she asked.

"Strawberry line? Somewhere with a bit of space and quiet so we can talk about stuff?"

"Ok," she replied, thoughtfully. "Shall we head for the boat?"

Jack let her go a little in front, and as they crossed onto the far side of the main road to go down past the goblin church, Jack could see the twins in their mum's car parked beside the pet food shop. He gave them a wave behind Poppy's back, and pedalled after her.

They cycled in silence over the high bridge, then turned along the gravel track to the boat field. They leaned their bikes in the hedge by the gate, and walked along the tractor ruts by the rhyne.

Poppy tilted her face up to the sun and stretched her arms out, stroking the long dry grass on either side of the track. "I wish we had a real boat, and could launch ourselves off across the sea. Row out to Steep Holm or something. Or even just an island in a lake, like Swallows and Amazons. Camp there all on our own. It would be wicked."

"Mum and dad took us camping in the lakes before Sam was born. We took a boat out on Coniston, but you couldn't get near Wildcat Island, there were boats and people everywhere. Should've probably gone in the rain, or something."

141

"I'd have loved that, just being on that lake, imagining the characters sailing up and down. Or even a boat on a river, like Wind in the Willows."

"We'll have to just pretend, then," said Jack as they crossed the log into the boat field. "I know, you can be the Lady of Shalott, and I'll push you off to float down the river."

"The Lady of Shalott didn't have any help, you idiot. We'll have to think of something else. I'm a disinherited princess about to be murdered by my mad uncle, and you're a kitchen boy -"

"A kitchen boy?!"

"Well, alright, then; a young knight, not yet tried in battle, but a champion of the training grounds."

"That's better," said Jack

Poppy Jumped into the boat and Jack put his hands on the stern and leant his weight into the wood.

"Here we go, m'lady," he said, then swung his legs over the side to join her.

"Ja-ack!" she cried, and as Jack sat down on the bench in the stern, the seat rocked beneath him, and he heard the sound of water slapping the sides of the boat.

They were afloat.

"What the...where are we?"

"I have no clue!" said Poppy, gazing about in astonishment.

They were on a vast expanse of water. The wind that had cooled them pleasantly before felt colder now, as they drifted at its mercy across the water. The trees where the boat usually sat high and dry were gone. The fields with all their hedges, the elevated strawberry line, all gone. Beneath Jack's whitening knuckles, the gunwales of the little boat were smooth and no longer weathered and flaky. The rowlocks were new and sturdy, and along the length of the boat, by his feet, were two oars.

"Are we dreaming?" he asked, looking up at the sky where a large hawk of some kind was gliding high overhead.

"This is insane!" said Poppy. "How is this possible?"

"I guess we ought to be past that sort of question after meeting the Elder-iche," said Jack.

"But why has it never happened before? All the hundreds of times I've sat in this boat. Is it the goblins' doing, do you think?"

"I suppose it must be, but I can't see how it could be. Or why. I can't see anything. Where do you suppose we are?"

"Look," said Poppy, pointing, "the Mendips are still there."

The wooded hills rose up out of the water, so familiar to Jack, now, that he hadn't registered the fact that they were still there. So they were still in the field where the boat was, were they? But where were the trees? And where had the water come from? And the oars? And why was the boat so new-looking? So many questions bombarded the children all at once, as they struggled to understand what was happening. This was weirder and more unexpected than meeting the goblins.

"Do you think we could have gone back in time?" asked Jack.

"Either that or another dimension," said Poppy, quite reasonably under the circumstances. "Have you read The Talisman by Stephen King? Or any of the Dark Tower books? They're all about kids moving between different universes or realities or whatever."

"But this isn't fiction. This is us. This is really happening. Isn't it? Are you sure it's not a dream?"

"Do you want me to come over there and pinch you?"

"No, you're alright. I think we should just go with it, you know. Go with the flow. Get it?"

"Yeah, I get it," said Poppy, "but if this is a lake, it won't be flowing anywhere, will it?"

"Yeah, alright, smart arse." laughed Jack. He knelt in the middle of the boat and picked up an oar, swinging it clumsily over the side and trying to fit it between the little wooden pins on the gunwale. The oar was heavy and the boat unstable, and his first couple of attempts missed.

"Rowlocks!" he said, giving Poppy a cheeky grin, not sure whether she knew what the pins were called.

"I'll kick you in the rowlocks in a minute," she laughed. "Do you even know how to row?"

"How hard can it be, once the oars are in place?" said Jack confidently. He finally got the balance of the oar and slotted it between the wooden pins. There was a sort of collar on the oar that kept it in position, and stopped it floating away while he dealt with the other one. Once both oars were in place, he sat on the central bench, facing Poppy, and gripped the oars.

"Wait," he said, "this isn't right. I'm supposed to row backwards. You'll need to sit in the stern and direct me."

So Poppy carefully climbed past Jack, taking care to keep her weight along the centre line of the boat, and Jack turned round to face her in the stern.

"Right, then, Jim Lad," said Poppy in a gruff, piratey voice, "heave away, me hearty."

It was hard work to begin with; Jack's arms strained to pull the boat through the water, and the long, heavy oars were cumbersome and difficult to control. Poppy very kindly said nothing, just gazed about them at their new

144

surroundings, looking deep in thought. Initially, Jack's right arm was much stronger and more controlled than his left, and he veered jerkily away from the Mendips, but soon he had found the knack of rotating the oars as they left the water so that they cut cleanly through the air like the blades of a helicopter, then twisting them back again as he dug into the water, bracing his feet against the struts in the bottom of the boat. Once he had established a rhythm, they moved quite swiftly, and Poppy said how well he was doing, and began to guide him to a point she had identified on the shore. It felt wonderful to be gliding through the water with the sun shining down on them, the unchecked wind in their faces. It was amazing how the landscape had changed. Jack had thought these fields had been flat before, but without the hedges and trees, the surface of the lake was flatter still. Not knowing when or where they were made the children feel quite exposed.

"Where are we heading?" asked Jack.

"I was aiming for the gap in the hills, there, where the road to Winscombe ought to be."

"I think we'd better be careful. If this isn't all some kind of illusion, then we must really be in another time or another dimension. Either way, I think it's safe to assume we will stand out as not belonging here. It could be dangerous." Jack was looking at Poppy in her denim shorts and Converse high-tops, and her t-shirt with 'Talk to the hand' printed on it. He was no better: knee length denim shorts, skateboard t-shirt and Nike trainers. In The Talisman, Jack Sawyer's clothes and belongings had changed to blend in with the world of The Territories whenever he flipped into them, but here they were going to need to find a disguise.

"I think we should avoid anyone we see until we can find

out what's going on. Treat this like a reconnaissance mission. Totally undercover, ok?"

"Yes, ok." said Poppy, feeling suddenly nervous now. This wasn't just some boating trip they had planned, after all. And it wasn't just the prospect of who they might meet that was worrying her. There was also the question of how they would get back. "Pull more with your left," she said, "the trees come right down to the water just there; we'll be able to hide the boat.

Jack ran the boat aground where a small copse came right down to within a meter or so of the lake. He stepped out of the boat onto the grass, and held it steady for Poppy to disembark. Together, they pulled the empty boat up the slope to the tree line, where they hoped it would be safe. During the fifteen minutes or so that they had been on the water, they had seen no sign of anyone. There had been no other vessels out on the water, and no signs of life on the shore. They crept carefully up the hill through the trees, listening to the sounds of the birds and insects. Ivy creeper covered the ground with shiny, dark leaves.

"Doesn't look like people ever come this way," said Jack, "no paths or tracks, look."

Poppy nodded. They walked further, stepping carefully over the creepers, listening hard, wondering if they were the only people left in the world. Maybe they hadn't gone back in time, but forward, to a point where global warming had flooded all the lowlands, and most people had perished. Gradually, they both relaxed slightly, and moved more quickly and naturally, until they came to a thin brown line of soil where the grass and creeper had been worn away. It ran diagonally up to their left, and the two children stood looking along the line it took through the trees, trying to make out any further signs of civilisation. As they were looking upwards, they heard a noise from behind them. The sound of running feet and swishing leaves. The children panicked. The widely spaced trees and low lying creeper didn't provide much cover at such close quarters. Whoever was coming up this path would be bound to see them. They quickly stepped back down the way they had come, and crouched low, each behind a tree, keeping as still and small as possible.

The noise came closer and closer, and now they could hear a heavy breathing, too, like a large man who wasn't used to running. Poppy and Jack waited, holding their breath, not daring to peer round the trees they were using for cover. The footsteps and the breathing came closer and closer, right up to the point where they had reached the path, and then stopped. Everything was still and silent for a few heartbeats, and Jack couldn't help leaning slightly round the tree and taking a peek. He looked up the hill to where he thought the man must be standing, but all he could see was branches. His heart racing, he let his eyes fall downwards, and there he saw a dark shape, low to the ground. With a sudden snort, the shape jerked and trotted off up the path.

"Did you see what it was?" asked Poppy when she heard Jack stand up.

"I think it was a boar. Like in the Asterix books. It was like a heavy set dog with tusks. When do you reckon boars last ran wild around here?"

"I have no clue," said Poppy. "Lucky it wasn't a wolf, though, eh?"

"Yeah, or we might end up in the bone caves, being trodden on by tourists in a thousand years' time."

"Don't!" said Poppy, rubbing her ear lobes.

"Why do you keep doing that?"

"What?"

"Fiddling with your ears. Are you feeling alright?"

"Oh, it's these new earrings. They feel hot, making my ears itch."

"Is that normal?" asked Jack.

"Not really. Sometimes cheap earrings can irritate the ears, but these are gold; they should be fine."

"They're the ones Django gave you. The ones he said to keep in that leather pouch when you weren't wearing them. Have you brought the pouch with you?"

"Yes, it's here in my pocket." Poppy dug out the black leather pouch.

"I'm just wondering," said Jack. "I think you should take them out and put them in the pouch. See what happens."

"See what happens? What do you think will happen?" asked Poppy, nervously.

"I don't know exactly. But they might be the key to this whole lake and wild boar scenario. Just try taking them out, can you?"

Poppy took the jewelled earrings that the gypsy had given her out of her lobes, and dropped them into the little pouch. Then she disappeared. Jack was all alone in the wood, with the birds and insects tweeting and buzzing as if nothing weird had happened. He had half expected, but not fully believed that that might happen, although part of him had also expected that they would both be taken back to reality at the same time. And now he was stranded.

"Put them back in, then, Poppy. Put them back in, now, and come back." he muttered, feeling anxious.

Nothing happened. Minutes passed slowly, and Jack was still in the wood, all on his own. He decided to go back to the boat. Maybe that's where Poppy would reappear. Maybe if he got into the boat himself, he would be transported back to normality. He set off down the hill, not bothering to go quietly anymore. He broke out of the trees and came to the edge of the lake. He looked all around him, but the little boat had gone. He walked a little way along the shore in both directions, getting more and more worried, wondering if, somehow, he had come out in a different place. But he hadn't. He found the mark the boat had made when they had pulled it up out of the water. Found the disturbed creeper where they had left the boat and tramped up the hill, but the boat was no longer there.

"Jack! Oh my god!" Poppy's voice came from behind him. He swung round to see her stepping out of the boat just at the edge of the lake.

"Poppy, what happened?"

"As soon as I put the earrings in the pouch, I was back in our world, in someone's back garden in Sandford. So I put the earrings back in, but nothing happened. Like when I put them in this morning, nothing weird happened until we got in the boat. So I thought about getting back in the boat, but of course the boat wasn't in the same garden, was it, because we had walked up the hill. So I had to sneak out of the garden I was in, and find a way through to where the boat was. Then I kind of did what you did before, pushed it and jumped in, and then there I was at the edge of the lake, staring at your back. Isn't this incredible, Jack?"

149

"Totally. Right, let me get my head around this, now. So we're in Sandford, but obviously there is nothing here apart from wild boar and forest. No settlement. And when you put the earrings in the pouch, you and the boat return to our world or our time or whatever."

"Pretty much," agreed Poppy.

"So, we kind of need to think where we leave the boat if you're going to take the earrings off. And I guess, we need to try and get it back to where we found it before we go home."

"I guess. That won't be easy, though."

"Ok. Do you want to go back up the hill, or should we take the boat further round the lake, see if we can see any settlements or anything?"

"Let's stay in the boat for now, shall we? I just feel that might be safer."

Jack pushed the boat off and jumped in, managing to keep his feet dry. He settled himself on the rowing bench again, and began to row in the direction of where Banwell ought to be, keeping about twenty meters from the shore.

"I think we must have gone back in time," mused Poppy in a quiet, thoughtful voice.

"I suppose that's really the most likely explanation." Jack replied. "And there's definitely some magical link between your earrings and this boat. Do you think we'll be able to make this happen at any time? I mean, the wardrobe didn't always lead to Narnia in the book, did it? There were certain conditions, weren't there?"

"I guess we'll just have to see. But what's it all for? I mean, why is it happening at all? Why would Django's earrings do this?"

"Good question. But it must be important. It must be something to do with finding the wimblestone. It must be goblin magic, and it will help us fulfil our destiny."

Poppy remained silent, and Jack put his effort into the oars. His unaccustomed arms were aching now, and his thighs hurt from bracing his feet so hard. At least in Swallows and Amazons they had used sails out on the lake. He stopped rowing and let the boat drift for a while, staring at the tree lined shore, and the hills behind. There was still no sign of any houses. No smoke from a chimney. The Hill where the quarry should have been looked intact.

"Let's row out a bit, see how big this lake is."

"I've got this horrible feeling that I'm in some kind of daydream," said Jack, "and any minute now the twins will find me sitting in the boat under the trees, pulling on a pair of pretend oars like some kind of idiot. Like, in primary school, I used to have these panic attacks in assembly thinking 'what if I've been sleepwalking, and I'm going to suddenly wake up in the middle of the school hall in my pyjamas or naked, with everyone laughing and pointing at me."

"You can be weird sometimes, you know!" laughed Poppy.

Jack rested on his oars again, holding them out of the water. His arms and shoulders were really aching, and he was starting to worry about the possibility of not getting back to the world they knew.

As the boat drifted round into the wind, Jack could see a clearing by the shore, and a sort of muddy beach area that looked like it saw regular use. His gaze followed a line in the trees that could have been a path, and then he saw the first sign that they weren't actually all alone here.

There was smoke, pale against the sky, drifting through the tree tops, clearly from a camp fire.

"Right," he said, flexing his shoulders and rolling his head on his neck, "I think we should head back now. Come again another day, maybe when we're a bit more prepared. Now, I want to make sure we can get home again."

Jack put every last bit of energy he had into rowing back towards where the boat field ought to be. Poppy tried to use her familiarity with the hills and her memory of where they had first appeared, to guide him, but it wasn't easy to judge distances over the water. She really had very little to go on. When they both agreed they ought to be somewhere near, Jack stowed the oars and held onto the gunwales, praying that they weren't going to end up caught in the branches of a tree. Then Poppy took out the earrings, placed them in the pouch and pulled the cord, and the boat landed with a heavy thud in the long grass of the field next to the one they had started out from.

"Well, I must say, that isn't bad going at all!" said Jack. "I think another three hundred meters that way should do it. Will we need to get out and jump back in, do you think, or will putting the earrings back in be enough?"

Poppy put the jewels back in her ears, but nothing happened. "I think it needs some momentum, some intention for it to work," she said.

Jack climbed out and gave the boat the same shove he had done earlier, and then they were afloat again. He tried to measure the approximate distance back to their starting point, mindful of not ending up in the trees, and when Poppy removed the earrings again, they were in the right field, just a bit closer to the strawberry line.

"Would m'lady care to disembark here?" asked Jack, with a smile. He had never experienced anything so amazing before in his life. He had completely forgotten to tell Poppy about the twins.

Poppy climbed out of the boat. The oars had disappeared and the wood was old and weathered again, the paint flaky and faded. Jack was flexing his arms and studying his sore hands.

"When we get up onto the strawberry line, we need to take a good look at the features of the hill and try and gauge the distance for next time," he said, practically.

"Next time? Are you sure?" She was smiling.

"I think this boat is somehow key to our whole quest. Maybe we'll even find the fifth one who is going to help us here."

They crossed over the log bridge and collected their bikes, pushing them up the steep bank of the old railway line.

"Listen, Poppy, I spoke to Kyle and Sean this morning at rugby."

Her mood changed immediately at the sound of the two names. "Oh yeah? I'm happy for you."

"They said the box car thing was an accident. They knocked over the lamp when they went in, and then the spilled oil caught fire."

"Just like that?"

"Well, not spontaneously. They lit it. But they only wanted to light the lamp to get a better look at the den. They said they didn't know it was yours. They thought it was sick."

"Really!" Her tone was still angry and sarcastic.

"Look, I think they're sorry about it. They were terrified when it caught fire. They could've died. Then I think they thought they'd get into trouble, so they just kept quiet about it."

"Typical! So, you're still friends with them, then?" She set off back along the strawberry line before he could answer. Or maybe it hadn't really been a question, more of a judgement. He would have to see what the twins had been up to during the last couple of hours. He was sure he could still turn things around.

He caught up with her at the main road by Humphry's garage. She was standing next to her bike, holding the handle bars, ready to push it across, and so Jack dismounted, too. "Listen, Poppy, I wanted to talk to you about something, you know, before the whole lake and wild boar thing took over."

She gave him permission with a look.

"Well, the thing is, it's all a bit crazy at home at the moment; mum and dad are always arguing. I thought things were supposed to get better when we moved here, but now I don't know. I think they might be going to split up."

"Grown-ups argue, Jack. It probably doesn't mean anything. And it's obvious they both love you all. You're still lucky in that respect. Could be worse." Poppy set off across the road, heading for the left hand pavement. Even with her gears, it was a steep hill to cycle up with no momentum.

Jack caught up with her again. "What I mean is, I'm worrying about it, and I think it's affecting Zander and Max, too, but I don't feel quite as worried as you look most of the time. You know, you're always alone at school unless we're talking, and you always seem to be glad to get out of the house. I just wondered...is everything ok?

You know, at home? I saw you put money in that charity tin in Yatton."

Poppy looked around her, then, without waiting for a response, said, "Let's cross the road," and headed towards a small parking area by the post box. Jack followed her, and they leaned their bikes against the stone wall and levered themselves up on top of it.

"No, everything's not alright, but I don't generally talk about it."

She paused and swung her legs, kicking her heels against the wall. Jack waited, then said, "You know I'm your friend, don't you?"

"Of course I do, stupid!" she said, sounding harsher than she had meant. "Sorry. It's just...my mum died earlier this year. Dad isn't really coping, he's drinking too much. Doesn't know what to say to me, doesn't know how to be a mum and a dad, you know. I confuse him. I think I remind him of her a bit, but then he doesn't know how to take her place, how to deal with girly stuff..."

"I'm really sorry, Scout."

"Jack, this is why I don't tell people. I don't want people to be sorry. Nobody can empathise with me, nobody else lost her as a mum, only me, and I don't need to be made to feel bad that other people are sorry for it, too. Do you understand?"

"I'm trying," said Jack, sincerely. "If I can do anything to help, just tell me. If you ever want to talk, I'll listen; about how you're feeling, about what she was like and the things you did together; I'm here for you, ok? But if you just want things to go back to how they were before you told me, that's ok, too. I won't go on about it, ok?"

155

Poppy wiped tears from her eyes and gave a half laugh, half sob. "Alright. Thanks, Jack. I know you care. I think I kinda felt that you were worried about me. It's ok, really. We just need time to adjust."

She gave him a smile as she hopped down off the wall. "Best get back."

"Yeah. Ok." He said, following her. "Listen, I thought we could maybe visit the cave again tonight, ask Sostror some questions, try and understand more about what we need to do –"

"And who the fifth saviours is!"

"Yeah. What do you think? I can text you later to organise it."

"Yeah, let's aim for midnight, see how the land lies."

"Great. Ok, see you later!" he called, as they reached the end of her road and parted ways.

"Bye!" called Poppy, heading home feeling lighter and happier than she had in months.

Chapter 12

Shadows

Jack listened to his brothers' snores and watched midnight creep nearer on the screen of his phone. All was quiet downstairs; he had heard his dad come home at about quarter to eleven, feigned sleep expertly as he had come up the stairs and stood in their bedroom doorway for a minute or so, before whispering something about sweet dreams. His dad had looked in on Sam, too, then paused outside his mum's door before going back downstairs to the sofa. Jack wondered if his mum also pretended to be asleep when she went to bed before his dad came home. There had been the low hum and babble of the television for half an hour as his dad channel hopped to unwind, then he had switched it off and settled down to sleep himself.

At five minutes to midnight, Jack messaged Poppy:

- YOU AWAKE, SCOUT? ALL CLEAR?

A message came straight back:

- NOT CLEAR. WITCH OF WOODBOROUGH PROWLING ABOUT. KEEPS WALKING UP AND DOWN IN THE SHADOWS. THINK SHES WAITING FOR US.

- WHAT???FREAKY! WHAT SHALL WE DO?

There was a pause, and Jack's room fell into darkness. He was dying to speak to Sostror again, and now that nosey old bat was going to spoil everything. What was she doing on Quarry Road at this time of night? Then his phone vibrated, and the screen lit up with a new message.

- I'LL SNEAK OUT AND COME TO YOUR HOUSE, MAKING SURE SHE SEES ME. YOU THREE GO UP THE MAIN ROAD AND ROUND TO SANDFORD REC. I'LL HIDE IN YOUR GARDEN UNTIL SHES GONE. YOU'LL HAVE TO SPEAK TO SOSTROR WITHOUT ME.

Jack thought about this plan. If the witch thought something was going on, then she might believe that Poppy was sneaking out to see him. But how long would she hang around, he wondered.

- BEST COME IN AND HIDE IN THE UTILITY ROOM. WE'LL LEAVE THE DOOR UNLOCKED, AND PUT SOME CUSHIONS IN THERE. OK? GIVE US 5 MINS.

Jack climbed off the top bunk and shook Alex and Max awake. They were expecting to be woken, but Alex was still deeply asleep. Jack couldn't understand why he hadn't been too excited to sleep at all. As they dressed, Jack told them about Poppy's messages, then he grabbed the pillows off his and Alex's beds, and the three of them crept downstairs, taking care to tread at the sides of the steps where they didn't creak. Jack left the pillows in the utility room, along with a chocolate roll and a carton of apple juice, then he sent Poppy a message.

- LEAVING NOW. GOOD LUCK!

The three boys quietly pulled the back door closed behind them, and crept out into the night, leaving the garden gate open. They scurried down the lawn and under the cherry trees, keeping to the shadows and the grass as much as they could. As they rounded the bungalow at the corner of the main road, Poppy crept out of her front door and, moving like a cartoon villain on tiptoes, made a show of taking extra care to tread quietly. As she opened the gate, she looked carefully all around her, up at her front

158

windows and along the road in both directions. She knew where the old woman was standing, but made it plain that she couldn't see her. She tiptoed along the path to the steps, and with a final look in all directions, disappeared into the darkness between the wooden fences.

On the main road, the three boys made their way nervously up the hill in the dark. There was no moon in the sky this time, and the difference to their first nocturnal adventure was immense. The street was not shining a luminous silver this time, and the boys could hardly see where they were walking. A street lamp half way up the hill shed a cone of light that did little but make the area around it darker still. Everywhere was black and quiet, except for the wind in the trees. The boys couldn't see the tree branches moving, and the sound they made didn't seem real; it sounded too close, and altogether sinister. The further the boys went, the more frightening the night became.

Taking care not to move too quickly, lest the witch lose track of her, Poppy felt her way down the steps in the dark. She was scared of being confronted by the witch, scared of being on her own, and scared of going into someone else's house at night. What if Jack's parents caught her? What would she say? And how would she explain that the boys weren't at home? She would far rather have been going to the quarry with the three of them. But she knew it was important to leave this false trail.

The boys ran in a crouch past the end of Quarry road, and their nerves kept them running past the big metal gates to the lower level of the quarry, and on past the chapel of rusty coloured stone. They took the footpath to the rec, and were plunged into utter darkness. Jack felt Max clutch at his arm, and they all stopped.

"Max, are you alright?"

"Yes," came a quivering voice from out of the darkness.

"If I had realised it would be this dark, I would have left you sleeping."

"You would not! I'm part of this, too, aren't I? You're not going to leave me out just because I'm seven. I'm one of the chosen ones, too!"

"Yes, you are, Max. I just didn't realise it would be quite this scary, that's all."

"What does dad say?" asked Alex.

"Courage isn't having no fear, it's overcoming the fear that you have" they repeated together.

Jack took out his phone and messaged Poppy.

- HOW'S IT GOING?

- IT'S WORKING. I'M JUST REACHING YOUR HOUSE AND SHE'S AT THE TOP OF THE ROAD, FOLLOWING ME. WHERE ARE YOU?

- ON THE FOOTPATH. TOTAL DARKNESS. WHY IS THERE NO MOON?!!

- LOL. TAKE CARE. I'M GOIN IN.

There was no danger of anyone seeing them now, so Jack used his phone to light their way along the path, Max still holding his left arm, making him feel braver having someone to protect. The path was narrow, and brambles stuck out from the hedge on their right, snagging at their clothes.

They emerged from the path at the edge of the rec, and light from streetlamps on Somerville Road opened up the space around them. They climbed over the fence, and up past the eerie shapes of the climbing frame, pirate ship

160

and the zip wire. Behind them, across the black expanse of the fields, the orange lights of Weston were visible, like Christmas decorations in a large window. At the top of the sloping playing field, the foreboding darkness of the woods awaited them. Jack took his phone out again, and increased the brightness of the screen.

"Come on!" he said, pushing his fear aside, and the three of them stepped down into the little ditch that marked the edge of the rec, and then climbed up through the wire fence and on through the dark maze of tree trunks and ivy creeper. They climbed diagonally because it was easier than going straight up the steep hill, and when they emerged from the trees they were on the track that sloped up to the top of the hill where the gypsies camped. The middle level of the quarry looked like a deep, black lake. If anyone were waiting for them beneath the tree this time, they couldn't see them. They couldn't even see the tree. Very carefully, they descended through the long grass to the floor of the quarry, and made their way to the mouth of the cave. Even though they had been in the cave at night before, and even though they knew what was inside, the children hesitated at the mouth of the cave, the light from Jack's torch barely reaching a meter inside.

"Do you think you can open the tunnel from here, Zander?" asked Jack quietly.

"Give me the phone," said Alex, and he led them slowly over the uneven, rock strewn floor. When they had gone a couple of meters, he burped the word that had opened the tunnel. The noise echoed around the cave, and was followed by a low rumbling. The green glow from the tunnel seeped into the darkness of the cave, and Alex gave Jack his phone back.

There were no goblins waiting to meet them tonight, and the boys each wondered whether it was too late. Perhaps they were all hibernating already, with not so much as a sentry standing guard. Jack led the way into the tunnel, still holding Max's hand, but once they were inside, surrounded by the comforting, soft green light, Max released his grip and walked confidently on his own. When they reached the chamber with the dais, they were pleased to see at least some goblins were awake; figures were seated in three of the alcoves, eating and drinking quietly, while two goblins seemed to be washing the cups and bowls in the stone trough. Jack was suddenly nervous about intruding like this, and a fear of embarrassment rose in his chest: what if he couldn't recognise Sostror after just one meeting? What if all the goblins looked the same to him, now? What should he say?

As the children stood nervously at the entrance to the chamber, two more goblins came out of one of the tunnels opposite, moving purposefully towards them. "Sostror and Bauzon," whispered Max, and Jack looked at him in astonishment. Then he remembered that his brother had special sight when it came to matters of the supernatural. He relaxed instantly, and began crossing the chamber to meet them.

"Uurobulock," burped Alex when they reached the goblins, and both little green figures bowed respectfully in response. Jack and Max did well not to laugh as they would usually have done when their brother burped like that.

"Greetings, chosen ones," said Sostror. "Why have you entered the hill? You do not have the stone." His voice was not harsh, Jack determined; it was merely curiosity, not an accusation.

"You can tell?" asked Alex.

"The stone is powerful. We would feel it. The gems in the walls would react to its presence. How goes your quest?"

"Well, we wanted to ask you some questions about that," said Jack.

Then Max spoke up: "Can't you feel the stone's power now? Do you have any idea where it is?"

"The stone has not been felt for centuries," said Sostror, sadly. "We Elder-iche have done all we can over the ages. I believe it is somewhere only you can find it. The prophecy on the wall is all we have, now." He looked at the three boys with his large, dark eyes.

"We hoped you could tell us a bit more about it; where it might be, how big it is, what it looks like; and some clue about the fifth saviour we need to find." Jack's voice sounded more desperate than he had intended. They just seemed to have so little to go on.

"The stone is like a large, dark emerald. But you will know it by its power more than its appearance. Even Awer-iche can feel the power of the wimblestone. King Arthur's enemies felt it; and his allies. Its force seduces men, feeds their greed, their dark natures. Merlin may have hidden it in some dense material to hide its power. Perhaps that is why we could not feel it when we searched and searched. But when you discover it, you will know. As for the fifth who must come to your aid, I can say only that you will know them when you find them, too. You must trust your instincts, Jack, reach for the senses that the Awer-iche have ignored for too long. Trust in yourselves, all of you; the strengths you need are within you."

163

Jack had been hoping for a little more clarity about their quest this time, specific details about the stone's location and who was going to help them, but somehow Sostror's words, combined with simply entering the chamber again, bolstered his confidence. He could tell that his brothers, too, were feeling more positive, as they crept back across the cave before the green glow from the tunnel faded. At the mouth of the cave, they stopped and scanned the darkness of the quarry, listening for any sounds of danger. Jack's phone vibrated madly as several messages from Poppy came through all at once. She was wondering how they were getting on, and worried that, from the utility room, she had no way of knowing where the witch was now. The last message read:

- BE CAREFUL ON YOUR WAY BACK!

"Right," said Jack, "We'll go back the way we came. And, Max, you keep a good look out in the shadows with those eyes of yours."

They set off, climbing up the bank to the track and then down through the trees on the north side of the hill, Max no longer holding onto Jack but vigilantly scanning the darkness all around them. They made their way along the narrow footpath below the rec, remembering to keep away from the brambles, and stopped when they reached the road. Cones of weak light from two lampposts made the road and the houses look like they had been inked in a comic book, but they could see no signs of anybody watching or waiting for them. Just as Jack led them out of the blackness and onto the pavement, they heard the sound of a car coming up the hill behind them.

"Quick! Get back!" whispered Jack, and he grabbed his brothers in his arms, pushing them into hiding like a rugby maul. Whoever was driving the car, it wouldn't look good for three young boys to be out alone at this time of night, especially if it was a patrolling police car. The boys crouched down, hearts beating fast, their breath coming in shallow gasps. They watched the car go past. It wasn't a police car, and Jack began to feel some relief; but then it stopped. The car pulled up by the curb, about twenty meters beyond where they hid, engine running and lights on.

"What do we do?" whispered Alex.

"We wait, but if they come this way, we run back to the woods, alright. I think that will give us the advantage."

As Jack finished his sentence, the car door opened. Jack strained to see who was getting out, taking care not to be seen. The driver closed the door, then walked across the road to the letter box, pushed something inside, and returned to the car. Seconds later, the car was pulling away and disappearing over the brow of the hill. All three boys exhaled together, standing up and smiling with relief.

"Phew! That was close!" said Alex.

"I thought we were really in trouble then," said Max.

"Well, we're not home yet. And it just shows: we need to be careful." Jack took out his phone and messaged Poppy.

- ON THE MAIN ROAD. BE BACK SOON. EVERYTHING OK THERE?

"Right," he said to the others, "I think we should run while we're on the street. Get back as quickly as we can, ok?"

His brothers nodded, and they jogged up the road past the chapel and the quarry at a pace that Max could manage, keeping into the shadow of the hedge as they came down from Quarry Road. When they reached the corner of Wimblestone Road, they stopped, looking for the witch.

"Can you see anything, Max?" asked Jack.

"No. No sign of her. I think we're safe."

Carefully, they advanced round the corner, bringing the line of cherry trees, their car, and finally their house into view. Checking up the lane past the bungalows, and the shadows of the quadrangle of garages, they jogged across the road and up the grass to their back door. Quiet as cat-burglars, they opened the door and crept inside. Poppy got up off the pillows and whispered, "How was it? Did you learn what we needed to?"

"It was helpful," whispered Jack, "I'm glad we went, but we're still none the wiser, really. Sostror said we'll feel the wimblestone when we find it; it's powerful, we'll sense it. He said we just have to trust our instincts. And I think I'm starting to; I feel more confident about it now."

"Ok." Said Poppy. "And any sign of the witch?"

"We couldn't see anything. I think she must have got bored. Do you want me to accompany you?"

"No, I'll be fine. I'll see you tomorrow, yeah?"

Jack watched Poppy run down the grass and onto the pavement. After a few seconds, she was visible over the fence, walking quickly up the cul-de-sac towards the steps. He closed and locked the door, picked up the pillows from the utility room, and crept carefully upstairs with his brothers. They undressed quietly, hiding their clothes under their beds again because the wardrobe doors made too much noise, and got into bed whispering "Goodnight" but saying nothing more. From his top bunk, Jack peeped round the edge of the curtain. In the shadows beyond the streetlight, a figure was crossing the road, heading towards the village centre.

- DID YOU GET HOME ALRIGHT?

Jack waited nervously for the reply.

- YES THANKS. FELT CREEPY IN THE DARK, BUT NOBODY ABOUT. GOODNIGHT.

- GOODNIGHT SCOUT.

Chapter Thirteen

Reparations and Preparations

"How did you get on?" asked Jack on the bus on Monday morning, as he sat in the seat beside the twins.

"We got all the wood up to the carriage thing with mum's help, not easy up that path, you know," said Kyle. "We made a good start, patched up all the holes around the sides, just need to do the roof."

"Yeah, didn't have anything to stand on to reach," said Sean.

"You didn't keep Poppy busy for very long, mate." Said Kyle. "We left the rest of the wood up there, inside the hut, but we had to take the toolbox home again."

"Felt like we'd been gone for hours," said Jack, beginning to wonder.

"That's women for you!" laughed Kyle.

The bus stopped again, and Poppy got on. She didn't look at the three boys, just sat down in her usual seat, and the bus set off again.

"Well, I can probably bring dad's ladder, or maybe just a chair or something from home," said Jack, quietly, as the bus turned right onto Greenhill road opposite the garage. "Is there enough wood for the roof?"

"Yeah, should be. We haven't got any felt left, though, to make it waterproof." Said Sean.

"Ok. Maybe we could get some varnish or something. Listen, what are you guys doing on Saturday? I'll be free in the afternoon."

"No can do, I'm afraid. We go to our dad's on Friday night. He brings us back for rugby on Sunday."

"Oh, right. What about Sunday, after rugby?"

"I think we're going back to Adam's to play in his garden," said Sean. "His dad's into archery, and Adam's got his own bow and everything."

"Look, we'll sort something out, yeah? Half term is coming up, isn't it?" said Kyle. "Anyway, we're here, now. Did you do the French homework?"

"Yeah," said Jack, swinging his rucksack up off the seat as he stepped into the aisle, "C'était trop facile!" he laughed.

"What?" said the twins in unison.

"How are your arms today?" asked Poppy when she saw Jack at lunch time.

"I feel like The Rock," laughed Jack, "but it reminds me that it really happened. I still can't believe it."

"I know. Do you think we should go back at the weekend? Where do you think we should go?"

"I don't know. I've been thinking about it. I want to bring Zander next time, but I think we need to prepare first. I don't think we should just go wandering blindly about. It could be dangerous."

"Boars, you mean? Or wolves?"

"I was thinking more about people. I just think we need a plan. Maybe half term would be best. Give us time to prepare."

"You're up to something, aren't you?"

"I've got some ideas, that's all. Listen, did you notice how long we were gone yesterday?"

"No, why?"

"I'm just wondering. Is it like Narnia, and no time passes while we're away, however long we spend on the lake? I mean, I've been thinking that that would make sense, if we travelled back to a time that had already passed, and had no control over what time we return to. It's not like we have a clock we can set like in Back to the Future, is it?"

"Yes," said Poppy, considering this for the first time, "I suppose we are 'outside of time' in effect, aren't we?"

"We ought to set a timer next time, so we know." Said Jack.

"Hey, wouldn't that be brilliant, though? I mean, we could do our homework in the boat, and it wouldn't take any time at all!" Poppy's eyes shone with delight. "You could spend hours on something, like an art project, then just casually say it took you a couple of seconds." She laughed.

"Yeah, that would be ace."

After dinner, Jack and Alex got changed into their Scout uniform, and cycled down to the Scout hut past the Spa shop. They leaned their BMX's against the hut at the side of the road, where a couple of other bikes had already been left, and joined the noisy throng of scouts inside the hut. After the opening of the meeting, the scouts were divided into two groups. The first group, which included Alex, were given a choice of activities through which they could earn a new badge. Howling Wolf took the second group over to the church hall to prepare for the fundraising jumble sale in half term. Inside the hall were bin liners and boxes full of donations that all needed sorting into categories, checking for fire safety labels, and in some cases putting on one side to be disposed of. Signs and price tags also needed to be made ready for the sale and a couple of children quickly volunteered to do this.

"We'll need some card and felt tips," said Howling Wolf. "Jack and Molly, I think there should be some art stuff in the store room, could you go and have a look, please? Jessica, here's a list of the signs we will need. Why don't you find a table and some chairs ready for when Molly gets back?"

The store room was next to the kitchen at the far end of the hall, and Jack had to follow Molly because he had never been inside the hall before.

"I wonder why Howling Wolf asked you to come and not Jess," said Molly, opening the store room, and reaching inside for the light switch.

"Egalitarianism," suggested Jack.

"Ooh, *egalitarianism*, get you!"

"The Scouts are all about equality and opportunity, aren't they?"

"Usually they're about hiking and raising money and collecting litter from beaches," said Molly, rummaging on the shelves at the back of the store room.

"I think it's a good balance of fun stuff, useful skills, and helping others," said Jack, looking in some of the cardboard boxes stacked up along the wall.

"You should be on the poster!" laughed Molly, with the slightest hint of scorn in her voice. Jack didn't know Molly or Jess very well, as they were both in Alex's year at school. He supposed he was still a bit of an outsider to the friends who had been at school for years and come through Beavers and Cubs together, so he didn't take any notice of her teasing. What he did notice, however, was a

171

large box of simple clothing in children's sizes; robes, cloaks, head scarves and so on.

"Right, I've got everything I need," said Molly. "You can turn the light off, I don't need any help carrying it."

Jack peered round the door after her. Everyone in the hall seemed to be busy, now, sorting through all the donations. There was a loud hubbub of chatter and noise as boxes were lifted, dropped, emptied, and the occasional battery operated toy activated. Jack crossed the corridor quickly and entered the kitchen. He quietly opened and closed drawers and cupboards until he had found an empty bin liner, then dashed back into the store room. He understood that Howling Wolf had chosen him to accompany Molly in order to make him feel part of the group and mix with more of the other children, and he was confident that he could engineer other special tasks quite easily, too.

When he had finished in the store room, he came back into the hall and joined Adam at one of the tables.

"How's it going, Adam?" he asked.

"Yeah, not bad. This side of the table is trousers in ascending sizes, look, and this is tops. Anything you don't think can be sold, you know like if it's ripped or got paint on it or whatever, just throw in that cardboard box, there."

And so Jack joined in, sorting the clothes into piles by size, checking for signs of wear and tear, hoping that there would be quite a few items to be discarded.

"The twins were telling me that you're into archery," said Jack.

"Yeah. My dad likes all the old sports like fencing and archery and axe throwing. I just got a new compound bow and target for the garden, it's really powerful."

"Wow, sick!" said Jack.

"The twins are coming round after rugby on Sunday. You could come too, if you like."

"Yeah, that would be awesome, thanks. I've never used a compound bow, only junior recurve ones."

"They feel a lot different. I've got recurves, too, but this compound one is amazing. Much more accurate over a long distance."

"It's an away match on Sunday, isn't it?"

"Yes. Clifton, I think. Somewhere in Bristol."

When all the items had been sorted, Jessica and Molly went round the tables with the signs they had made, and the clothes, toys and bric-a-brac were placed in boxes and bin bags, and labelled accordingly.

Jack approached the Scout leader. "Howling Wolf, would you like me to collect all the things for disposal, and take them out to the bin?"

"Er, yes, that's a great idea, Jack. Thank you. I think you will find the back door key on a peg in the kitchen. It should be labelled."

Jack quickly gathered up everything that people had weeded out of the jumble, and stuffed it into a bin bag. Then, as nonchalantly as possible, he went through to the kitchen and found the key. He opened the door to the store room, leaving it blocking the view of the back door from the hall, and collected the other bag that he had filled earlier. Then he unlocked the back door and pushed it open.

"What are you doing, poster boy?" asked Molly, standing in front of the store room with the pens and remaining coloured card.

"I'm just taking the rubbish out."

"And what's in that bag?"

Jack looked at her with an exaggerated frown. "The rubbish?" he said sarcastically.

Molly gave him a quizzical look in return, but said nothing more. She switched on the store room light and went inside. Jack went out into the yard. He found the big commercial wheelie bin, and slung the bag of unsuitable items inside. The other bag, he hid behind the bin, checking over his shoulder to ensure Molly wasn't watching from the doorway.

When they got back to the scout hut for the closing ceremony, Alex showed Jack his Emergency Aid badge. "I wanted to do the Digital Maker one like Gabe, but that was the most popular. Standing Bear said I can do that one next time."

"That's great. Zip it in your pocket before you lose it, and mum can sew it on for you before next week."

They collected their bikes and turned on the front and rear lights. The evenings were becoming noticeably darker now. They said goodbye to their friends and the scout leaders, and set off past the Spa shop and down the hill to the Co-op.

"Shall we carry on along the road, now, or take the Strawberry line? There's no traffic." Alex asked.

"No, I need to go this way." Replied Jack, indicating the way to the old railway track.

They rode up the path behind the public toilets and onto the cycle path, then just as they were passing the old

174

station, Jack stopped and dismounted, leaning his bike against a tree.

"Wait here a minute," he said to Alex.

"What for? Where are you going?"

"Back in a sec. Just wait there!"

He disappeared down the steep bank along what Alex could just make out was a narrow path through the trees. It led onto the driveway past the church hall, but Alex couldn't see where Jack had gone. He waited nervously, looking around in case any adults were passing who might wonder what he was doing. He thought he would say that his brother was just taking a leak in the trees. There came a rustling from the bank, and soon Jack re-emerged carrying a black bin bag.

"Where did you get that? What's in it?" whispered Alex.

"Just some stuff we need. All will be revealed, but it's a secret, ok? You mustn't tell anybody about it."

"Is it to do with...you know what?"

"Yes. Now, come on, let's get home. I'll need you to help me smuggle this inside."

Jack was very preoccupied over the next few days, and the mysterious bin liner that he had managed to sneak into the house lay unmentioned behind the storage box of sports kit under his and Alex's bunk bed. He spent break times in the school library, poring over history books, and kept Mr Pearson's copy of Le Morte D'Arthur at the bottom of his bed, reading it by torch light late at night. Along with the darker evenings, it rained almost every day. Mr Pearson had developed an obsession with Somerset rain.

"It's incredible," he would say, "it's like nothing I've experienced anywhere in the world. I've never known such torrential, localised showers. It must be the hills and the proximity of the sea. This morning, on the way to work, I actually had to pull over and stop the car for five minutes. I literally couldn't see the road in front of me, with my wipers on full tilt. It was ridiculous. And then half a mile up the road it was as dry as a bone. There's something about these hills," he said to Jack, conspiratorially. "I think there must be radioactive rock in the Mendips; a couple of times, now, in the early hours, I've seen a green glow coming from the hills. Most peculiar." Jack tried to look casually interested, hoping his dad wouldn't see anything like recognition in his eyes, as he thought of the green glow that illuminated the tunnels of the Elder-iche, of the crystals set in the walls, and of their green skin.

After the rugby match on Sunday, Jack rode down to the twins' house, and they all cycled along the strawberry line to Adam's. Adam lived in the old part of the village. On the opposite side of the valley to Wimblestone Road, St James' church stood half way up the hill which culminated in Crook Peak. Below the church was the village green, surrounded by big old houses and farms, and little narrow lanes to Barton and Loxton. Adam lived in an old stone cottage with a modern extension on the back that overlooked a meadow with a large oak tree and a copse of silver birch. When the three boys arrived, Adam and his dad were already in the meadow where they had set up the archery targets.

There were enough bows for each of the boys, but only two targets, so they had to take turns at shooting. There was a small target set about thirty meters from the Oak tree, and a larger target another twenty meters beyond that. Adam was standing in the shade of the oak, using his new compound bow on the larger target. He was a consistent shot, Jack could tell, as there were three arrows all grouped together, just to the right of the bullseye. As Adam's dad showed the twins how to grip their bows and nock their arrows, Adam showed Jack his new bow. It was shorter and heavier than the traditional recurve bows, with a series of pulley wheels that augmented the force applied to the string, so that the bow was more powerful even though the lower tension in the string meant it was easier to pull back and aim. It also had a sighting arm that you could adjust to your eye, and made it more accurate over long distances. Jack was very impressed by the look of the weapon, and also by Adam's knowledge.

The twins were laughing at each other's first attempts with the traditional bows. They were wearing arm guards, or leather bracers as Adam called them, but somehow, Sean kept managing to hurt his wrist on releasing the arrow. Of all the shots that Jack had heard fired, there were only three arrows stuck in the small target. Adam's dad called Jack forward, and fitted him with a bracer that extended from his thumb to his elbow. He had done archery a couple of times before, and the bow felt good in his hand. He patiently listened as Adam's dad explained the technique and warned him of the dangers of using such a weapon, even in sport. He didn't want to brag about his experience in case he made a fool of himself. Guided by Adam's dad, he nocked his first arrow and drew the string back, the arrow just resting on his finger. He suspected that the twins' mistake had been in trying to hold the arrow and pull it back with the string instead of letting the string pull the arrow itself. Keeping both eyes open, he took aim just above the bull, held his breath, and released his fingers. The bow was a powerful one, and the target quite close, so the arrow lost hardly any of its trajectory, and hit the target about a centimetre above and right of the bullseye.

"Wow! Nice one, Jack!" said Adam, impressed.

"Fluke!" cried Sean, and Kyle laughed. "Betcha can't do it again!"

Jack nocked another arrow, adjusted his stance, drew the string back, and with held breath, aimed at the bottom left of the bullseye. Once again, the arrow flew straight, and this time hit the bottom of the bull.

"Very good, Jack," said Adam's dad. "I think you must have done this before. Let's move you over to the other target. Adam, you can supervise Sean and Kyle on this one for a minute."

When they had all had several turns on both targets, and the twins had got the hang of releasing the arrows, Adam let them have a go with the compound bow. The twins thought it was great, and found it much easier, once they had got the hang of keeping the target in focus through the sight. However, Jack found the lighter tension of the string at odds with the expectation of his arms, and couldn't quite get to grips with it.

"I think I must be a traditionalist," he said, and Adam's dad laughed.

"I must admit, I'm the same," he said, "but you've certainly got the strength in your arm for the traditional bow."

"Would you boys like a drink?" Adam's mum called, as she came across the meadow carrying a tray with two glass jugs and several frosted glasses. "It's home-made lemonade," she said, placing the tray on the picnic table under the tree, "and the glasses have been in the freezer, so it will taste beautifully cool. How are you all getting on?"

"I think Jack's a natural," said her husband, "and these two are showing promise."

They all took long draughts of the lemonade, which was cloudy, sweet, and delicious, with strands of lemon pulp giving it a really home-made touch. Jack took in the view of the meadow; the long grass growing pale and thin near the birch trees, the afternoon sun slanting through the oak leaves dappling the table gold and black; the targets stuck with arrows, all clustered more closely around the centre, now, with no sound but the breeze and the sloshing of lemonade from jug to glass. It seemed to him that this scene was timeless. This could have been a hundred years ago, with boys drinking the same home-made recipe from similar jugs, boys whose names were now probably listed on the memorial in the churchyard up the road. He wasn't really sure what he was feeling; a sense of happiness, a sense of nostalgia, of timelessness and peace? He knew he wouldn't have felt this in London, that was certain. And, looking at the crumbling old wall that surrounded the meadow, covered in ivy and honeysuckle, he felt certain, too, that there would be an Elder-gate in it somewhere, and that thought made him both happy and sad at the same time.

After their refreshments, Jack got a text to say that it was nearly dinnertime, and so the three boys thanked Adam and his parents for the afternoon, and wheeled their bikes to the road with assurances that they were welcome back any time.

"That was ace!" said Kyle, as they freewheeled down the road.

"Tell me you'd done it before, though, Jack!" pleaded Sean.

Jack admitted that he had, once or twice, and they all laughed. When they had joined the Strawberry line, Jack brought up the subject of finishing the old railway box car. "I thought I might have a go at the roof with Alex this week," he said, "but it would be great if you could come and help."

"Yeah, we want to. It really should be us, seeing as it was our fault it burned down."

True to their word, the twins did most of the work on the box car, fixing panels in the roof, and coating it with some green paint they found in an abandoned garage opposite their house. While they were happily occupied with that, Jack got Alex to help him with another part of his plan. He showed Alex the sort of saplings to choose, cutting them with the saw blade on his penknife, and then how to strip the shafts and whittle the tips until they had made three sturdy spears.

When the box car was finished, the four of them pulled some of the ivy from the undergrowth around it and trained it up over the sides and the roof. Around the back, where Poppy had squeezed in through a hole in the original woodwork, the twins had screwed a piece of ply wood in place with hinges and a proper clasp. Inside, they had even put up some shelves. Jack was really impressed, and secretly pleased that he had been right about the twins, who weren't as bad as Poppy was convinced they were. He had been with his dad to fill the car up with diesel, and had noticed an offer on a battery operated camping lantern, which he asked if his dad could buy for him. He even offered to use his pocket money, but Mr Pearson had just smiled and said it was no trouble. He put the lantern inside the den, and Kyle locked it with a new padlock. Sean produced an envelope on which was written:

> To Poppy
> Sorry
> Sean and Kyle

Kyle popped the padlock keys into the envelope and sealed it shut. There then followed an argument about who was going to put it through her door, which ended in the revelation that neither of them knew which door was hers.

"Give it here," said Jack eventually, and he took the envelope from Kyle.

"Are we going to hide in the bushes and watch her open it?" asked Sean, clearly pleased with the work they had done.

"We don't even know if she's in. Could be ages before she comes to look at it," said Kyle. "What do you reckon, Jack?"

"Yeah, I think you're right. I'm sure she'll be mega delighted, but I don't fancy just sitting around here all night waiting to see. We ought to be getting back, now, anyhow."

"Gotcha," said Sean. "No worries. Let us know if she says anything to you ok? See ya!"

"Hey," called Kyle, as Jack and Alex dropped down from the gravel track to the little footpath, "what are those spears for?"

"Just for something to do, you know," Jack called back. "See you guys!"

"What *are* they for, Jack?" asked Alex.

"You'll find out soon enough," said Jack, skipping down the steps and pushing the envelope through Poppy's letterbox.

"Ugh! And you call me annoying! You're always saying that!"

"Well, this time I guarantee it's true."

Over dinner that evening, Mrs Pearson raised the subject of a party that Max had been invited to the following day. Mr Pearson would be at work until the afternoon, and Ashah's mum had said she could stay and let Sam join in.

"Will you two be alright for a couple of hours?" she asked.

"Of course we will," said the boys together.

"What will you do? I think the weather is going to be dry."

"Oh, we'll probably go down to the rec, or see what the twins are up to," said Jack. "We'll be fine. You guys enjoy the party."

"Why do I get the feeling I should be suspicious?"

Two faces of angelic innocence looked at her in unison and shrugged their shoulders.

Chapter Fourteen

Hunters

When the Galaxy had disappeared round the bend by the wizard's house, Jack pulled a sports bag out from under the bunk bed. He told Alex to put his school shoes on, and disappeared into the utility room, taking the bag with him. They locked the back door, and then opened the shed. Alex made to take his bike out, but Jack said they would have too much to carry, and would have to walk. He handed his brother the three spears they had whittled, and slung a long, thin, canvas case over his shoulder. He refused to answer any of Alex's questions, and would only smile and say that he and Poppy had a surprise for him. As they passed Poppy's house without stopping, Jack explained that they would meet her there as she would be on her bike.

"Typical!" said Alex.

It was another mild day in spite of the recent rain, and the patches of blue sky around the innocent-looking clouds suggested it would stay fair. As they dropped down to the rhyne from the old railway line, they saw Poppy's bike leaning against the hedge, and Poppy herself was waiting for them at the little log bridge over the clear water.

"Hey, the boat's moved!" exclaimed Alex.

"Yep," said Jack.

"How did that happen?"

"It really is too difficult to explain," said Poppy. "Come on, keep close to the hedge."

They reached the part of the hedge closest to the boat, and Jack slung his bag onto the ground. "Right, Zan, put this on." He took out the costumes and handed one to his brother and one to Poppy.

"What the gubbins?" said Alex, holding the garment up. "This looks like a nativity costume."

"Shepherds, that's right."

"'What the gubbins'?" queried Poppy with a chuckle.

"It's something dad says. He comes out with all sorts of weird alternatives to swearing, to try and protect us," explained Jack. "It's how I know what rowlocks are."

"It's because of the little ones, mostly," said Alex. "But why are we dressing up as shepherds? What's going on?"

"You'll see," said Jack, taking three medium sized potatoes out of the bag. He unzipped Adam's bow and arrows from their case, then pushed the bags under the hedge.

"Where did you get that?"

"Borrowed it." He stood up and put his own shepherd's costume on. "Now, I think we should roll around in the grass a bit, make these look lived-in."

Poppy and Alex watched as Jacked lay down and started to roll and writhe about as if he was being bitten all over by ants. At his insistence, they both did the same, then Jack made sure that the rope belts were tight, and any signs of their modern clothing were hidden.

"I think we'll need to muddy our shoes a bit, too, but we can do that later. Let's go to the boat. Poppy, can you bring the potatoes, please. Alex, you bring the spears. This really is going to blow your mind, but I'm afraid I can't really prepare you for it beforehand." He picked up Adam's bow, and set off.

"I have done archery before, remember?" said Alex, following him. "We did it at Center Parcs. But what are we going to be shooting at?"

They waded through the long grass to the boat, and Alex jumped in, sitting on the bench in the stern.

"You'll have to sit in the prow this time," said Jack, placing the archery equipment and Poppy's potatoes in the bottom of the boat before climbing in to sit on the rowing seat. He turned to face his brother in the prow; he wanted to watch his face.

"Are we going to throw the potatoes in the air and shoot them? Like clay pigeons? They're not very big, are they?" said Alex. Jack just grinned.

"Right, shipmates," said Poppy, resting her hands on the gunwale near the stern. "Are you ready for this?" And she gave an imperceptible shove to the boat as she swung her legs over and sat on the bench seat.

"Holy moly! What the heck!" cried Alex. His face was a picture. "What's happened? Where are we?" He gazed around at the vast lake. In his nativity costume, he looked like one of the Disciples in their illustrated children's bible, when Jesus walked on the water. Jack didn't think he could look any more surprised even if somebody did walk across the lake.

Jack slotted the oars into the rowlocks. "We think that there is some kind of magic connection between this old boat and Poppy's new earrings. We're still in the same place, but just in a different time, and we think it's all to do with the wimblestone."

"So what's with the potatoes? And the bows?"

"You'll see." Said Jack, and he began to row them towards the shore, with Poppy giving directions. He glanced up and smiled to himself as the hawk he had seen previously flew overhead.

"Jack," said Poppy, "you wouldn't happen to know anything about a set of keys, would you?"

"Keys? Keys to what?"

"Keys to a newly refurbished railway box car?"

"Maybe," Jack grinned, "But the twins did most of it. I told you they were alright, deep down."

"Yeah, ok. Maybe you're right. But, thank you. I know it wouldn't have happened without you."

"Do you like it?"

"It's fantastic. Absolutely amazing. Better than before, in a way, although it was kinda special and, like, my own little discovery before. But, no, it's ace, really."

"I helped with it." Said Alex, feeling a little left out.

"Thank you, Zander. It's ace."

They came ashore in roughly the same spot as before. There was no sign of their previous visit, no marks in the earth from where they had dragged the boat up the bank, but Poppy and Jack recognized the tree formation. The three of them pulled the boat up to safety, and Jack gave Alex a spear. He picked up Adam's bow and slung the quiver of steel-tipped arrows over his shoulder.

"Poppy, do you want to stay with the boat? I don't know how long we'll be."

"Why would I want to stay here? I'm coming with you two. For sure."

"Ok, then. Grab a spear, and can you carry the potatoes again, please?"

"Why do I always get to carry the potatoes?" she muttered to herself.

Jack led them up through the trees to where the little track crossed their path. He looked around at the trees and creeper, then pointed to a spot on the track. "Put the potatoes down there," he said to Poppy, "and maybe stand on the two bigger ones, squash them a bit, break them open. That's it. Excellent." He turned, and descended the hill a few meters. "Alex, you come and hide behind this tree, here. Poppy, I think you'll be safe over there, look."

"Safe? What do you mean, 'safe'? Safe from what?"

"Just in case anything goes wrong."

"What are you playing at, Jack?" asked Alex.

Jack took an arrow from the quiver and nocked it onto the string. He gave a couple of pulls on the bow, stretching his shoulders and feeling the tension in the shaft, aiming at the spot where the potatoes were lying on the track, then he crouched down behind the tree he had chosen.

"Wait. You're not going to do what I think you're going to do, are you? You're not going to shoot the boar?" asked Poppy, incredulously.

"We need something to take to the camp fire. We need an excuse to talk to people, a way to blend in and make the locals grateful to us, so they are less suspicious."

"Couldn't you shoot some pigeons instead?"

"I'm not Robin Hood, you know. It's going to be hard enough to hit a pig, let alone a bird flying through the branches."

"But killing an animal..." Poppy was genuinely horrified.

"Look, as far as we're concerned, this animal died a thousand years ago. This is all in the past, already. The boar as we know it is dead and gone, probably shot in this very wood by someone else who needed to eat. That's

187

how life was back then. Here. Whatever. And I have a theory about where we are. This will be a good test of it."

"What theory?" asked Poppy.

"I'll explain later. We need to keep quiet, now. Everybody stay still and out of sight. You ok, Zan?"

"Yeah. Think so."

"Right. Get ready with the spear."

"What for?"

"Just in case."

"Just in case what?" asked Alex, nervously.

"I wish you'd stop saying 'just in case'," said Poppy.

"Shh! Here it comes!"

The boar came trotting up the path as it had the time before. Jack adjusted his grip on the bow, and tested the nock of the arrow on the string. He was tense; nervous but ready. The animal stopped where they had left the potatoes. It stood for a moment, sniffing in every direction, then bent its head to the food. Jack rose slowly and silently behind the tree, drawing back the string and lifting the bow to sight the boar. The place he had chosen to shoot from was just downhill enough to expose the boar's ribs to his arrows without the undergrowth getting in the way. As its head came back up, Jack loosed the arrow and reached into the quiver for another. He had been aiming behind the boar's front leg, hoping the arrow would go straight to the heart, but he had caught the beast in the shoulder, and it squealed and stamped, flaring its nostrils and turning to face the children. Without hesitation, it began to charge at them, the arrow firmly lodged, catching at the creeper beneath the trees.

"Oh my god!" cried Poppy.

"Jack. Jack!" shouted Alex, pointing the spear, which seemed very flimsy and insubstantial all of a sudden, at the charging pig.

Jack, however, remained steady behind his tree, fixing the advancing boar in his sights, the second arrow at full tension. The boar had chosen Alex as its target, and was about three meters from him, squealing in rage, when Jack's second arrow went right through its left eye and stopped it, dead.

"Oh my god!" cried Alex with relief.

"That. Was. Amazing!" said Poppy. "You were fantastic. I mean, look at that shot, right through the eye! And if you'd missed… what might have happened to Alex… You saved his life, I reckon! That was brilliant!" She was suddenly very excited, overcome by the drama of the moment, all qualms about killing an animal forgotten.

Jack felt like jelly. All the nervous tension had washed away leaving him feeling almost dizzy. It had been a stupid and reckless idea. He had seriously endangered his brother. What if it had gone wrong? He didn't like to tell them that he had been aiming for the animal's chest. The shot through the eye had been sheer dumb luck.

Jack retrieved the arrows, then took the spear from Alex and poked the tip into the arrow holes. He told Poppy to do the same with her spear, then he took some brown garden twine from his jeans pocket and with Poppy and Alex's help, tied the boar's front and rear legs together. Hoping Alex's spear could take the weight of the animal without breaking, Jack passed it between the boar's tied legs and he and Alex lifted it onto their shoulders. Poppy picked up the bow and arrows, and they trooped down the hill to the boat.

189

When they reached the water, Jack thoroughly cleaned the two Arrows he had used, and put them back in the quiver, then they placed the boar in the boat between Alex and Jack, and pushed away from the shore. Jack rowed them hard towards the dip in the hills where the main road in their time ran up past the castle and down past the garden centre, where he and Poppy had seen the little beach and the smoke from a camp fire rising. His strokes had become much more purposeful and clean since his first efforts, and now he looked like he had been at the oars all his life. He was much more evenly balanced, and the rhythm he set himself seemed effortless.

As they approached the beach, Jack became more cautious. He made Poppy and Alex scan the trees for any signs of people. Poppy guided them in to the edge of the beach, and Alex jumped out onto the mud. Together, they pulled the boat out of the water and hid it in the trees, just enough to conceal it from thieves, but no further from the water than necessary.

"Look!" said Poppy, pointing to the stern of the boat, where Silver lettering spelled out 'Nymue'. "I can't believe I've never noticed that before."

"Nymue," said Jack, "King Arthur's Lady of the Lake. Amazing. I suppose we've never seen the back of the boat out of the water here, that's why. And the paint has all worn away in our time."

Jack made them all get their shoes and the shafts of their spears muddy, then he stuck the end of his own spear between the pig's ribs, to make it look like the three of them had fought and killed the animal.

Jack and Alex put both their spears through the boar's legs, and hoisted them onto their shoulders, with the boar suspended between them. The spears could have done with being longer and a little thicker; the weight of the animal bent them, and as they walked, the carcass swung and nudged each of them in turn. Poppy carried her spear, and used it as a walking stick, or for swatting aside branches and creepers. Slowly, they followed the track through the woods, up the unrecognisable Banwell hill towards the brow where the castle would stand, and where they could see the smoke rising.

"I think this track must be Dark Lane," said Poppy, gazing around her at the slope and their rough trajectory.

When they reached the brow of the hill, the trees cleared, and the valley of pastureland lay before them, similar to the view they were familiar with. The boys laid the boar down at their feet and gazed at the scene before them. Small brown cattle grazed in herds along the bottom of the valley. There were no hedges marking the boundaries of fields, no orchards of fruit trees, no St James' church visible on the hillside opposite. More smoke and some dark thatched roofs indicated that the oldest part of Winscombe had been settled, but what caught the children's attention stood over to their right, at the very end of the ridge that faced them.

"Look over there!" said Poppy, pointing.

"Woah! Look at that!" exclaimed Jack.

"Is that Crook Peak?" asked Alex.

"Yes it is, but what's that?"

Where the rounded hill they knew bore a hump of exposed rock, there now stood a tall stone tower. The children couldn't tear their gaze from it.

"Has anyone ever mentioned a tower there before, Poppy?" asked Jack.

"Not to me. I'm sure there would be some sort of sign or plaque or something. Or somebody would have had a story to tell about it. There's not even any mention of it in A Somerset Sketchbook."

"No." Mused Jack, deep in thought.

"You don't think that little mound of rock is all that's left of that tower, do you?" asked Alex. "I mean, it does kind of look like an ancient pile of stones, doesn't it?"

"And it's in exactly the right place," said Poppy. "Bit of a coincidence."

"Right," said Jack, "let's find this camp fire, see what we can find out. Let me do the talking, ok? People in these times would have been wary of strangers; nobody really travelled very far, so don't be too friendly. Look like you don't trust anyone."

They could smell the wood smoke of the fire, but whose fire was it? Were they woodsmen? Farmers? Cowherds? Or were they the first settlers of Banwell? This, more than the boar, was what Jack was most nervous about: encountering people who would be suspicious of them, who would know instantly, makeshift medieval costumes aside, that they didn't belong. Maybe it wasn't so easy for aliens to infiltrate humanity, after all. Maybe they did need the power of invisibility to make their observations.

"Remember, let me do the talking, ok? Keep your hoods up. I don't want them to know how young we are, and I don't want them to know Poppy's a girl, ok? If anything goes wrong, we head back to the boat as fast as possible. If it means you two pushing off into the water without me, that's fine, I'll swim out to you if I have to. Ok?"

"Ok."

"Try and look comfortable in your costumes, and as if you've been carrying spears and killing pigs all your lives."

Jack looked at the two of them in their hastily dirtied nativity costumes. Was this going to work? What had he been thinking? He motioned to Alex to help him with the boar, and then the three of them made their way in the direction of the fire.

The fire was enclosed by a circle of stones fitted expertly together like a dry stone wall, and a blackened iron frame was fixed across it. A large black cauldron similar to Bethany's sat on the far side, and log seats, some like Bethany's, some long like benches, formed a rough circle. The fire was in the centre of a clearing of bare earth, on the edge of which sat two huts and a covered stack of logs. On a log bench outside one of the huts, a man was sitting mending a leather apron. As the children came into the clearing, he stood up warily.

"Greetings, friend." Hailed Jack in a deep voice. Alex had to stifle a laugh.

The man put the apron down on the bench and walked slowly towards them, bringing a long staff that had been leaning against the hut beside him. He didn't exactly look menacing, but on the other hand he didn't look friendly. He was short and thick set, with long, dirty hair and a thick, black beard. It was impossible to guess how old he was, but he certainly wasn't young. Jack noticed that his clothes were at least similar in appearance to what he had achieved with the shepherds' outfits, but the material was much coarser and thicker, and filthier. He looked strong and fit, used to living in the forest, and his attention seemed to be focussed on the boar.

The man's voice was like a bear growling, growling that almost sounded like words similar to English. "What business have you here, strangers?"

Jack looked round at Alex and Poppy. "What do we do now?" he asked in an urgent whisper.

"Tell him we want to use the fire, I suppose," said Alex.

"What good will that do?" asked Jack, exasperated.

"Well, he asked what our business was. I thought we were going to share the boar in exchange for information."

"You mean you understood him?" asked Poppy.

"Course. Didn't you?"

The man came a little closer, holding his staff at the ready.

"You talk to him. Say 'greetings friend', then say we've caught the boar but don't have a fire to cook it with. And make yourself sound older."

"Greetings, friend," said Alex in his gruffest voice. "We caught this boar. Perhaps we could share your fire." He took the spears from his shoulder, and he and Jack lowered the boar to the ground.

"Make a fine meal, that will, no mistake. When it's hung and skinned. Got stew in the pot. You can all have stew and bread, hot from the fire, in exchange for that boar."

Jack and Poppy looked at Alex, who couldn't understand why he was having to translate for them when they were all speaking the same language as far as he could tell.

"Where are you from?" asked the man, coming forward and feeding his staff through the boar's bound legs and hoisting it over his shoulder."

"Say we're from the north," said Jack, when Alex had translated.

"You're not Welsh?" asked the man, with a stern look. He hung the boar from a hook under the eaves of his hut, and leant his staff back against the wall. He clearly trusted the strangers now that they had shared their kill. He pointed at the log seats, and nodded, inviting them to sit down, then, with no explanation, he went inside the building, and re-emerged after a couple of minutes with a crusty loaf of bread, and three wooden bowls with wooden spoons. He lifted the cauldron and hung it on a hook on the iron frame over the fire, then, muttering a few words, he went back inside the hut.

"What did he say?" asked Jack.

"Can you honestly not understand him?" asked Alex. "He said that the others will be back soon."

"Others," said Poppy, nervously. "I wonder how many." She looked round at the circle of logs, estimating how many bottoms they could accommodate.

"Best ask his name and introduce ourselves. I think we might need Saxon names. I'll be Ector, you can be Dunstan, and Poppy can be..."

"Arwen," said Poppy. "Always wanted to be Arwen."

The man came back out with four horns with leather bindings, and a large jug. As he handed a horn to each of them, Alex said,

"Thank you, friend. I am Dunstan, and my friends here are Ector and Arwen. What do they call you?"

"They call me Wulfren." The man filled their horns with mead from the jug, then gestured for them to sit down. "How is it that your friends don't speak the Saxon tongue?" he asked Alex.

"Erm, they have never travelled so far from our village," he replied. "We speak a little differently in the north."

"And what has brought you south to these woods, then?" asked Wulfren.

"He wants to know what we're doing here, so far from the north," whispered Alex.

"Tell him we are seeking something that was stolen by raiders," said Poppy.

The children sipped their horns of mead, trying to look as if this was the most natural thing in the world. It had a sweet taste, but left a dry feeling in their throats. As Alex was explaining their story to Wulfren, three large, shaggy dogs came trotting into the clearing, followed by two more men and a woman, all carrying staffs like Wulfren's. Wulfren stood up to greet them and explain the presence of the children. As the newcomers settled themselves on the logs around the fire, giving their names as Glodwin, Oeric and Myldred, Wulfren stirred the cauldron, then went back into the hut for more bowls and bread.

The adults sat looking at the children, as the dogs settled themselves at their sides, protective but not threatening. An awkward silence fell about the fire.

"Have you been tending the cattle in the valley?" asked Alex, and the newcomers said that they had, and spoke about the herds and their dogs, and the weather. As they spoke, Jack and Poppy began to understand more and more of the language they used. Apart from the strong and unfamiliar accent, many of the words were recognisable, with a little effort and close listening. Jack, however, didn't let on that he could understand. He found it useful to make Alex translate because it gave them all more time to think, and slowed the stream of information down.

"Tell me, friends," said Alex at his brother's prompting, "for we are strangers to these parts; what is that stone tower on the other side of the valley?"

"Tis Merlin's tower," said Oeric, sullenly, breaking off a hunk of bread from a loaf that Myldred passed him.

The children tried not to let their interest show. After a few agonising seconds that felt like minutes, Alex asked "The wizard, Merlin?"

"Heard of Merlin in the north, have you?" asked Wulfren.

"I think everyone has heard of Merlin," said Alex, trying to sound nonchalant.

"Wizard!" spat Oeric. "Trickster, Merlin. Charlatan, Merlin."

"He's a crook, he is," said Glodwin.

The children couldn't help themselves at that. They each looked at the other with mouths open, then quickly tried to recover. Merlin, the wizard from Arthurian legend, being called a crook, and his tower standing on what was now known as Crook Peak. It was as if they had each been struck by lightning.

"It's not him is bad, it's that Morgana. Merlin's just an old fool," said Myldred. "Since the death of Arthur, there's been nothing checking her reins. She's the evil one, and Merlin's no match for her."

"That's enough of that talk," said Wulfren, looking sternly at all of them as he returned to the cauldron. He began to ladle stew into the wooden bowls and pass them round, first to the children as they were his guests and had brought the boar, then to his companions. The stew was piping hot, and the children dipped their hunks of bread in, sucking up the juice as the strangers did, before attempting to eat the meat and vegetables with the wooden spoons. The meat was chewy, but the juice was well flavoured, and the vegetables were fresh and tasty.

"Good stew this, master Wulfren." Said Alex, and the others all nodded and made appreciative noises.

The three cowherds were evidently hungry, and the conversation died down, replaced by the scraping of the bowls and the sounds of sucking, slurping and chewing. When they had cleaned their bowls, Myldred took the ladle and dished out a small portion for each of the dogs, who set about lapping them up as hungrily as their owners, and with very similar noises.

Jack gathered up the bowls from Poppy and Alex, and handed them to Wulfren, who took them over to a stone trough between the two huts, and sloshed water on them from a wooden barrel.

"We ned to get going before they see which way we go," whispered Jack to Alex, "otherwise we'll have a long walk just to convince them of our story. We've got no business having a boat on the lake if we've walked here from a village in the north."

"We thank you all for your generous hospitality, friends, but now me must make haste," said Alex, and the three of them retrieved their spears and nodded their gratitude.

"Fare well on your quest," said Wulfren, and the children stopped in panic. "Are you far behind these raiders you seek?" he asked.

With relief, Alex said, "we expect to catch them on the south coast. Fare well, master Wulfren. Fare well, friends." And the three children raised their spears and left the clearing via the track to the brow of Banwell hill.

They stopped to take one more look at the tower that dominated the view of the valley, then they jogged down what would become Dark Lane to the muddy beach, and launched Nymue. When they were safely on the water and

Jack was rowing them steadily back towards the boat field, they all began to laugh with the release of tension.

"Wow! This has been incredible!" mused Alex. "I mean, absolutely unbelievable. What a wicked adventure! I can't believe it! And that tower! And Merlin, actually Merlin from the legend of King Arthur! I can't wait to tell Max all about this."

"Yes," said Jack, more soberly, now. "We've got a lot to tell Max, and a lot to think about. And I somehow need to get these costumes washed and returned to the church hall before anyone notices they're missing." He sounded so serious and like an adult, that the other two burst out laughing again.

Chapter Fifteen

Petra Vita

"So, Jack, do you think the stone is at Crook Peak, under those rocks?" asked Poppy. She, Jack and Alex were in the old box car den. It was once again her favourite place to chill.

"I reckon it could be." Jack replied. "If Merlin took the stone from Excalibur before it was thrown back into the lake, and kept it instead of returning it to the goblins, then he would have taken it to that tower, wouldn't he?"

"But it wouldn't be there now, just lying among the rocks, would it? Surely? After all this time?" asked Poppy.

"I don't know," said Jack. "I bet the tower had a cellar. People throughout history have kept their most valuable possessions or treasure in cellars. Much harder to break into, and safe from the rest of the building catching fire. What do you think?"

"Makes sense, I suppose."

"No harm in looking," said Alex.

"Shouldn't we go to Merlin's tower while it's still standing? Wouldn't that make more sense?" asked Poppy.

"I don't really want to tangle with Merlin if we don't have to," said Jack.

"Or Morgana." Added Alex.

"Anyway," continued Poppy, "how are we going to get into this cellar, if it exists? It will be like digging through rock, now, after all these years."

"Zan can open it, like he did the cave." Said Jack.

"I don't know. That was goblin magic. That was their secret entrance. This is just stones." Objected Alex.

"But if the wimblestone is inside, the goblin magic might work." Jack smiled, encouragingly.

"Worth a try." Said Alex.

"You've really thought about this, haven't you?" said Poppy, smiling too.

"And," said Jack, "I think we should bring Max."

"Oh, what? Why?" moaned Alex.

"Because he's a part of this; he's one of the chosen ones, and we might need his eyes. This quest is bigger than your petty squabbles with your brother."

"But he's just so annoying!" Alex complained, theatrically.

"Learn to deal with it." Implored Jack.

"Ugh!"

"But what about the fifth painting?" asked Poppy. "If we need Max, don't we need the final saviour, too? We still don't know who or what that is, do we?"

Jack looked down at his hands, the fingers twining restlessly together. He knew Poppy was right; the missing piece of the puzzle was still bothering him.

"I don't see what else we can do until we work out what that painting means," he said. "I just know we need to be doing something. We need to do what we can for the time being, and hope that the rest of this puzzle falls into place, somehow. Who knows, maybe we won't discover the meaning of the fifth figure until we've explored beneath the tower." He looked from Poppy to Alex. "I just think we should be doing everything we can before it's too late."

After lunch, Jack asked their mum if he, Alex and Max could go for a bike ride with Poppy.

"Where to?" asked their mum, wiping down Sammy's high chair.

"We thought we would go to Crook Peak, along the strawberry line."

"Well..."

"Is a hole in the ground. You get water from it." Said Jack.

"Don't you be cheeky, young man, or you won't be going anywhere, do you hear me? That's not how you talk to an adult."

"Sorry mum. But can we go, please?"

"I just don't know if you should go all that way on your own, especially with Max."

"We'll be fine, honestly. I thought this was why you wanted us to move to the countryside, so we could be out in the fresh air, safe from traffic and the dangers of the city. Why we joined the scouts and everything. This is what scouts do, they go out into the wilderness, scouting about, exploring, having adventures. Why shouldn't Max be allowed to go? We'll look after him. Won't we, Zan?"

"Of course. Mum, I really want us all to go. We don't fall out as much as we used to, honest." Said Alex.

Their mum drew in a deep breath and sighed. "Oh, alright, then. But be careful. And promise me you'll look after Max, you won't just go off with Poppy somewhere and abandon him!"

"Of course we won't! What do you take us for?" protested Jack.

"Well. Don't let him go near the edge. And don't be late home, it gets dark earlier now, remember."

"Yes, we remember!"

"Bye!" the three of them called as they went to get their bikes out of the shed. "Bye, Sammy, bye, mum!"

The four children emerged from the long tunnel, and pushed their bikes up the narrow path that led up to the woods by the Crook Peak car park. Then Poppy had to wait while the three boys took their rucksacks off and tried out the natural half pipe formed by the ravine amidst the trees, until she finally decided to have a go herself. Eventually, she reminded them why they were there, and they all leaned their bikes up against the car park wall and chained their wheels together.

The walk up to the peak didn't take them very long, as they didn't have to wait for any parents pushing buggies, and soon they were standing by the rocky outcrop where Merlin's tower had stood the last time they looked at the hill.

"Over to you, then, Zander." Said Jack, when they had made sure that no one else was enjoying a walk on the hill.

"Aarlubbock." Burped Alex. It never ceased to amaze Jack how he could burp at a moment's notice.

There was a rumbling like thunder, and a tremor beneath their feet, and then, slowly, the stones started to move, shaking off the soil that surrounded them cementing them in place, and parting like tumbling dice to reveal a set of stone steps leading downward in a spiral.

"I don't believe it!" said Jack. "It worked! I mean, I know it was my hypothesis, and all, but I still don't believe it actually worked."

They took out their torches, and carefully descended the steps. At the bottom was an oak door, studded with black iron squares. Jack eyed it closely, then, with his torch between his teeth, turned the heavy iron handle and pushed the door open. Alex was beside Jack, shining his torch through the widening gap. Max stayed back, holding Poppy's hand. The beams of light from the torches passed over an eerie scene. The room was like a cavern, with no other light penetrating the gloom. A solid wooden table and chair stood in the middle of the room, laid out with thick candles, pots and jars, and other objects covered in thick grey dust and dense, silvery spider webs. The stone floor was also covered in dust, giving the impression of looking at an old black and white photograph, water marked by occasional drips that had seeped through the ceiling.

Jack pointed his torch upwards to inspect the ceiling. He had been expecting it to be made of wood, stout oak beams and boards that would have been rotten and dangerous by now, but it seemed as though the cellar had actually been carved out of the rock, with just the floor and the doorway made of cut stone.

"I think it's safe to go in." He said. "Zander, I think you'd better close up the entrance."

"No! Wait! What if we can't get out again?" cried Max in a panic.

"Look," said Jack, calmly, "Zander has opened it once, and if he can close it now, he'll be able to open it again, ok? And we'll be fine in here, this room has been untouched for centuries, look. The rocks only covered the staircase. We'll be safer if we're hidden, just in case anyone comes up the hill, yeah?"

Max and Poppy stepped into the cellar, and Max nodded bravely. Alex gave another of his burped words, and Jack pushed the door closed as the stair case started to fill up with fallen stones. When the rumbling stopped, it was deadly silent in the chamber. The children swept their torches around the room. As well as the table and chairs, there were shelves containing a multitude of pots and vessels and small caskets, heavy stone bowls and small tin dishes, and bulbous jars of glass and copper with long spouts. 'Alembics' muttered Jack in awe; this really was Merlin's laboratory.

Next to the shelves was a large chest which instantly caught Jack's attention. Beneath its covering of dust, it was made of a rich wood, edged and decorated in what looked like bronze. Jack gave the metal a rub, but it was too tarnished to shine. The others were exploring the room, now, too, and while Jack tried to open the chest, Poppy was blowing the dust off the things on the table. Max came over to Jack, and bent down to examine the chest. It had lasted extremely well underground for such a long time, and Jack's efforts at prizing the lid open were proving futile.

"I'm sure the stone will be in here," said Jack, "it's a proper treasure chest, isn't it, Max?"

Max didn't speak, but reached out and pressed a bronze decoration shaped like a crescent moon. Nothing happened. With his thumb, he pushed it up, down, then left, as if the crescent had been a gently curved arrow, and there was a satisfying mechanical click from inside the chest. The lid sprang open half a centimetre under Jack's hand, and he opened the chest with a smooth, easy action.

"Max! You're a genius!"

At this exclamation, Alex came over to see what was inside. The boys shone their torches over a stack of scrolls of parchment, some bound with cords of leather, some loose. Once again, they seemed to be very well preserved.

The inside of the chest was lined with leather, which must have kept out the damp. Carefully, the boys removed the scrolls. The edges of some were brittle, and broke under their thumbs as they tried to unroll them, but the ink was still clear on most, although none of them could read the elaborate swirls of italic script.

"Is this even English?" asked Max, looking at a scroll he had opened.

"I doubt it," said Jack. "I think these are foreign works that Merlin collected. Doesn't look like Arabic, though, or Greek. Could be Latin or early German, maybe."

"Is there anything else in there?" asked Alex, eagerly.

Underneath the scrolls was a thick, leather bound book decorated with the same crescent moon as the front of the chest. Beside it were some small leather pouches and larger velvet bags with braided silk drawstrings. The bags were heavy, and clinked when Jack and Alex reached in and picked them up.

"Maybe the stone is in one of these!" cried Max excitedly.

They opened all the bags, and found an assortment of gold, silver and bronze coins, some Roman, some Saxon, others possibly Egyptian or Byzantine.

"Wow! Look at this!" cried Alex. "This is awesome!"

Inside the last bag were gemstones of all different colours, many with their own iridescent glow, but nothing like the wimblestone that Sostror had described.

"Oh my god! We're rich!" laughed Alex.

"We can't keep them," said Poppy, coming over to have a look. "We can't just steal them."

"It's archaeology," corrected Jack with a grin, letting the coins run through his fingers back into a purple velvet bag, "not theft."

"They don't belong to anyone now," said Alex. "Merlin has been dead for a thousand years."

"I don't know," said Poppy, "I'm not comfortable with this. Finding the wimblestone for the goblins is one thing, but keeping all this treasure..."

"We could give it to the museum," suggested Max, "donate it. Or most of it." He added, grinning at the others.

"Anyway," sighed Jack, standing up and looking around, "the wimblestone isn't here."

"But it was," said Poppy. "Come and look at this." She went back to the table, and showed them a leather bound book similar to the one in the chest. The pages were still dusty from where the book had been left open on the table, and Jack could see a quill and a small pot in the gauze of dust and cobweb by the side of the book. On the left hand page, in capital letters clearly legible were the words PETRA VITA. There were more Latin words underneath, and a drawing of a stone that fitted the goblins' description of their Stone of Life.

"That's it!" said Jack. "Petra, stone, from where we get the word 'petrified', and Vita, life, where we get the word 'vital'. The stone of life. Merlin was making notes, studying it. Quite possibly the last time he was in this room!"

"But look here," said Poppy, pointing to the right hand page. There was another picture of the stone from a different angle, but this one was more of a diagram. There was a line drawn through the tip of the stone, and below that, a drawing of a ring with the severed tip of the wimblestone set in it.

"Do you think he was going to take a bit off and keep it? To harness its power?" Jack asked Poppy.

207

"Looks like it." She replied.

"What a crook!" said Jack. "But where is it now?"

He shone his torch around the room again, passing over each of the shelves, the chest, right round to the wall behind them.

"Hang on!" he cried. "Look there!"

In the corner, on the same wall as the door to the stairs, was another oak and iron door. They approached it like the altar of a temple, unable to believe that none of them had noticed it before. Jack turned the handle and pulled, but the door just juddered in its sturdy frame. "Of course," he said, "it would be locked!"

Alex and Poppy gave the door a rattle, too, but it was definitely locked. There was a keyhole in the ironwork by the handle, but no key. Jack took his torch back over to the table, and started blowing dust off everything there. "I don't suppose anyone brought an axe?" he asked. Beside a pestle and mortar on the table was a wooden box, which Jack opened in hope, only to reveal three clay pipes and a wad of what must have been tobacco. Max walked around the far side of the table, and something metallic skittered across the stone floor.

"They key!" he shouted, and picked it up out of the grey dust. He handed it to Jack.

"What's up, Max? Scared there'll be a skeleton in the closet?" jeered Alex.

"No!" said Max, defiantly, his triumph at finding the key suddenly dissipated. "I just think it should be Jack who opens the door."

"Unless you want to, Zander?" suggested Jack, pointedly. He did wish Alex could just leave Max alone sometimes.

"No, go ahead. I was only joking."

"Right. Here goes." Jack fitted the key into the lock, and looked round at the eager faces fixed on the door in the reflected light of the torches. They seemed to contain the same emotions of excitement, anticipation and trepidation as he was feeling himself. He turned the key, and a gust of stale air assaulted their nostrils. He pulled the door slowly towards them, and three beams of light speared the darkness beyond.

They were looking into a store room. Shelves of jars, pots, vials of coloured glass, wooden caskets and more scrolls, not so well preserved, lined the walls. On the floor was a mess of broken pottery, fallen scrolls, the remains of whatever had been in the jars, and what looked like some woven material. Jack's torch joined the other beams raking the darkness. One by one, they all settled on something leaning against the bottom shelf at the far end of the small room.

"What's that?" asked Alex.

Jack's torch crept along the floor towards them, and came to rest on what they were all expecting, and dreading, to see.

"Oh my god!" shrieked Poppy, and she turned away from the doorway.

In the light of Jack's torch was a skeletal foot, the bones dusty and clothed in webs, while Alex and Max's torches illuminated the dusty grey dome of a skull.

"Is that Merlin, do you suppose?" asked Alex.

"I reckon it could be," replied Jack.

"Do you think he's still got the stone on him?"

"If this were a film, we'd be able to see it clutched in his bare finger bones," said Jack. "As it is, we'll have to see if there are any pockets in this garment he's wearing."

"We?" exclaimed Alex. "How about Max and I hold the torches steady?"

"Great idea," muttered Jack. He took a tentative step into the store cupboard, shifting the debris to get his foot firmly on the floor. He bent down and brushed the dust and cobwebs off the prone figure with one of the sturdier scrolls. The material seemed to be a robe of dark blue, edged in a golden thread. Jack patted it carefully, trying not to look at the staring eye sockets of the ancient skull. The robe was empty.

"What do you think happened, Jack?" asked Max.

"I don't know."

"Well, obviously someone locked Merlin in the cupboard, threw away the key, and stole the stone." Said Poppy. "So now what do we do?"

"I felt sure the wimblestone would be in here somewhere." Said Jack. "I suppose we ought to check everywhere, to make sure he didn't hide it. Maybe he hid himself in the cupboard when the thieves came, and had time to hide it in one of the pots. Maybe he knocked all these things off when he climbed up the shelves. We need to be thorough."

"True," said Poppy, with determination. "Come on then, we'll search every shelf, every jar, every box and every corner until we've either found it or we're one hundred per cent certain that it's gone."

While Poppy and Jack searched the store room, Alex and Max searched the shelves in the main chamber, and double checked the table and the chest.

"Maybe there's a secret floor in the chest," suggested Alex. "What did you fiddle with before, to get the lid open?"

Max showed Alex the crescent moon, and pressed it to the right this time. It slid easily as it had done when the lid opened, but there were no more clicks, and nothing happened to the chest.

"Hang on," said Max. He felt the leather lined inside of the lid, and pulled it down to examine the top. The lid of the chest was curved, like a barrel lying on its side, but the inside was flat. With the lid closed, Max pushed the moon to the right again, and the lid sprang up with a click, revealing, not the open chest, but a shallow tray lined with rich velvet.

The brothers' delight at this discovery soon evaporated, however, when they saw what the tray contained.

"Hair?" Alex looked at Max, incredulous at the neatly preserved locks capped in wax, and laid out like a museum exhibit. One long pony tail of deep auburn, with copper and gold highlights and an almost aqua-green sheen, and two small, wispy curls, one blonde and one jet black. "Why would anyone keep hair like this?"

"Mum's got bits of our hair from when we were babies," said Max, "and these two could be from babies. They're very fine, and only short."

"Not this one, though. I've never seen hair like that. Is it human, do you think? Or maybe from a horse's mane?" Alex wanted to stroke the long tress of richly coloured strands, but the idea of them laid out like this in a secret compartment made them feel like sacred religious relics. "Well," he said, closing the lid gently, "it's not the stone, anyhow."

Poppy and Jack had no more success in the store room, and after an hour of meticulous searching, including the underside of the table, the children had to accept that the wimblestone was not in the cellar.

"Looks like we'll have to face Merlin after all," said Jack with resignation.

"Maybe we could lock him in the store room!" laughed Alex.

"Yes, maybe!" said Jack, lightly, but then he frowned in thought, and muttered to himself: 'maybe…maybe.' "What we're going to do now, though, is take some of this treasure back with us. Poppy, why don't you take the precious gems, and we'll all take a bag of coins each. I'm not saying we'll keep them, but there's no point leaving them here. And I'll take this, too," he said, picking up the book with the drawing of the Petra Vita. He closed the door to the store room, and asked Alex to open up the way out of the cellar.

"Aarlubbock!" burped Alex, and they all listened to the shifting of the stones out of the stair case. He opened the door, and let Jack, Poppy and Max go through, before closing it behind them all.

The sky above them had clouded over during the afternoon, but the light still made them squint after the subterranean gloom of the cellar. They climbed the steps cautiously, shielding their eyes with their hands. When they reached the top, Alex turned and burped the word to close the hill again. Before the rocks had finished resettling, the other three stopped, and Max cried out in alarm: "It's the witch!"

The old woman that Max had seen with Stephen, the one the school children called The Witch of Woodborough Drive, was standing about ten meters in front of them, her hands in the pockets of her coat, glaring at the children, and by her side was a malevolent looking black cat. Her clothes and hair looked normal, like any other woman her age from the village, but there was something in her eyes that made her look unmistakably witchlike. She seemed to radiate a dark force, and the clouds swirled and darkened behind her like a cinematic effect. Seeing her unexpectedly like that, realising that she had been waiting for them, struck the four of them with fear. Alone on the hill, they felt rooted to the spot by her penetrating gaze.

"So," hissed the witch, walking slowly towards them with her cat at her side, "it *is* you! How long I have waited!" She stood two meters from them and looked from one to the other, a lingering, searching look. She settled her eyes on Jack in a way that he could almost feel them clutching him like the talons of an eagle. She extended her right hand. "Give it to me," she croaked.

None of the children moved.

"Give me the stone," she cooed, as if Jack were a baby, or a puppy with a ball.

"We, we haven't got it," he stammered.

"But you've been into his lair. How did you do that? You would need the magic of the Elder-iche to do that." The witch's gaze and voice were hypnotic. The children were spellbound. She turned her attention to Alex. "You closed up the hole. How? Tell me. What magic did you use, and who taught it to you?" Her head moved like a cat watching a butterfly, as if she were trying to see inside every hidden corner of Alex's mind.

"We haven't got what you want!" said Jack vehemently. It was much easier to think and speak when the witch's stare wasn't directly upon him.

The witch rounded on Jack in an instant, one finger pointing between his eyes, the rest clenched tightly, and on her middle finger, jack noticed a ring of dull gold set with what might have been an emerald.

"You do know what I want, don't you? I know. I've been watching. Yes. We've been watching you." Her cat gave a choked sort of meow, showing its sharp teeth, and rubbed itself against her leg. "Tell me what you found in Merlin's cave. Is the old man still there?" At this, her mouth twisted into an ugly smile, then she turned back to Alex, ignoring Poppy and Max. "I will discover your secrets," she said, in a sickly voice, her hypnotic eyes fixed on his.

Max was crouching down, rubbing his thumb and finger in the direction of the cat, making chirruping noises with his lips and saying: "Puss, puss, puss! Here, puss, puss!" The cat ignored him for a few seconds, then took three paces forwards and allowed Max to tickle its chin.

"Show me what's in your back pack," the witch was saying to Alex, so close to him, now, that they were almost touching.

The cat bowed its head, allowing Max to stroke its ears and back, then in one swift, smooth movement, he had picked it up and hugged it to his chest.

Instantly, the witch's trance was broken, and she shrieked at Max to let the cat go.

"Run!" shouted Jack and Poppy together, as they found their legs again and put them into motion. Max swung the cat away from the witch in a perfect under-arm rugby pass, and raced after the others, who were running half turned towards him, their hands stretched out in encouragement.

"Alex! Alex, come on!" screamed Poppy.

214

"Dammit! What's wrong with him?" asked Jack, coming to a halt when he heard Poppy shout.

Alex hadn't moved a muscle. He was still entranced by the witch, who seemed to be laughing at the children's predicament. Without hesitation, Poppy ran back up the hill towards Alex, calling his name as she went. The witch was still laughing, and the cat was prowling angrily around her, while Alex stood calmly before her. Poppy quickly took off one of her gypsy earrings and pushed it forcefully through Alex's left ear lobe.

"Ow! Poppy!" Whether it was the magic in the gemstone or the pain in his ear that brought him round was impossible to tell, but his eyes were suddenly alert, and he was back to normal.

"Run, Zander! Run for your life!" Poppy shouted, and pulled him down the hill after the others, the witch shouting vengeance after them. The children ran full pelt on adrenalin, all the way to the woods, where they slowed, panting, to a hurried walk. They could hear some people through the trees, riding bikes in the ravine near the car park, and felt a bit safer. They looked over their shoulders, but couldn't see any sign of the witch.

"That was scary!" said Poppy.

"Freaky!" gasped Jack.

"I told you she was a witch, didn't I?" panted Max.

"Yes, you did," said Jack with a smile, patting his brother on the back, "and good thinking with the cat. You saved us!"

"And thanks for this," said Alex, rubbing his bleeding ear lobe and handing the earring back to Poppy. "I was in another world, it seemed. I wasn't aware of anything around me but her."

They slowed their pace to a normal stroll as they neared the car park. Five teenagers were drinking cans of energy drink and watching each other do jumps out of the ravine. As the children unlocked their bikes, Jack asked in a hushed voice: "Did any of you see her ring?"

"Not really, no. To be honest, I can't really remember much about what happened until Max picked up the cat," said Poppy. "Why? Do you think it's where she gets her power? Like it's her wand, or something?"

"I think it's the ring from the book; the one with a piece of the stone in it. I think she's...I think she's Morgana." Jack looked at their astonished faces. "We'd better go. We can talk about it at home."

As Poppy and Max wheeled their bikes down to the gate between the woods and the path onto the strawberry line, the adrenalin rush wearing off and making them feel a little shaky, Jack and Alex couldn't resist one swoop down the ravine, jumping out between two trees that leaned away from each other in a V formation.

"Nice bike!" said one of the teenagers; "Sick!" said another.

"Thanks!" Jack shouted back, his heart pounding. Poppy just shook her head.

Chapter Sixteen

A Gift from the Gods

The next couple of days were tense, as the children felt perturbed by their encounter with the witch. Jack in particular was concerned about what she knew, and how she knew it. The hole in Alex's ear lobe and the resulting blood on his tee shirt had taken some explaining, and Mrs Pearson was worried about their sudden change in behaviour, their hanging around the house and garden, constantly looking up and down the road, not venturing out on their bikes.

"Have you had a run in with some of the local children?" she asked pointedly. "Alex, are you being bullied again? You would tell me, wouldn't you? We talked about how important it is, didn't we?"

"Yes, mum. It's fine, honestly. I just caught my ear on a bramble bush in the woods. There's nothing for you to be panicking about."

"Then why do you three look worried all the time? I know something's going on. You've not been getting into trouble, have you? Trespassing or stealing or anything?"

"Of course not, mum!" they all said.

"That Poppy hasn't been leading you astray, has she?"

"I thought you liked Poppy," said Jack.

"Well," said his mother, and the word hung in the air for a moment, all on its own. "If you're all going to be sitting around the house today, you could tidy your room up, couldn't you?"

With exaggerated sighs, the boys trooped off upstairs.

"Morgana must have been following us," Jack said to Alex and Max, when they were alone in their room. They were once more looking at the haul of coins they had 'rescued' as Jack liked to put it, from Merlin's cellar, sorting through them all, and wondering what they should do with them. None of them thought the room looked particularly untidy at the moment, but their mum always seemed to see things with different eyes.

"She could have just been out walking," said Max.

"No, I don't think so. And I mean she must have been following us for a while. Remember when she was hanging about Poppy's house that night? She must know about the boat and the quarry and everything. She certainly knew why we were under the tower; she thought we had found the stone. Maybe she thinks we still have it."

"So what should we do?" asked Max. "You don't think she'd really come to the house, do you? Maybe tell mum that we'd been in her garden and stolen something from her?"

"What, a stone? Nobody would believe that we would want to steal a stone, would they?" said Alex

"We just need to be very careful. Lie low for a bit. And stay together as much as possible."

"What about Poppy?" asked Alex. "Won't she be vulnerable? We can't all stick together all the time, can we?"

"She's used to being on her own and keeping out of the way. I might just text her and tell her to stay out of the box car for a while, she could easily get trapped in there."

Max was silent for a minute or so while Jack sent Poppy the message, then he plucked up his courage to say what he had been thinking about for a while.

"I think she uses the cats as spies," he said, hesitantly.

Jack and Alex looked at each other with a flash of recognition. They had all observed the number of cats around the house and garden, and up on Quarry road, outside Poppy's house, but none of them had seen the connection except Max.

"Of course!" said Jack. "Oh, how could we have been so dumb?! I'd better tell Poppy to beware of cats, too."

"Maybe we could ask mum for a dog," suggested Alex.

"Yeah, right! Like that would ever happen!" laughed Jack.

"So, what are we gonna do with the treasure, anyway?" asked Alex. "It's pointless keeping it hidden, isn't it?"

"I really think we should show dad," said Jack.

"What?" exclaimed the others with one voice.

"We can just say we found them. He doesn't have to know everything. But he might know what's best to do with them."

"I don't know," said Alex.

"Maybe we could show him one coin. Tell him we found it in the woods. Then, after a week or so, say we've been digging and found some more."

"Good call, Max," said Jack. "That's not such a bad plan, is it, Zander?"

"Best wait until we've been to the woods, or even out of the house again, though, first."

"Not sure I'm ready for that just yet," said Max. "I never thought I'd say it, but I'll be glad to get back to the routine of school next week."

The others laughed. "Just watch out for cats in the playground, alright," warned Jack.

They put the coins back behind the water tank in the airing cupboard, and made an attempt at tidying up their games and books. Jack's phone beeped, and he suddenly looked serious again.

"It's Poppy. She says there is a big ginger cat sitting on the roof of her dad's car right now."

The three boys looked at each other. They went to the window and looked out into the street. Two cats were sitting in the shade of the cherry trees, and from Sam's room they could see the one that liked to sun itself on the roof of the shed. It was going to be almost impossible to go anywhere without alerting the witch.

"Anyone fancy a game of Monopoly?" asked Alex.

"Go on, Jack! Down the line!" shouted Mr Pearson on Saturday morning, standing with the other parents at the side of the football pitch. "Lovely pass, well done, Jack!"

"You're Jack's dad, are you?" asked the man standing next to him.

"Yes, that's right," said Mr Pearson. "Which is your son?"

"Henry, the centre, there."

"Right. Yeah, he's a good player." Making casual conversation with strangers was not Mr Pearson's strong point, but he was keen to make friends with the local community, particularly where his sons were involved.

"Henry tells me you work up at the airport."

"That's right."

"Doing what, exactly?" Henry's dad didn't seem to have the most natural people skills, either, unless he was being direct on purpose.

"Air traffic control." Said Mr Pearson, trying to keep an eye on the game.

"And you've moved up from London. Heathrow, was it?"

"Yes, that's right."

The crowd of parents suddenly erupted in cheers as Henry's shot found the back of the net.

"So, it's true, then?" asked Henry's dad, as the game restarted.

"What's that?" replied Mr Pearson, his eyes still following the ball.

"They're planning an expansion."

There was another spontaneous burst of applause as the keeper saved a good shot at goal, and Jack cleared it to safety.

"There is a proposal for an expansion," said Mr Pearson, "and, yes, if it becomes a reality, then I will be in place to cope with the changes and manage the staffing and so on, but between you and me, I can't see it happening."

"No?" The other man didn't sound convinced. "I can't imagine they'd transfer you unless there was a reason."

"More of a precaution than a reason, and really more of a lucky bit of timing, to be honest. A vacancy appeared at the right time, and we wanted to move the family out of London. This way, I got a promotion and a more relaxed position at the same time. Even with the expansion, Bristol will be a fraction of what Heathrow is, but like I say, I don't think the proposal is practical."

"Not for me it's not, certainly, living in Wrington."

"No, I guess it wouldn't be. Coventry went through the same rigmarole a few years ago. I think people get paid to look at various options, keep the shareholders happy. Nothing came of that, though, and I don't suppose Bristol will be any different."

"Well, that's good to know, I suppose. I'm Bill, by the way." Henry's dad seemed to relax, and a friendlier persona emerged from the gruff man he had been before.

"Nice to meet you, Bill. I'm Matt," said Mr Pearson, shaking Bill's hand, and smiling too.

After that, the talk turned to general chat about the game, the academy, the local area. Mr Pearson got the impression that an opinion had been formed about him, and that Bill would now be instrumental in altering the other parents' perception of him. He thought this might also be helpful to the boys, particularly Jack, who had been looking very withdrawn and preoccupied recently. As they got into the car after the match, Mr Pearson congratulated him on another great performance by the team.

"Thanks, dad. It's great when you can make it to the games."

Mr Pearson gave Jack a well-earned bar of chocolate, their little ritual when he was able to watch the boys play.

"I was talking to Henry's dad today; do you get on alright with him?"

"Henry's dad?" asked Jack, deliberately misinterpreting the question.

"Henry," laughed Mr Pearson, proud that Jack was criticising his imprecise wording as he so often did with his sons. "None of the boys are funny with you, are they, because you're new, or," he added after a slight pause, "because of the airport business?"

"No, everyone's been friendly," replied Jack, swallowing a mouthful of chocolate.

"At school, too? And to Alex? He hasn't mentioned anything, has he?"

"Not to me," said Jack. "I don't think there's anything to worry about like before."

"It's just that cut to his ear. Looks so clean and, er, deliberate somehow. I really don't believe it was done by a stray thorn." Jack made no reply to this, and just looked out of the side window. "You boys would tell me, wouldn't you, if there was something going on? Me or your mum; you'd talk to one of us, wouldn't you?"

Jack wanted to say 'and you'd believe us, would you? Whatever we told you? About goblins and wizards and saving the world with some kind of human arachnid?' but he didn't. He just said "everything's fine, I promise."

Mr Pearson smiled, and ruffled Jack's hair as he changed gear approaching some traffic lights.

Slanting sweeps of rain chased Jack and the twins across the tarmac to the doors of the history block on Wednesday morning. Once inside, they joined the dozen other students who were shaking their limbs and sodden fringes, and wiping their faces with wet sleeves.

"Ugh!" said Kyle, "I'm soaked down to my socks!"

"Yeah," said Sean, "I hope sports are cancelled this afternoon."

"You know they won't be," said his brother.

"Doesn't bother me," laughed Jack, "I've got swimming."

"Jammy git!" said the twins in unison.

The boys entered the classroom and took their seats, opening their wet rucksacks carefully. Small lakes were already forming around everyone's chairs, and the windows were beginning to mist up. Beyond the glass, people were still running and splashing through the downpour.

"Right, everyone," said Mr Cooper, "Roman gods, week three, taking up where we left off at the end of the first semester. Turn to the illustration on page 149, please. Without looking over the page, I said WITHOUT looking, Benny, thank you, can anybody tell me who this god is? Anybody seen him before?"

Pages turned, throats cleared, water dripped from clothes and bags; faces stared at the book, eyes looked at other faces, but no arms were raised, and eventually Mr Cooper was forced to answer his own question.

"This is Janus. Can anyone tell me what is special about him?"

"He's got two faces, sir," said Benny, trying to redeem himself.

"Well done, Benny. Yes, unlike Sean and Kyle here, who are essentially two men with one face," Mr Cooper paused, ever so slightly, in case anyone wanted to appreciate his joke, "Janus was one man with two faces, one looking forwards and one looking backwards. What might have been the purpose of that?" he asked the class.

"To make him a better teacher?" suggested Oscar from the back of the room, and everyone joined in the appreciation of that joke. Everyone except Jack. Jack was staring at the twins, and hadn't heard anything since Mr Cooper had called them two men with one face. He turned to the back cover of the book, and with his biro, drew a rotund stick man with four arms and four legs. One man with two sets of limbs, or two men with one face; identical faces. His heart was racing, and he was still deaf to Mr Cooper's words. He couldn't wait to talk to Poppy. And then they would have to talk to the twins.

The rain had stopped by lunch time, but it was too cold and wet to spend it outside. There was nowhere indoors that Jack could talk confidentially to Poppy except the library, so after they had finished their paninis in the canteen, Jack took Poppy and his history books to the reading area in the library, as if they were discussing an assignment.

"Have you studied Janus yet in history?" asked Jack.

"Yes, we did it with Mr Cooper yesterday. Why?"

"And you didn't think anything of it?" Jack was finding it hard to suppress his excitement.

"No, not really. The god of doorways and gateways, who gave his name to January, the turning point of the calendar. Able to see the past and the future. Why? What's so special about him?"

"I had Mr Cooper today. And so did the twins."

"So? What did they get up to?" she asked, sensing some mischief in Jack's expression.

"Nothing. They didn't get up to anything. But Mr Cooper said that unlike Janus, the twins were two men with one face. Just a flippant little joke, but look!" Jack opened his textbook at the back cover, where he had drawn the cave painting. "One face and two bodies. The fifth saviour is the twins. It's got to be!"

Poppy stared at Jack's drawing, remembering the original version in the cave. How else would you draw two identical people; two people with one face? But, the twins. Why did it have to be Sean and Kyle, of all people?

"What do you think?" asked Jack impatiently, as Poppy still hadn't said anything aloud.

Poppy groaned. "It's just, Sean and Kyle, I mean, you know. Can we trust them?"

"I thought you were ok about them now, after they fixed the box car up."

"Yeah, I am." She gave a sigh. "Old habits die hard, I guess. But what good will they be, do you think? I was expecting the final saviour to have some kind of magical powers or abilities. What's so special about the twins?"

"It's obviously the fact that they are twins, isn't it? One face. They are identical. They could be used in subterfuge."

"How?"

"I need to speak to Max. I'm sure dad read some books to him where there were twins who tricked an ogre or a witch or something. But I'm sure that's the key."

The bell rang, signalling five minutes to the start of afternoon lessons. Jack and Poppy gathered up their things and left the library.

"So, shall we all talk to the twins together? I think that would be more convincing. We've got Karate tonight, but maybe we could talk to them at youth club tomorrow? What do you think?"

"We'll need to keep an eye out for the witch," warned Poppy. "School's probably the safest place."

"Yes, we could do without her knowing about Kyle and Sean. Much safer if she thinks it's just the four of us."

"Well, let me know ok. Catch you later." And Poppy dashed off to her next lesson, before the bell rang again.

Jack decided that Friday would be the best time to get the twins' attention in secret, where Morgana wouldn't be likely to spy on them. School usually finished half an hour earlier on Fridays, and Jack asked Sean and Kyle to meet him and Poppy in the hard court behind the swimming pool before the busses arrived. He had brought some of the coins and Merlin's book as proof, but he really didn't know where to start with the explanation. He sat on one of the low benches mid-way down the side of the court, the furthest point from any of the gates or footpaths, and waited nervously, scanning the court for any lurking cats.

"What's up, Jay?" and "What's this all about?" The twins came over to the bench and stood looking expectantly at Jack.

"Alright, guys. Sit down for a minute. Poppy will be here soon."

"You two engaged, are you?"

"Want us to be your best men?"

The twins laughed good-naturedly.

"Look, this is deadly serious, ok?" Jack reached into his rucksack. "I mean, it's crazy, I know, and you'll think we're totally bonkers, but –"

"We did warn you not to hang around with her. Said she was away with the fairies, didn't we, Sean?"

"Listen," said Jack, in a tone of voice that cut through their teasing in an instant. "You know at the start of films, when you watch something incredible happen to the main character, like they meet an alien, or they find a gateway to another world, and they try to tell someone about it but nobody believes them? And you're like, 'why doesn't anyone believe them? We've seen it, it's true, why won't you believe them,' yeah?"

"Y-eah?" said Sean, uncertainly.

"Well. This is that moment, okay. Poppy and I discovered something, and now we're going to tell you, and you won't really want to believe it, but you've got to, okay?"

There was a nervous laugh from the twins. Jack left his rucksack alone for a minute, as Poppy sat down next to him, and asked if he had said anything yet.

227

"So," he began, "you know your tour shirts, with the green goblin on? Well, Poppy had some books and stuff about Goblin Coombe and all these folk tales. So, first of all, goblins are real."

Jack and Poppy looked at Sean and Kyle, whose faces were blank with bewilderment.

"Not only that," continued Jack, "but we met them. My brother, Alex, can speak their language or something, he did it by accident the first time, but anyway, there are goblins living in the quarry."

"You have got to be kidding!" said Kyle. "This is a wind-up, isn't it?"

Jack and Poppy looked at each other, then shook their heads at the twins.

"It's all true," said Poppy. "We went into the goblins' cave, and they showed us an ancient painting on the wall, of five figures, each with some special gift or power. They explained that me, Jack, and his two brothers were the first four figures, and then the fifth one we couldn't work out. Not for ages. It was a person with two sets of arms and legs."

Poppy looked at Jack, and he took over. "When Mr Cooper said you were different from that Roman god because you had two bodies but one face, it suddenly struck me that you guys are that fifth figure."

"Ok," said Kyle, "so what are our special powers, then?"

"Well, you're not going to believe this," said Jack, "but I think your special power is that you're twins."

"No way!" said Sean in mock astonishment. "Now you're really having us on!"

"No, just listen for a minute, and look at this." Jack pulled Merlin's journal out of his rucksack. He flicked through the pages of Merlin's symbols and writings, arcane diagrams and lists of potions.

"Woah, that looks well old. Where did you get that?"

"Ok. Look at this." He turned to the diagram of the wimblestone. "The goblins have lost this stone, right. It's their life stone. Now, they gave the stone to King Arthur, in the sword Excalibur, but when Arthur died, they were supposed to get it back. Merlin kept the stone for himself to try to harness its power. Look, he wanted to make a ring from it, see?"

"Are you telling me that's Merlin's book? THE Merlin? Where did it come from?"

"We have discovered Merlin's cellar. It's on top of Crook Peak, where his tower used to be. We opened it up, and we found this book, and these coins, but we didn't find the stone." He let the twins examine the old coins. "Now, are you ready for the next bit?"

The twins looked at each other, then back to Jack, as if it really didn't matter what else he said now.

"Poppy's got these earrings. We think they are also made from a goblin stone similar to the wimblestone. They can take us back to Merlin's time; we've seen the tower from the site of Banwell Castle."

"What? Time travel? No way! Earrings?"

"Listen, just listen, ok? I know it's far-fetched, believe me, I know what it sounds like, but just think of all those films, like E.T and The Chronicles of Narnia and whatever, where the audience knows the truth but nobody believes it, ok? My little brother Max was the first one to see the goblins, and I didn't believe him at first, but now I do. I believe we have to go back in time and trick Merlin out of the stone, and I think it is the fact that you two look identical that is the way we'll do it."

"How?"

"I'm not sure about exactly how yet, I only thought of this after Wednesday's history lesson. But we needed to prepare you for it. I mean, we couldn't just spring all this on you one minute, and then say 'right, let's go!' could we?"

"And there's one more thing," said Poppy. "Merlin's acolyte, Morgana. She stole the ring that Merlin made, and she wants the stone. The ring has let her live for the past twelve hundred odd years, and she's been watching us. She's dangerous, so you mustn't discuss this outside of your own bedrooms, ok? Do not tell anyone, seriously. The sorceress Morgana is the Witch of Woodborough Drive."

"Wow, ok, well that's, I mean, ha –"

"What my brother means is, that's quite a lot to take in, and we really need to catch the bus now."

"Look, we know it sounds crazy, but honestly, it's the truth, and we need your help. You're mixed up in it, too. You're the fifth person in the cave painting. Look at these coins. Feel the book. We couldn't fake this."

"Any more where these came from?" asked Sean, indicating the coins.

"Please, just think about what we've said, ok?" said Poppy. "Don't say a word to anyone, but just let it sink in a bit. You're part of our gang, now, anyway, yeah? The box car gang?"

They all picked up their bags and walked to the front of the school in silence, where other students were chatting and the fleet of buses was pulling in off the road. Other friends were calling to them, and conversations about the weekend, football and rugby matches, and homework assignments took over, and the twins drifted away slightly, as they normally would.

"Do you really think we can trust them, Jack?" asked Poppy.

"Yes, I really do. I've always kind of clicked with them, even when you said you hated them. I think I've always had a connection with them, and I think this is the reason. They were wearing the first goblins I ever saw, after all," he laughed. "If only the goblins weren't hibernating; it would really help if we could just show them."

"Maybe we could show them the tunnels," suggested Poppy, suddenly excited. "We could open the cave and show them where the goblins live; show them the paintings, couldn't we. There wouldn't need to be any goblins awake to make our point, would there?

"No," said Jack cautiously, as he thought the idea over. "But it's risky. We'd have to take great care not to be seen."

"We can all meet up in the woods above Sandford rec: you and Zander, the twins, and me, we can all come separately and meet among the trees. We can coordinate it through texts. Sunday afternoon? What do you reckon?"

So, on Sunday afternoon, Poppy sent Jack a message to say that she was going to cycle onto the strawberry line, and then circle round to the Rec. Sean sent a message to say that his mum was going to drop him and Kyle off at a friend's house on Somerville Road, and then they would walk up to the rec from there.

Jack and Alex fetched their bikes and set off down the hill, pretending not to notice the cat that watched them from the roof of the garages across the road. They turned up past the bungalows, and then turned left into Sandy Lane. They could sense that more feline eyes were watching them, but felt sure the diversion would work. They quickened their pace, and raced along the narrow lane to the footpath signs, where the flat verge widened out and dog-walkers parked their cars on evenings and weekends. They leaned their bikes against a couple of standing stones at the entrance to the path, then doubled back to the previous corner of the road, where a track led down to some holiday cottages, and there was another footpath up the hill past the farm.

Poppy and the twins were talking quietly when Jack and Alex arrived. They set off up the hill, pulling themselves up on the tree trunks. They kept to the trees as long as they could, until they were almost level with the wall of the upper level, then scurried down the bank towards the mouth of the cave.

"Haven't been in here for years," said Sean.

"No," said Kyle. "Smaller than I remember it. Where's this door, then?"

Crouching under the low ceiling, they made their way to the back of the cave.

"Aurrlubbock" burped Alex.

The twins laughed, and then stopped abruptly, as the cave wall rumbled and the opening to the goblin tunnel appeared. Jack and Poppy smiled with satisfaction at the look on their faces, or, as Jack now thought of it, their one face.

"Come on," he said, waving his arm in encouragement, "it's quite safe, you know."

Once they were all inside the tunnel, Alex closed the portal again, and the five children made their way along the tunnel by the pale green light of the glowing gemstones.

"This is incredible!" whispered Kyle.

They came to the chamber with the alcoves and the stone seats. It was completely quiet and empty now. When the children stopped and stared around, the sounds of their breathing and the water splashing into the trough were all they could hear. Jack led the twins up to the dais at the far side of the chamber, and explained the identities of the first four figures on the wall.

"And you think this one is meant to be us?" asked Sean, indicating the figure with the extra limbs.

Now that Jack was looking at it again, he had to admit that it still bore no resemblance to Sean and Kyle. It had been pure chance that he had made the connection between the twins and the bizarre looking figure. But somehow he knew he was right. "You'll just have to trust me," he said.

Poppy came to stand beside them in front of the paintings, carrying two dishes of water from the spring in the alcove. "Drink this," she said, holding them out to the twins, "I think it will help. The goblins gave us a drink when we first came here, and, I don't know, it made me feel different, somehow."

"Where are all these goblins?" asked Kyle, taking the dish from Poppy's outstretched hand and having a tentative sip.

"Hibernating. They don't have the strength to get through the winter without this precious stone. That's what we need your help to find, so we can return it to them and save them from extinction."

"What's through these tunnels?" asked Sean, pointing to the two large holes either side of the dais.

"Their sleeping quarters, I guess," said Jack. "We weren't invited to go through there." He took the empty dishes from the twins, and stepped down off the dais. "We should probably be going. I take it you believe us now?"

"Yeah, I guess. Not sure about all this prophetic hero stuff. Do you know what we need to do to find the stone?"

"Not exactly, but I'm working on it. Do you two have any identical outfits, by any chance?"

"Outfits? We're not eight!" objected Sean.

"No, sure. Clothes, then. Tops, shirts, I don't know."

"Got our uniforms?" said Kyle.

"Alright. Come on. I'll tell you what I'm thinking on the way back."

"Jack?" said Sean, putting a hand on his arm before he could walk away, "how do you know we can trust these goblins? I mean, what if those tunnels lead to an armoury or something, and as soon as we give them this stone of power, they come marching out of the hill with swords and axes glinting in the sunlight?"

"I just know. You'll see when you meet them. This isn't Mordor, you know. They're the good guys. We're the ones who waged war on them and on the natural world. Humans. We're the bad guys, not them. We can trust them, you'll see."

As they left the tunnel and Alex sealed the cave wall behind them, Poppy gave a little shiver of excitement. "Can you feel it?" she asked Jack. "Something's going to happen soon. It's all coming together. It's like I can feel all this energy. Can't you?"

Jack felt very on edge and unprepared. His excitement at discovering the twins was fading and being replaced by the reality of what they had to do next. This wasn't like reading a book; nobody was writing the script for what they were facing. He had no idea if his plan was going to work, if the twins could accomplish what he needed them to do. And he had to admit that what Sean had said about trusting the goblins had occurred to him over the last two months. Was he sure they were doing the right thing? Were they right to trust Sostror? He hoped he was, in spite of the doubts in his mind. But all he said to Poppy was: "Yes, I can feel it. I think now we've solved the riddle of the fifth saviour, the prophecy is upon us."

Poppy looked at Jack and smiled. "It's going to be alright, Jack. Everything will work out. I know it."

Chapter Seventeen

Kidnapped

The grey October sky was dark with clouds and the early approach of dusk. From the floor of the valley below, the ridge and the tower were just darker shapes against the clouds, and nobody, had any of the shepherds been inclined to look, would have seen the small dark figure that emerged from the trees and approached the tower, the unsteady orange light of flames warming its windows.

The iron ram door knocker boomed three times on the oak door. The visitor waited patiently, full of a nervous excitement, shifting the weight of their bundle for comfort, taking in the silence of the dying afternoon. Nothing bigger than a cow nor faster than a cat would be moving anywhere below. The visitor gave a nostalgic sigh, and stepped back a pace from the door as she heard the wizard's footsteps. The door opened, and the once familiar entrance hall of the tower came into view, bathed in the living light of the torch in the sconce on the wall.

"Yes?" enquired Merlin, peering out into the gloom at the stranger with the bundle in her cloak.

"Have you forgotten me, Merlin?" asked the stranger.

The old man stared anew, hearing the voice. "Morgana?" he said, incredulous. "Morgana? But...but what has happened to you, child?"

"Might I come in?" asked the witch. "You seem less hospitable than I remember."

Merlin opened the door wider, and stood back to let her enter. "But what has happened to you?" he asked again. "When I saw you yesterday..."

"Your yesterday is not mine, Merlin. But I still remember of what we talked."

"Yes?" Merlin closed the door, staring at Morgana in the flickering torchlight.

"I have brought you something." Morgana unfastened her cloak, and showed Merlin the bundle that nestled sleepily in her arms.

"Where did you get this?" Merlin's hands trembled as he held them out towards the child. "What have you done? I don't understand."

"No, that was always the trouble, old man," said Morgana, coldly. "Now, I have brought you what you wanted, a child of your own to replace Arthur. Do you not have something for me?" Her cold eyes fixed on Merlin in a penetrating stare. She still held the child firmly against her chest. "You know what it is I have come for. I think it is a fair exchange."

Merlin let his hands fall back to his sides. He looked from Morgana's blazing green eyes to the sleeping child, and the ring on the hand that cradled its head.

"Where did you get that?" he asked hoarsely, then with more force as fear rose in him: "What is that ring, and how did you get it?"

Jack and Alex raced each other to the side gate, and came crashing into the utility room together, breathless and laughing. They kicked their trainers off in the general direction of the shoe rack, and went into the kitchen, swinging the Co-op bags up onto the worktop.

"Mu-um! We're ba-ack!" called Jack, taking out the milk and cheese to put in the fridge.

There was no reply; no sounds of anyone upstairs.

"Mum?" called Alex, heading down the hall towards the lounge, listening up the stairs as he went.

"Max?" called Jack behind him.

Alex entered the lounge, followed by Jack. Their mum was slumped on her side on the sofa, asleep.

"Mum, we're home," said Alex. He put his hand on her shoulder, usually enough to wake her, but she continued to sleep, her breathing slow and steady. He gave her shoulder a shake. "Mum!" he said, a little louder.

Jack turned and galloped up the stairs, two at a time. In the front bedroom, Max was lying on the floor, still in his school uniform, next to his bed. Just like their mum, he was unshakable from his deep sleep.

"Sam!" breathed Jack, suddenly, and ran to the box room. The window was open, and the cot was empty. "Oh, no. No, no, no, no, no!" he said, beginning to panic.

Alex came running up the stairs. "I can't wake mum. Where are Max and Sam?

"Max is asleep too, and Sam's missing."

"Missing?"

"Gone. Not here. Missing. Vanished."

"Have you looked everywhere? Have you looked in mum and dad's room? Maybe he's hiding."

"No. He's gone. The window's open. She's taken him."

"Who's taken him? What do you mean?" Alex's voice was shrill with fear.

"The witch; Morgana. She's kidnapped Sam because we didn't give her the stone!"

"What are we going to do? Why won't mum wake up?"

"She must be either drugged or bewitched, and Max, too." Said Jack. "Either they will wake up in a few hours, or we'll need to break some sort of spell that they're under. I'm calling Poppy."

"Shouldn't we call dad?"

"There's no time. This is getting serious, now. Come on, Poppy! Pick up! Answer your –"

"Hello? Jack? Everything alright?"

"No. Nothing's alright!" said Jack into the phone. "The witch has kidnapped Sam. I think she's going to the tower. We need to tackle her and Merlin, now."

"Alright. I'll meet you by the bridge."

"Right. Listen, I'm bringing the twins. This is when we need them."

Jack and Alex quickly dragged their bikes out of the shed, knocking over the rake, garden fork and a collection of bamboo fishing nets. They left them lying half out of the open door in their haste, and pedalled like maniacs down the hill and past the bungalows. Jack's mind was turning as fast as his wheels, going over the plan he had been forming since his discovery a week ago about the fifth saviour being both Sean and Kyle. Could it work? Had he read all the clues correctly?

Poppy waited for what seemed like an age for the others to reach the bridge. She knew it would take time for Jack to organize Sean and Kyle, but the suspense was torture. Finally, she saw four figures pedalling furiously towards her.

"Where's Max?" she asked as Jack reached the top of the bridge, and they all cycled down the far side towards the railway line, squeezing past a black car that was parked on the gravel by the field gate.

Jack explained what had happened to Max and his mum.

"And what about your dad?"

"He'll be at work. Hopefully we can get this all resolved before he gets home."

"Should have plenty of time!" grinned Poppy.

They all threw their bikes down at the side of the track by the stream, and ran to the log bridge. But even before they were all across, Jack knew it was hopeless.

"It's gone." He said.

"What?"

"Look, the boat's not there. She must have taken it. It must work with her ring, just like your earrings."

"That was her car by the bridge!" exclaimed Sean.

The five of them stood on the bank, hands on hips, catching their breath. Jack felt broken. Poppy could see the pain in his eyes as he looked from her to Alex, then at the twins.

"Don't give up yet, Jack," she said, "I've got an idea."

"What is it?"

"Come on! Follow me! Back on your bikes!" And she was off, over the log bridge and sprinting along the track.

The others followed, pushing their bikes back up the embankment, then cycling frantically back towards the bridge. Once they were speeding down the other side, Poppy took them past the turn for the strawberry line, down the narrow lane to the main road opposite the church. As the boys caught up with her, she turned and grinned at Jack.

"The door!" he exclaimed. "Do you think it will work?"

"I think it will have to. It's got to be worth a shot, right?"

They all crossed the road and pushed their bikes into the church yard, up the cobbled path, and leaned them round the back of the church where the door to the vestry was.

Poppy took the big iron ring in her right hand, looked round at the boys' expectant faces, and then turned it, pushing the old door firmly with her left hand on the ancient centre section. The church door swung inwards, but not in the way doors usually opened. Around the edges of the doorway, the empty church was visible, but the centre of the opening, where the older piece of wood had been fixed, showed a dim stone hall lit by flickering flames. The vision was most surreal. Poppy stepped carefully through the aperture into the stone room, then turned to face the others.

"It's ok, come on through. Just mind you pick your feet up and step over cleanly. And mind your head, Jack."

The boys carefully stepped across the threshold of the past. Then Poppy slowly closed the door, which was smaller on this side, just the ancient centre piece. They were standing in a square hallway, paved with flagstones, with stone steps leading down into the cellar on their left, and another staircase climbing up to the living quarters on their right.

The twins looked about them in utter astonishment "Wow! What is this place?" asked Sean.

"I think this is Merlin's tower, still standing. The only thing I don't know is when."

"Freaky!" said Kyle. "No offence or anything, Jack, but I don't think me and Sean quite believed you before."

"That's understandable," said Jack. "Now. Can you remember what I told you? You understand the plan?"

"Yes, mate. No worries, we're good to go."

"Right. You guys go down into the cellar, and we'll go up there and look for Sam. Good luck, and be careful. You might have trouble understanding him at first, but you kind of get used to the language after a while. And I think Merlin will be easier to talk to than the shepherds were, anyway."

"No problem!" said Kyle.

"Leave it to us!" said Sean.

The twins descended the cellar steps out of sight, and Jack led the others over to the stairs on the right, treading as silently as possible over the smooth flagstones. At the bottom of the cellar steps, Kyle knocked loudly on the solid oak door while Sean hid in the shadows. There was the sound of muttering and pacing, then the footsteps came nearer, and the door opened just enough for one pale blue eye to peer through.

"Well, what is it?" came a sharp voice.

"Greetings, Master Merlin. I have travelled from afar to speak with you." said Kyle, in a voice like the sorcerer in Disney's Aladdin.

"What? Who are you?"

Without even the merest hint of a pause, Kyle said "My name is Cristiano Ronaldo. I am a wizard like yourself."

"What sort of a name is that?" croaked the old man through the gap in the door.

"Where I come from, it is a name that encapsulates all the talent a man can possess. I have travelled over land and sea to give you instruction, Oh Master Merlin."

"You? Instruct me? But you're just a boy!"

Now Kyle raised an imperious finger. "Do not make that mistake, old man. It is not wise to underestimate what you have not tried and tested."

The old wizard opened the door wider to get a better look at his visitor. "What can you teach me that I, Merlin, do not already know?"

"I left Zanzibar but a few minutes ago, and now I stand at the very door to your cellar. I can teach you that, old man." Kyle was really enjoying this masquerade, now.

"How is that possible?" asked Merlin, no longer in his disparaging tone, but genuinely interested.

"I am a skilled practitioner with orbs of air," said Kyle, as mysteriously as he could. Sean found it very difficult not to laugh. "Might I be permitted to enter, and give you a demonstration, Master Merlin? I assume you have a cupboard or store room which you can lock? Somewhere you can secure your most valuable items?"

'Don't overdo it, Kyle,' thought Sean. 'Don't get carried away with yourself!'

But the vain old wizard was intrigued, and desperate for the promised knowledge. He stood back from the door, and motioned for the boy to enter, turning to cast an eye over his bench of alembics and manuscripts.

"Yes, yes, come in," he muttered.

Kyle gave the signal, and as he entered and then closed the door, Sean dashed into the room while Merlin's back was turned, and kept close behind him.

The old man crossed the room to another oak door. "Now, here is my store, where I keep all my potions, and, as you said, valuable things."

"Perfect." said Kyle. "Now, I want you to lock me in. Close the door on me, and turn the key to secure it, yes?"

"Yes," said Merlin, doubtful but excited. He unlocked the door, and opened it to reveal a small, stone room with shelves of bottles and boxes and rolls of parchment, and no windows. Kyle stepped serenely into the room, and turned to face the door, smiling at the old man. Merlin closed the door and turned the key. Behind him, unobserved, Sean crept a couple of paces back, then jumped into the air, stamping his feet down flat on the floor as he landed.

Merlin turned in astonishment, as Sean stood there with the same serene smile that Kyle had given him on the other side of the door. He came over to Sean and gripped the tops of his arms, shaking him to make sure that he was not an illusion, then he looked back at the door in wonder. "How did you do that?" he asked.

"Elementary, my dear Merlin," said Sean, doing his best to imitate the voice and manner that his twin had adopted for the charade. "A simple incantation, and a good dose of concentration. Would you like to try it yourself?"

"Yes, oh yes!" said the wizard, his excitement mounting in the wake of the little demonstration.

"This is how it works: you must repeat 'Akabusi, Akabusi, Pelé, Lamborghini', and you must focus your mind on where you want to be. That is the hardest part. You must imagine your destination with your whole being, let your mind and body forget where you are. 'Akabusi, Akabusi, Pelé, Lamborghini', and then when you say 'ghini', jump in the air. When you've mastered the incantation and the concentration, that jump will take you across any distance. But to start with, just try coming back into this room."

"Yes, yes," muttered Merlin, practicing the phrase over and over.

"Let's get you in the store room," urged Sean, and as Merlin excitedly opened the door, Sean pushed him firmly into the tiny room as Kyle dashed past into the laboratory.

He placed a small barrel he was carrying onto the floor, and the two boys pushed the door shut and turned the big key in the lock before the old man had stopped staggering. The twins high-fived, laughing and whooping in their elation.

"You found it?" asked Sean.

"No."

"So, what's in that barrel?"

"Doesn't it look familiar? Like, from a cartoon or a cheesy movie?"

"Is it gunpowder? It can't be? Can it?"

"Yep. Just like in the movies. And I used to think that A-Team program we watched with dad was a joke, always getting locked in a tool shed or a barn full of machinery," laughed Kyle.

They could hear Merlin banging on the door and raving at them angrily.

"Right. Jack said the stone might be on the table. Let's grab it and get back upstairs."

"Yes, here it is!" cried Kyle. The table was just as it would be when Alex opened up the cellar steps in the future, apart from the lack of dust and cobwebs. The stone lay next to the book where Merlin had been making his notes and diagrams. Kyle picked it up and put it in his jacket pocket, then began to look at the rest of the things on the table.

"Come on!" urged Sean, "Jack said to leave everything else as it is. Let's see if they've found the baby yet.

"What about the gunpowder? I reckon we should take it. Maybe that's how the tower collapses and the cellar goes undisturbed for all those years?"

"Maybe, I suppose. Alright, bring it with you. Come on."

High above the twins, Jack, Alex and Poppy were reaching the top of the tower. They had discovered a room half way up with a fire burning in a large fireplace and a cauldron like Bethany's standing beside it, a wooden table with benches either side, and a dresser full of herbs and vegetables and dried meats, but no sign of Sam nor anyone else. As they crept to the top floor, they could sense that someone was there. Jack held up his arm as a signal for them all to stop. He could hear what sounded like the noises little Sammy made when he was asleep. He crept slowly up the last few steps, and into a sleeping chamber. There was a four poster bed with thick curtains all around it, rugs of sheepskin and woven cloth covering the floor, a wardrobe, and a crib.

Jack ran to the crib, and the others followed him into the room.

"Sam!" whispered Jack, then, turning to the others, he said "it's Sam, and he's alive, sleeping like Max and mum. But he's safe." He picked his brother up and cradled him in his arms. Then the children froze where they were, for the curtains around the bed were suddenly pulled open from within, and there was Morgana, her face terrible with triumph.

"So," she said, "you've come to rescue the little one. And you think I'm just going to allow you to take him out of here?" She stepped down off the bed and advanced towards Jack. "Give me the stone, boy!" She hissed harshly.

"We haven't got the stone!" said Jack, truthfully, backing away from her and holding Sam tight.

"None of you will leave here alive until I have that stone. I know you can get it. The old fool never trusted me, but you three seem quite resourceful –"

"We wouldn't give it to you, even if we had it," said Poppy, angrily, her fear making her bold.

The witch turned on Poppy in an instant, the ring on her finger blazing as green as her eyes. Poppy could neither move nor speak. Alex moved quickly away and stood behind Jack. Then, before the witch could do anything else, there was a shout from the kitchen room below.

"Guys! We've got the stone! Come on, let's get out of here!"

The witch's trance was broken, the green light faded, and Poppy fell back against the wall, gasping.

"Who's that?" muttered Morgana, as she ran to the stairs.

"Poppy, are you alright?" asked Alex, helping her back to her feet.

"Come on, quick, let's go," said Jack, and he followed the witch down the stairs.

"You!" They heard the witch scream. "Give me that stone, now!"

When they reached the kitchen room, it was empty, but for the sounds of receding footsteps coming from the stairs to the ground floor. The three children raced across the room and down the steps after them, Jack carrying Sam, who was growing heavy in his arms now.

When they reached the entrance hall, they saw that one of the twins was standing by the wall, with the underside of the steps arching over his head. The other twin was engaged in a tussle with Morgana. For her age, she was clearly very strong, and her rage was making her even more powerful. The young boy in her grasp was soon

247

overpowered, and then the witch was staring at them all, her green eyes glowing in the light from the burning torch on the wall. She held the boy before her, his arms twisted up behind his back. She glared at them, malevolently.

"Now. One of you twins has the stone. I know it. Which one?"

None of the children breathed a word.

"WHERE IS THE STONE?" screamed the witch, jerking her captive's arm painfully.

"Ow! Ok, ok!" Jack could tell now that it was Sean who was the prisoner. "Here's what we'll do, alright? I've got the stone, it's in my inside pocket. I'll give it to you, but you have to let the others go, first."

"No, I want the stone first," said the witch, twisting Sean's arm again.

"Look, if Merlin didn't trust you, why should we? Let them take the baby outside, and I'll give you the stone."

"You are no match for my magic! Give me the stone now, or you will all perish!"

She released Sean's hands, but turned him round to face her, and with her finger pointed menacingly at him, held him in her green fiery gaze. Sean reached slowly into his inside jacket pocket. Jack, Poppy and Alex couldn't believe what they were seeing.

"Sean, no! How could you!" screamed Poppy, but Kyle pushed her and Alex towards the door.

"Run!" he shouted, as he reached up and took the torch from the sconce on the wall.

The witch took her eyes off Sean to see what the commotion was about, and suddenly, Sean's empty hands were reaching for her.

Alex pulled open the door, and he and Poppy ran through it, followed by Jack with Sam clutched to his chest. Kyle pushed the door shut behind them and ran to where he had stashed the barrel of gunpowder beneath the rising stairs. He shoved the burning torch into the corner, where he had left a trail of powder leading to the barrel.

Meanwhile, Sean had pulled the ring with the green stone from Morgana's finger, and was running towards the door. He pulled it open and dashed through as first the witch and then his brother followed him. Sean burst through the door, and ran into the church noticeboard. He turned to see Morgana, screaming with rage, fly at him through the centre of the church door, and then evaporate into dust before his very eyes, her shoes, skirt, blouse and coat falling to the floor of the church porch, and a second later, Kyle ran right over the empty clothes and crashed into him. The twins watched through the aperture in the church door as the barrel of gunpowder exploded with a bright flash, and the centre of the door slammed back into place with a loud bang.

On the hilltop that would become Crook Peak, Poppy, Alex and Jack waited tensely for the twins to come out of the tower. They had no idea what was going on inside since Kyle had shut the door. Had they planned what they were doing, or were they just winging it on the spur of the moment? Had Sean really had the stone, or was he just bluffing? They stood and stared at the door, willing the twins to come through it, grinning, wimblestone in hand. But nobody came through the door. Instead, there was a sound like a bomb going off, and the right hand side of the tower exploded outwards in a shower of rock.

The children felt every second that elapsed after the explosion, but nobody came through the door. The light through the first floor window was becoming brighter, and smoke was climbing into the night sky.

"What do you think has happened to them?" asked Poppy. "Should we go back inside and help?"

"It doesn't look safe in there," said Alex.

Jack was trying to piece the events together. "What if the twins went back through the church door?" he said. "If they had the stone, maybe they opened the portal back to our time. It's possible, isn't it?"

"Yes!" cried Poppy, "of course! They're already back in 2014. We need to get back there, too, right away!"

"How are we gonna do that?" asked Alex.

"We go back in, and then I open the door." Said Poppy. "Look, the tower is still standing at the moment. It won't take two seconds to get in and out."

"I suppose it's either that or we try and find the boat somewhere along the lake shore," said Jack.

"I think we should decide quickly," said Alex, looking at the burning tower.

"Alright, then," said Jack, adjusting his sleeping brother in his arms. "I say we try the door. Alex, you open it first, then Poppy opens it from inside, ok?"

A minute later, Poppy, Alex and Jack stepped over the witch's clothes in the church porch, and saw the twins picking themselves up off the floor.

"Where is she?" Poppy asked Sean and Kyle.

Sean pointed to the empty clothes and the dust that was eddying around the porch.

"She just disintegrated," said Kyle.

"How?" asked Alex.

Sean held up Morgana's ring. "I took this off her before we opened the door; I guess, without it, she would have been over a thousand years old. She just turned to dust as she chased us over the threshold."

"Oh my god!" breathed Poppy, staring from the witch's clothes to the four boys, "we've done it. We've actually done it. We've got the stone, and Morgana's dead. I think I need to sit down."

Sam rubbed his eyes and looked around him. He was used to waking up in a different place to where he fall asleep, but even he seemed to be a little confused by his present surroundings.

"I need to get Sam home," said Jack. "Zan, we'll have to leave our bikes, and just tell mum that we took Sam for a walk while she was asleep."

"Do you guys want to come to my den?" Poppy asked the twins. "I want to hear about how you tricked Merlin. And we'd better take these clothes and hide them."

"Shall we take your bikes with us?" Sean asked Jack and Alex.

"Yeah, thanks. We'll pick them up from Poppy's later."

"Who's gonna bring these clothes?" asked Alex.

"I ain't touching them!" cried the twins in unison.

"Zan," said Jack, "just scoop them all up inside the coat and roll them into a bundle. They won't hurt you. After everything we've been through, you're not scared of some clothes, are you?"

Everyone laughed, and Alex did what his brother suggested.

"Not scared," he muttered, as he rolled the shoes, skirt and blouse inside the dusty coat. "Just creepy, that's all."

Chapter Eighteen

The Return

The children wheeled the bikes up the hill to Quarry Road together, not talking, all lost in thought, replaying the past hour over and over in their heads. Poppy, Sean and Kyle took the witch's clothes up to the box car, while Jack and Alex took Sam back home down the narrow steps, taking turns carrying him on their shoulders. Sam laughed and garbled away in his own little half language, and the boys were pleased that nothing seemed to be wrong with him. Morgana must have put them all to sleep before taking him, they thought. They hoped he wouldn't have nightmares. Coming down the road, they could see all the lights were on in the house.

"Mum must have woken up when Sam did, I suppose," said Jack. "I hope she's not going to be too mad."

When they got to the back door, Mrs Pearson came running into the kitchen, phone in hand and tears in her eyes. She took Sam from Jack and hugged him tight. "Where have you been?" she asked the two boys, her voice a mixture of relief, fear and anger, "I was worried sick! I was just about to call the police!"

"We just took Sam out for a little walk," said Jack. "When we got back from the Co-op, you and Max were both asleep, and we didn't want Sam to wake you."

"Well, next time, leave a note or something, ok? I didn't know what had happened to him. I was thinking all sorts of things." Mrs Pearson put the confused, wriggling Sam down and wiped her eyes. Behind her, a terrified looking

Max crept gingerly into the kitchen. Mrs Pearson hugged him, too, and said "mummy's sorry for shouting, Maxie. It's alright, now. I was just scared, that's all."

"Sorry mum," said Jack, giving her a tentative hug.

"Yeah, sorry. We didn't think to leave a note. Thought we'd probably be back before you woke up," said Alex, rather convincingly. Jack supposed that whatever lie they made up would be more believable than the truth. Clearly, their mum had no idea that she had been bewitched into sleeping in the afternoon.

"Right, boys, what do you fancy for tea? Did you manage to get everything from the shop? Have you got my change?"

While their mum put the oven on and arranged frozen pizzas on an assortment of baking trays, Jack and Alex took Max upstairs to tell him about what had really happened.

"So, it's all over now? We've really done it?"

"Yes. We just have to take the stone back to Sostror, and everything will be ok."

"I can't believe I slept through the final adventure!" Max said, slumping onto his bed in frustration.

"You couldn't help being put under a spell, Max. And anyway, it was quite scary in the tower. If it hadn't been for the twins and the gunpowder, I don't know how we would have escaped." Said Jack.

"And what about Sam? Is he really ok? Why did the witch have to take him, anyway?"

"I don't know. Maybe to lure us to the tower to steal the stone for her. She said Merlin never trusted her, so I don't think she could have got it herself."

"She was powerful, though," said Alex. "I mean, she nearly killed Poppy."

253

"Poppy's not a wizard, though. She's just a girl," said Jack.

"Don't let her hear you saying that!" laughed Alex.

"I didn't mean it like girls are inferior; I meant she's not a wizard like Merlin."

"She's just a muggle."

"Exactly," laughed Jack.

"What are we going to do about the witch's clothes? Aren't the police going to be looking for her?" asked Alex.

"Eventually," said Jack. He sat on Max's bed, next to his brother. "I think it's time we told Dad. I know he'll believe us. We need to tell him everything. Maybe he'll know what to do."

Mr Pearson came home at twenty to eleven. He sometimes took his time leaving the airport, and chose to take scenic routes home to avoid any arguments that might occur if his wife were still awake, but this time he had had an inexplicable urge just to get home and see that his children were all safely tucked up in bed. He came in quietly through the back door, hung up his coat in the utility room, and eased himself into the kitchen. He could hear the sound of the television in the lounge, and popped his head around the door. Mrs Pearson was watching an American crime program over the top of her phone. Of all the annoying habits she complained about him having, her inability to concentrate on any one thing, always on her phone when they were talking or watching a film – 'multi-texting' as he called it - was his biggest bugbear about her. He sighed inwardly, then asked how her day had been.

She beckoned him into the room, and told him about waking up and finding Sam missing.

"They obviously thought they were doing you a favour by distracting him for half an hour," said Mr Pearson.

"I know, I know, but I thought they would know better than to take him without leaving a note. I mean, what was I supposed to think? If you had woken up to find him gone, how would you have felt?"

"I understand completely," said her husband, "and I understand how you feel now." He added, kindly.

"I was so scared, Matt. I really think I frightened Maxie half to death, too. I let them all have pizza for tea, and Sam ate half of one. Seems to like pepperoni."

"I'll just pop up and take a peep at them."

When he pushed the bedroom door gently open, Jack was leaning on his elbow, looking at him.

"Hi, dad!" he said, and the other two boys sat up and grinned at him, too.

"Why aren't you all asleep?" he asked, coming into the room.

"We need to talk to you. It's really important."

"Is it about Sammy this afternoon? I – "

"It's about everything." Said Jack. "Sammy, Poppy, what we found in the quarry, what we know about Crook peak, Merlin and Morgana. You're going to need to sit down."

Mr Pearson looked at the faces of his children, their eyes sparkling with some strange excitement. "Alright," he said, "just give me five minutes, ok, or mummy will come up wondering what's going on."

"Ok," said three voices.

Back in the lounge, Mr Pearson said "they're all wide awake, even Max. I'm going to take them some warm milk and read to them for a bit, ok?"

"I'm not surprised Max is awake. He slept like me this afternoon; most unusual, really. Are they alright, though? They're not still upset, are they?"

"No, they seem ok. Just wide awake. Anyway, I'll read a couple of chapters and settle them down."

He warmed up a jug of milk, and poured it into three small beakers, then, with practiced hands, carried them back up to the front bedroom, pushing the door closed behind him.

"Can somebody switch the light on, please?" he asked, and Alex pulled the cord that hung down beside the bunk beds. "Right, I've told mummy I'm going to settle you all with a story, so take these, and then tell me what's all this about the quarry and, did you say Merlin?"

"Yes. Merlin and Morgana. It's not going to be easy, but you've got to believe us. We do have proof." And so Jack, with the help of his brothers, told their dad all about the quarry, the cave, the goblins, and the wimblestone; about the prophecy, the twins, Poppy's gypsy earrings, and Nymue; about killing the boar, meeting the shepherds and learning about the tower on Crook Peak.

"Look, these are the coins we found in Merlin's cellar," said Alex, bringing the coins out from under his duvet.

"And this is Merlin's book of experiments," said Jack, handing the book down from the top bunk.

Then they explained about meeting Morgana, about spotting her ring, and the true story of how Alex's ear got pierced, and then they came to the part about Sam being kidnapped, and Max and their mum being put under a spell. When they had finished, with Morgana turning to dust, and Sam, Max and Mrs Pearson waking up from their enchantment, they waited, hardly breathing, all eyes fixed on their father's face, willing him to believe them, wondering what it must sound like to an adult.

Mr Pearson looked at the coins, holding them up and examining them closely. He turned over the pages of Merlin's book, studying the writing and the diagrams, feeling the parchment carefully. What his children had told him was utterly preposterous; and yet, they had all been agreed, all been certain of the details, telling the story as one. And these coins looked genuine, and they felt old; they were worn and aged, different weights, different metals. These were not the sort of souvenirs they sold in castle gift shops. And the book. Nobody could have forged this book. The material, the ink, the language; all definitely hand written with a real quill. Nobody could have invented these pages of notes and diagrams, studies of plants. He wanted to believe them; all his open-mindedness about U.F.O.s and intelligent extra-terrestrial life urged him to be open-minded about this, too. And how, or rather, why would his children want him to believe what they were telling him? Was all this something they had concocted this evening to explain why they had taken Sam out while their mum was asleep? It made no sense at all. Like the old professor in The Lion, the Witch and the Wardrobe, he knew that the most logical explanation was that they were telling the truth.

"And this stone, the wimblestone," he said at last, still examining the book and the coin in his hands, "where is it now? And the ring?"

"Poppy has taken the stone home, and I think the twins still have the ring." Jack explained. He had been texting the other three since they hadn't been able to get back up to the box car after returning their brother. "But, dad, we don't know what to do about Morgana's clothes and her car. What will happen if she's reported missing, and the police find her car by the strawberry line? What if we're all on CCTV?"

"I don't think there's any CCTV around here. It's not exactly Hounslow, is it?" said Mr Pearson, reassuringly. "What clothes are we talking about, and where are they?"

"A rain coat, shoes, skirt, shirt, cardigan and underwear. Her car keys were in her coat pocket. Don't remember there being a phone or anything else. Poppy has hidden them in her den in the woods. It's got a lock on it. They'll be safe there for now, but if there is a police search with dogs –"

"Alright. Let's remain calm. I'm hoping it won't come to that. Right, thank you for telling me all this; for trusting me with your secret. We'll talk more about it tomorrow. Right now, I want you all to settle down and get to sleep, ok?"

"Ok. Thanks dad. For believing us," said Jack.

"Are you going to tell mum?" asked Alex, a little apprehension in his voice.

"No, I don't think that's necessary right now. Good night, boys. And no sneaking out of windows tonight, alright?" Mr Pearson smiled at them all before turning off the light, and taking the milk beakers back down to the kitchen.

The next morning, the boys came downstairs for their porridge without having to be called twice. Mr Pearson was on the late shift again, so he would be taking Alex and Max to school while Mrs Pearson had a lie in. Sam was in his high chair serving himself messily with porridge and mashed banana; he looked none the worse for his ordeal the previous day, but Mr Pearson looked as if he had hardly slept. Jack closed the dining room door before asking what all three boys wanted to know.

"Have you decided what to do about the clothes, dad?"

"And the car?" asked Alex.

Mr Pearson looked at his children's faces. From the worry on Jack and Alex, the expectation on Max, and the concentration on Sam. He was immensely proud of all of them. They had looked after each other, been incredibly brave, acted in secret with good reason, and achieved something incredible, something he could never have imagined.

"Let's just say it's all been taken care of." He said, enigmatically.

"How? What have you done?"

"It's best you don't know, for the time being. Just forget all about the witch."

"But how can you have sorted it already? The clothes were locked away in the box car."

"A cheap padlock is no match for an accurate strike with a hammer, or a decent pair of plyers," said Mr Pearson with a wink. "Always opt for a lock like the one on our shed, if you actually want to keep something safe. We can buy Poppy a new one, ok?"

The boys looked at their dad with sudden respect. Whatever he had decided to do, he had solved their problem of a missing person, and had clearly been up most of the night doing it. Now all that remained was for the six of them to take the wimblestone back to the goblins.

"Right," said Mr Pearson, "almost time for your bus, Jack. Is it a home game on Saturday? Will Henry's dad be there, do you think?"

"Umm, yes it is. And I should think so. He usually is. Why?"
"Just that it's my weekend off and I thought I would come along. Want to put something to him. Come on, you two, brush your teeth while I get Sammy dressed."

In spite of their excitement, there was a solemnity to the group of children crossing the middle level of the quarry on Sunday afternoon, like a procession along the Mall or down the aisle of Westminster Abbey. For some reason, although there was plenty of space in the vast hole in the hill, the children had naturally fallen into a column two abreast, Jack and Poppy at its head, Alex and Max in the middle, and the twins bringing up the rear. Poppy carried the wimblestone safely in her rucksack, along with the other gemstones that they had found in Merlin's cellar.

"Do you think it will work?" she asked Jack, quietly. "Do you think the stone will wake them? What if we have to keep it safe until spring? I don't think I could handle the worry!"

"I'm sure they will wake up. Sostror was very clear on the power of the stone. He said even the cave will feel it and respond."

"I can feel it," said Poppy. "I'll be glad to hand it over, to be honest. I think it has been affecting my earrings, too. They make me feel peculiar when I wear them, now."

The procession reached the cave and stopped. Poppy and Jack turned to face the others. "Zander, you go first and open the tunnel," said Jack. They all followed Alex into the cave, and then paired up once more, with no discussion, to file down the tunnel to the main chamber. Around them, the gemstones in the walls pulsed like the beating heart of an animal, filling the tunnel with a much brighter, clearer green light than before. The walls almost appeared to be contracting, flexing, as if the hill were coming alive around them. When they reached the chamber, it was brightly lit, with no shadows in the alcoves. The painting behind the dais stood out more boldly, the colours more vibrant, and the children could see that there were other decorations around the rest of the walls; there were more of the symbols that were clearly the written language of the Elder-iche over the alcoves. The light was accompanied by a sound which the children had not heard before; the chamber had always been eerily silent. Now, there was a rumbling, chittering noise, growing ever louder, a noise the children could both hear and feel. They looked nervously at each other, and towards the tunnels either side of the dais, as goblins began to stream into the cavern, their bare feet and eructating chatter making the noise that now echoed around the chamber like the roar of a crowd in a stadium. Some of the goblins looked half asleep, plodding dazedly along and rubbing their faces, while others were clearly excited, gazing at the glowing chamber, and talking rapidly.

As the Elder-iche settled expectantly on the stone seats in the centre of the cavern, furtively looking round at the children standing in the mouth of the tunnel, Sostror, Bauzon, Tibigar and Minador came to greet the chosen six. "Greetings, saviours, and welcome. You have returned the wimblestone. We cannot thank you enough!" said Sostror, as he and the other emissaries gripped the children by the tops of their arms in a traditional Elder-iche embrace. When he reached the twins, he looked from Sean's face to Kyle's and back again, then he gripped each of them by their arms and introduced himself and his companions. "It is a great honour to meet such special Awer-Iche. Now all becomes clear!"

A change in the atmosphere in the cavern made them all look around. All the goblins had settled onto the stone seats, and a hush had fallen over them. The children felt nervous once more.

"We will lead you to the front, and then I will officially thank you for this courageous act that you have done, and then I will return the stone, in view of all my people, to its rightful place, which has been bare for so long. Come, do not be afraid. The worst is over."

With Sostror and Tibigar leading the way, and Bauzon and Minador bringing up the rear, the children once more processed solemnly towards the dais. Sostror stood at the front, with the six children in a line behind him, and the remaining guard of honour at the back, then he addressed the silent throng in their own tongue.

Standing in the middle of the children, Alex quietly translated what the goblin was saying so that the others could follow the speech. "He says 'at long last, after centuries of darkness and…something like lethargy or a dulling of spirits…the stone of life has been returned to us by our brave saviours from the overworld, righting the wrongs done to us in the time of Merlin, and restoring our source of life and power that we may continue to thrive for centuries to come.' Now he's going to ask us to hand the stone over; Poppy, are you ready?"

Poppy slipped the rucksack off her shoulders and unzipped it, trying not to fumble with nerves as she reached inside for the wimblestone. This was far worse than being called up in assembly at school. Sostror turned to her right on cue, and there was a surge of chattering and murmuring

262

from the crowd. Sostror thanked Poppy quietly, then holding the stone above his head, he turned back to the seated company and paraded the stone from one end of the dais to the other. After a minute or so of letting the stone take all the glory, he began to speak again.

"He's saying 'these humans selflessly risked many dangers and overcame many difficulties to return the stone to us today.' Now he's asking them to show their appreciation," said Alex.

Sostror stood to one side and beckoned the children to step to the front. In one movement, all the goblins in the chamber stood up and began ululating deeply, stepping from one foot to the other. The glowing gems in the chamber walls pulsed in rhythm with their chanting, and the children felt their chests contract with a strong emotion, like hypnosis, making them feel joyful, proud, loved and invincible all at once.

"Come!" said Sostror, and he lead the children, followed by his emissaries and all the goblins in the chamber, into the tunnel at the right hand side of the dais.

"We're going to put the stone back in its secret place," whispered Alex, "we're very privileged."

"Now we'll see if there's an armoury in here!" said Kyle to Sean and Jack.

Half an hour later, the chosen six returned to the cave, where Sostror, Minador, Bauzon and Tibigar bade them farewell.

"What did he say to you?" Jack asked Poppy, as the cave wall sealed itself, and the green glow faded to a grey shadow.

"I showed him the gems that we took from Merlin, and asked if he wanted those as well, and he told me to keep them. He said I could use them for healing, and that the gypsies would teach me how. He said he could trust me not to sell them as jewels, although they would be worth a fortune, but I think they will be more valuable as healing stones."

Jack nodded and smiled, and gave Poppy's shoulder a squeeze. He could tell that she was wishing she had been given them a year or two ago. He wished it, too. He would have liked to have met Poppy's mum, and seen Poppy smile more.

They emerged from the cave under the bare branches of the tree, a darkening grey sky forming a low roof over the dark grey walls of the quarry, but inside, the children felt like it was a bright summer afternoon. Each of them was grinning although none of them knew why, and then all together, unaware of who had made the first move, the six of them ran together as fast as they could, their grins turning to smiles, turning to outright laughter as they raced towards the lime kilns and home.

Epilogue

The following Thursday, Mr Pearson was at home when Jack came in from school. He was reading the Weston Mercury at the dining room table.

"Hi dad! Don't usually see you reading the paper. Anything interesting?"

"A couple of articles," said Mr Pearson, "come and have a look."

He closed the paper so that Jack could see the front page:

'Missing Woman Feared Drowned,' declared the headline. 'A Woman from Winscombe, who has not been seen for almost a week, may have drowned after walking unaccompanied over Brean Down. The woman, who at this stage cannot be named, left her car in a car park near the local beauty spot, where it remained for six days. A search of the area was conducted, but all that was found was a size five shoe on some rocks near the headland. This morning, however, a couple walking their dog along Brean Sands spotted a raincoat caught on some driftwood. In the pocket of the coat were the keys to the abandoned car.'

"Did you arrange all that, dad? The car and the shoe and everything?"

"I did," said his dad, matter-of-factly.

"And what about the rest of her things?"

"Well, the underwear I put in a bin in one of the toilets at the airport the following day, and her other clothes I put in a charity clothes skip on the other side of Bristol. The police won't connect any of these things, even if they're looking. I suspect all their attention is focussed on finding a body somewhere in the Bristol Channel, and they may

265

not have much hope of finding that. No, I'm sure they will conclude that all the evidence points to her slipping and falling into the water, struggling out of her coat to try and stay afloat, and then being carried out to sea, while the coat was brought in by the tide or got snagged on the piece of wood first, and that's how it ended up on the beach. Anyway, nothing for you boys or Poppy to worry about."

"That's amazing. Thanks, dad."

Mr Pearson smiled at Jack. "And look here, the other article of interest, on page five: 'Roman Remains Stop Airport Expansion.'"

Jack took the paper and read it for himself. "'An exciting archaeological discovery on the proposed site of the new runway at Bristol Airport has put paid to the developers' plans. Mr Kinnon, 45, of Wrington, made the discovery after his son' - hang on: Mr Kinnon? That's Henry's dad! 'After his son found some coins while playing soldiers in the fields surrounding the airport. Mr Kinnon did some digging himself, and found a considerable stash of very early currency. Experts have now declared the site one of the most important in the country, and plans to excavate more extensively over the next few years are being discussed. In the meantime, a spokesperson from the airport has confirmed that the proposed expansion is no longer an option.' Wow, that's incredible, dad!"

Mr Pearson tried to look nonchalant for a moment, then smiled broadly at his son. "I think we'll keep this paper for posterity, what do you reckon? Just as a reminder of these extraordinary events."

"Definitely," said Jack, and then he laughed. "Something to show the grandchildren one day."

"Do you think you will take your children to meet the goblins? Will you all have much to do with them now that the quest is over?"

"I expect we will. I think they could teach us a lot. But, you know, I've been wondering..."

"Wondering what?"

"Well...they asked us to find the stone and to return it; and we ended up finding it in Merlin's time, and returning it in the present day. So, really, it's our fault that it went missing in the first place, isn't it?"

"Hmm, yes, I see your point. I suppose, initially, the mural could have been a record of who stole the stone, not who was going to return it. Strange how things turn out."

"But do you think we should have made the effort to find the goblins in Merlin's time, so the stone would have stayed where it belonged?"

Mr Pearson took a deep breath and pondered his son's question. "Jack, I don't think you could have done anything other than you did. From what you've told me about the legend of the stone reaching the ears of power-hungry men, and their subsequent attempts to dig for it in the hills, I think the stone was probably safest where you took it – outside of time. Perhaps if you had taken it into the hill straight away, it would have been found, and the era of the goblins would have been terminated long ago. You can't mess with history, Jack. I think if you had returned the stone then, the history of our world would have been changed beyond recognition. No, you all did the right thing, believe me. The stone needed to vanish for all that time, for man to forget about finding it, and now it's safe."

"Between the dream time and the now," mused Jack, quietly, "never and forever."

The End

Or just the end of the beginning?

Acknowledgements

This story suggested itself to me in 2013 when I moved my family to Somerset and rented the house described in this book that backs onto the wooded hill and the quarry. I made several notes for the story, and began the opening chapter, on a cheap tablet during my limited spare time. By 2015, my tablet had broken, holding on to all my ideas, and leaving me with just their memories and a frustrated yearning to one day write a story about the wimblestone.

My thanks are primarily due, then, to the Covid-19 pandemic and the lockdown restrictions of 2020, for two reasons: with no evening and weekend activities for my children to attend, I had the time I needed to think and put my thoughts on paper (no tablet this time!); with no evening and weekend activities for my children to attend I hardly saw them, and writing them into my story was my way of connecting with them, being part of their lives and having them a part of mine during the isolation.

In addition to the time and the incentive provided by the pandemic, I also received much needed support and encouragement from my parents, and my friends in the Weston-based writing group Writers in Stone. Writers in Stone have been a great source of encouragement for the last four years, keeping my hand in with short pieces of writing each month, and providing valuable feedback. Particular thanks are due to Fenja Hill, Lois Elsden and Elizabeth Lawrence who proof read the full story at various stages, and to Ashah and Gabe, the invaluable critics who provided an independent, children's perspective.

The extracts of *A Somerset Sketch-Book* are included by kind permission of Forgotten Books, for which I am duly grateful. The song about the fart is an old playground chant, of which many different versions exist, and can be found online.

Finally, I would like to thank my four sons four being who they are, particularly Ellis whose interest and attention to detail were crucial in correcting errors. This book is my monument to their childhood, and none of the events in it would have happened without them.

Hamish MacNeil, November 30th 2020

Further Reading

You may be interested to track down and read some of the books that the children in the story have read and discuss, the books which helped to build the story itself, and some which may appeal to you if you have enjoyed this one.

To Kill a Mocking Bird by Harper lee

Stig of the Dump by Clive King

The Harry Potter series by J. K. Rowling

The Chronicles of Narnia by C. S. Lewis

The Hobbit by J. R. R. Tolkien

The Lord of the Rings by J. R. R. Tolkien

The Hitch Hiker's Guide to the Galaxy by Douglas Adams

Five Go To Mystery Moor by Enid Blyton

The Wind in the Willows by Kenneth Grahame

Swallows and Amazons by Arthur Ransome

The Talisman by Stephen King and Peter Straub

The Spiderwick Chronicles by Holly Black & Tony Diterlizzi

Tom's Midnight Garden by Philippa Pearce

The Watch House by Robert Westall

The Shrinking of Ralph Perfect by Chris d' Lacey

The Graveyard Book by Neil Gaiman

A Somerset Sketch-Book by H Hay Wilson (Forgotten Books, 2012)

Printed in Great Britain
by Amazon